# *the* BOOK *of* UNKNOWN AMERICANS

## CRISTINA HENRÍQUEZ

CANONGATE

This paperback edition published in Great Britain in 2019 by Canongate Books

First published in Great Britain in 2014 by Canongate Books Ltd, 14 High Street, Edinburgh EH1 1TE

First published in the United States in 2014 by Alfred A. Knopf, a division of Random House LLC

canongate.co.uk

1

*British Library Cataloguing-in-Publication Data*
A catalogue record for this book is available on
request from the British Library

ISBN 978 1 78211 122 1

Printed and bound in Great Britain by Clays Ltd, Elcograf S.p.A.

*For my father, Pantaleón Henríquez III*

*Let us all be from somewhere.*
*Let us tell each other everything we can.*

—BOB HICOK, "A PRIMER"

*the* BOOK *of* UNKNOWN AMERICANS

# Alma

Back then, all we wanted was the simplest things: to eat good food, to sleep at night, to smile, to laugh, to be well. We felt it was our right, as much as it was anyone's, to have those things. Of course, when I think about it now, I see that I was naïve. I was blinded by the swell of hope and the promise of possibility. I assumed that everything that would go wrong in our lives already had.

THIRTY HOURS AFTER crossing the border, we arrived, the three of us in the backseat of a red pickup truck that smelled of cigarette smoke and gasoline.

"Wake up," I whispered, nudging Maribel as the driver turned into a parking lot.

"Hmmm?"

"We're here, hija."

"Where?" Maribel asked.

"Delaware."

She blinked at me in the dark.

Arturo was sitting on the other side of us. "Is she okay?" he asked.

"Don't worry," I said. "She's fine."

It was just after sunset and darkness bled in from the outer reaches of the sky. A few minutes earlier, we'd been on a busy road, driving through four-way intersections, past strip malls and fast-food restaurants, but as we neared the apartment building, all of that had given way. The last thing I saw before we turned onto the long gravel lane that led to the parking lot was an abandoned auto body shop, its hand-painted sign on the ground, propped up against the gray stucco facade.

The driver parked the truck and lit another cigarette. He'd been smoking the whole trip. It gave him something to do with his mouth, I guess, since he'd made it clear from the moment he picked us up in Laredo that he wasn't interested in conversation.

Arturo climbed out first, straightened his cowboy hat, and surveyed the building. Two stories, made of cinder blocks and cement, an outdoor walkway that ran the length of the second floor with metal staircases at either end, pieces of broken Styrofoam in the grass, a chain-link fence along the perimeter of the lot, cracks in the asphalt. I had expected it to be nicer. Something with white shutters and red bricks, something with manicured shrubs and flower boxes in the windows. The way American houses looked in movies. This was the only option Arturo's new job had given us, though, and I told myself we were lucky to have it.

Silently, in the dim and unfamiliar air, we unloaded our things: plastic trash bags packed with clothes and sheets and towels; cardboard boxes filled with dishes wrapped in newspaper; a cooler crammed with bars of soap, bottles of water, cooking oil, and shampoo. During the drive we had passed a television set on the curb, and when he saw it, the driver braked hard and backed up. "You want it?" he asked us. Arturo and I looked at each other in confusion. "The television?" Arturo asked. The driver said, "You want it, take it." Arturo said, "It's not stealing?" The driver snorted. "People throw away everything in the United

States. Even things that are still perfectly good." Later, when he stopped again and pointed to a discarded kitchen table, and later again at a mattress propped up like a sliding board against someone's mailbox, we understood what to do and loaded them into the truck.

After we carried everything up the rusted metal staircase to our apartment, after we found the key the landlord had left for us, taped to the threshold of the door, Arturo went back down to pay the driver. He gave him half the money we had. Gone. Just like that. The driver put the bills in his pocket and flicked his cigarette out the window. "Good luck," I heard him say before he drove off.

INSIDE THE APARTMENT, Arturo flipped the light switch on the wall and a bare bulb in the ceiling flashed on. The linoleum floors were dingy and worn. Every wall was painted a dark mustard yellow. There were two windows—a large one at the front and a smaller one at the back in the only bedroom—both covered by plastic sheets held in place with tape, the wood casings warped and splintered. Across the hall from the bedroom was a bathroom with a baby blue sink, a toilet ringed with rust, and an upright shower stall with neither a door nor a curtain. At first glance, the kitchen was better—it was bigger, at least—though the stove burners were wrapped in aluminum foil and bedsheets had been stapled over the lower cabinets in place of doors. An old refrigerator stood in the corner, its doors wide open. Arturo walked over to it and poked his head inside.

"Is this what smells?" he asked. "¡Huácala!"

The whole place reeked of mildew and, faintly, of fish.

"I'll clean it in the morning," I said, as Arturo closed the doors.

I glanced at Maribel standing next to me. She was expressionless, as usual, clutching her notebook to her chest. What did she make of all this? I wondered. Did she understand where we were?

We didn't have the energy to unpack or brush our teeth or even to change our clothes, so after we looked around we slapped our newly acquired mattress on the floor in the bedroom, crawled on top of it, and closed our eyes.

For nearly an hour, maybe more, I lay there listening to the soft chorus of Maribel's and Arturo's long, even breaths. In and out. In and out. The surge of possibility. The tug of doubt. Had we done the right thing, coming here? Of course, I knew the answer. We had done what we had to do. We had done what the doctors told us. I stacked my hands on top of my stomach and told myself to breathe. I relaxed the muscles in my face, slackened my jaw. But we were so far from anything familiar. Everything here—the sour air, the muffled noises, the depth of the darkness—was different. We had bundled up our old life and left it behind, and then hurtled into a new one with only a few of our things, each other, and hope. Would that be enough? We'll be fine, I told myself. We'll be fine. I repeated it like a prayer until finally I fell asleep, too.

WE WOKE in the morning bewildered and disoriented, glancing at one another, darting our gaze from wall to wall. And then we remembered. Delaware. Over three thousand kilometers from our home in Pátzcuaro. Three thousand kilometers and a world away.

Maribel rubbed her eyes.

"Are you hungry?" I asked.

She nodded.

"I'll make breakfast," I said.

"We don't have any food," Arturo mumbled. He was sitting bleary-eyed on the mattress, his elbows on his knees.

"We can get some," I said.

"Where?" he asked.

"Wherever they sell food."

But we had no idea where to go. We stepped out of the apartment into the bright sun and the damp early-morning air—Arturo wearing his hat, Maribel wearing the sunglasses that the doctor had suggested she use to help ease her headaches—and walked down the gravel drive that led to the main road. When we came to it, Arturo stopped and stroked his mustache, glancing in both directions.

"What do you think?" he asked.

I peered past him as a car sped by, making a soft whooshing sound. "Let's try this way," I said, pointing to the left for no reason.

Between the three of us, we knew only the most minimal English, words and phrases we had picked up from the tourists that traveled to Pátzcuaro and in the shops that catered to them, and we couldn't read the signs above the storefronts as we passed them, so we peered in every window along the way to see what was inside. For the next twenty minutes, flat glass fronts, one after another. A beauty supply store with racks of wigs in the window, a carpet store, a Laundromat, an electronics store, a currency exchange. And then, finally, on the corner of a busy intersection, we came to a gas station, which we knew better than to pass up.

We walked past the pumps, toward the front door. Outside, a

teenaged boy stood slouched against the wall, holding the nose of a skateboard. I could feel him watching us as we approached. He had on a loose black T-shirt and jeans that were frayed at the hems. Dark brown hair, bluntly cut, brushed forward past his hairline. An inky blue tattoo that snaked up the side of his neck from beneath the collar of his shirt.

I elbowed Arturo.

"What?" Arturo said.

I nodded toward the boy.

Arturo looked over. "It's okay," he said, but I could feel him pushing my back as we passed the boy, ushering Maribel and me into the gas station with a certain urgency.

Inside, we scanned the metal shelves for anything that we recognized. Arturo claimed at one point that he had found salsa, but when I picked up the jar and looked through the glass bottom, I laughed.

"What?" he asked.

"This isn't salsa."

"It says 'salsa,'" he insisted, pointing to the word on the paper label.

"But look at it," I said. "Does it look like salsa to you?"

"It's American salsa."

I held up the jar again, shook it a little.

"Maybe it's good," Arturo said.

"Do they think this is what we eat?" I asked.

He took the jar from me and put it in the basket. "Of course not. I told you. It's American salsa."

By the time we finished shopping, we had American salsa, eggs, a box of instant rice, a loaf of sliced bread, two cans of kidney beans, a carton of juice, and a package of hot dogs that Maribel claimed she wanted.

At the register, Arturo arranged everything on the counter and unfolded the money he'd been carrying in his pocket. Without saying a word, he handed the cashier a twenty-dollar bill. The cashier slid it into the drawer of the register and reached his open hand out to us. Arturo lifted the blue plastic shopping basket off the floor and turned it over to show that it was empty. The cashier said something and flexed his outstretched hand, so Arturo gave him the basket, but the cashier only dropped the basket behind the counter.

"What's wrong?" I asked Arturo.

"I don't know," he said. "I gave him the money, didn't I? Is there something else we're supposed to do?"

People had lined up behind us, and they were craning their necks now to see what was going on.

"Should we give him more?" I asked.

"More? I gave him twenty dollars already. We're only getting a few things."

Someone in line shouted impatiently. Arturo turned to look, but didn't say anything. What must we look like to people here? I wondered. Speaking Spanish, wearing the same rumpled clothes we'd been in for days.

"Mami?" Maribel said.

"It's okay," I told her. "We're just trying to pay."

"I'm hungry."

"We're getting you food."

"Where?"

"Here."

"But we have food in México."

The woman behind me in line, her sunglasses on top of her blond hair, tapped me on the shoulder and asked something. I nodded at her and smiled.

"Just give him more money," I said to Arturo.

Someone in line shouted again.

"Mami?" Maribel said.

"I'm going to take her outside," I told Arturo. "It's too much commotion for her."

A bell tinkled as Maribel and I walked out, and before the door even closed behind us, I saw the boy again, still slouched against the wall, holding his skateboard upright. He shifted just slightly at the sight of us, and I watched as his gaze turned to Maribel, looking her up and down, approvingly, coolly, with hooded eyes.

I was used to people looking at her. It had happened often in Pátzcuaro. Maribel had the kind of beauty that reduced people to simpletons. Once upon a time grown men would break into smiles as she walked past. The boys in her school would come to the house, shoving each other awkwardly when I opened the door, asking if she was home. Of course, that was before the accident. She looked the same now as she always had, but people knew—almost everyone in our town knew—that she had changed. They seemed to believe she was no longer worthy of their attention or maybe that it was wrong to look at her now, that there was something perverse about it, and they averted their gaze.

But this boy looked. He looked because he didn't know. And the way he looked made me uncomfortable.

I pulled Maribel closer and edged us backwards.

The boy took a step toward us.

I moved back again, holding Maribel's elbow. Where was Arturo? Wasn't he done by now?

The boy picked up his skateboard, tucking it under his arm,

and started toward us, when suddenly—¡Gracias a Dios!—the gas station door opened. Arturo walked out, holding a plastic bag in one hand and shaking his head.

"Arturo!" I called.

"Twenty-two dollars!" he said when he saw me. "Can you believe that? Do you think they took advantage of us?"

But I didn't care how much money we had spent. I lifted my chin enough so that Arturo caught my meaning and glanced behind him. The boy was still standing there, staring at the three of us now. Arturo turned back around slowly.

"Are you ready?" he asked Maribel and me a little too loudly, as if speaking at such a volume would scare the boy off.

I nodded, and Arturo walked over, shifting the bag as he clasped Maribel's arm and put one hand on the small of my back.

"Just walk," he whispered to me. "It's fine."

The three of us started toward the road, doubling back in the direction from which we had come, heading toward home.

# Mayor

We heard they were from México.

"Definitely," my mom said, staring at them through our front window as they moved in. "Look at how short they are." She let the curtain fall back in place and walked to the kitchen, wiping her hands on the dish towel slung over her shoulder.

I looked, but all I saw was three people moving through the dark, carrying stuff from a pickup truck to unit 2D. They cut across the headlights of the truck a few times, and I made out their faces, but only long enough to see a mom, a dad, and a girl about my age.

"So?" my dad asked when I joined him and my mom at the dinner table.

"I couldn't really see anything," I said.

"Do they have a car?"

I shook my head. "The truck's just dropping them off, I think."

My dad sawed off a piece of chicken and stuffed it in his mouth. "Do they have a lot of things?" he asked.

"It didn't seem like it."

"Good," my dad said. "Maybe they are like us, then."

WE HEARD FROM Quisqueya Solís that their last name was Rivera.

"And they're legal," she reported to my mom over coffee one afternoon. "All of them have visas."

"How do you know?" my mom asked.

"That's what Nelia told me. She heard it from Fito. Apparently the mushroom farm is sponsoring them."

"Of course," my mom said.

I was in the living room, eavesdropping, even though I was supposed to be doing my geometry homework.

"Well," my mom went on, clearing her throat, "it will be nice to have another family in the building. They'll be a good addition."

Quisqueya took a quick look at me before turning back to my mom and hunching over her coffee mug. "Except . . . ," she said.

My mom leaned forward. "What?"

Quisqueya said, "The girl . . ." She looked at me again.

My mom peered over Quisqueya's shoulder. "Mayor, are you listening to us?"

I tried to act surprised. "Huh? Me?"

My mom knew me too well, though. She shook her head at Quisqueya to signal that whatever Quisqueya was going to say, she'd better save it if she didn't want me to hear it.

"Bueno, we don't need to talk about it, then," Quisqueya said. "You'll see for yourself eventually, I'm sure."

My mom narrowed her eyes, but instead of pressing, she sat back in her chair and said loudly, "Well." And then, "More coffee?"

WE HEARD A LOT of things, but who knew how much of it was true? It didn't take long before the details about the Riveras began to seem far-fetched. They had tried to come into the United States once before but had been turned back. They were only staying for a few weeks. They were working undercover for the Department of Homeland Security. They were personal friends with the governor. They were running a safe house for illegals. They had connections to a Mexican narco ring. They were loaded. They were poor. They were traveling with the circus.

I tuned it all out after a while. School had started two weeks earlier, and even though I had told myself that this would be the year the other kids stopped picking on me, the year that I actually fit in for once in my life, things already weren't going exactly as planned. During the first week of school, I was in the locker room, changing into my gym shorts, when Julius Olsen tucked his hands into his armpits and started flapping his arms like wings. "Bwwaak!" he said, looking at me. I ignored him and cinched the drawstring on my shorts. Actually, they were my older brother Enrique's shorts that had been handed down to me, but I wore them because I thought that maybe they would make me seem cooler than I was, like maybe some of Enrique's popularity was trapped in the fibers and would rub off on me. He'd been a senior the year before, when I was a freshman, and every single person in the school had adored him. Soccer stud. Girlfriends by the dozen. Homecoming king. So opposite of me that when I tried to earn points with Shandie Lewis, who I would have given just about anything to hook up with, by telling her that I was Enrique Toro's brother, she said that was a really stupid thing to lie about.

"Bwwaaaak!" Julius said louder, jutting his neck toward me.

I balled up my jeans and shoved them into my locker.

Garrett Miller, who had basically made picking on me last year his special project, pointed at me, laughed, and said, "Fucking chicken legs." He flung his boot at my chest.

Julius snorted.

I took a deep breath and shut my locker. I was used to this kind of abuse. Last year, whenever Enrique caught wind of it, he'd tell me to stand up for myself. "I know you don't want to fight," he said once. "But at least have the balls to tell them to fuck off." And in my head I did. In my head, I was Jason Bourne or Jack Bauer or James Bond or all three of them combined. But beyond my head, the most I ever did was ignore it and walk away.

"How do you say 'chicken' in Spanish?" Garrett asked.

"Pollo," someone answered.

"Major Pollo," Garrett said.

The kids at my school loved changing my first name to English and then tacking insults onto it. Major Pan (short for Panamanian). Major Pan in the Ass. Major Cocksucker.

Julius started cracking up, and he squawked at me again. A few of the other guys in the locker room snickered.

I started walking—I just wanted to get out of there—but when I did, I bumped Garrett's boot, which was on the floor in front of me.

"Don't touch my shoe, Pollo," Garrett said.

"Kick it over here," Julius said.

"Fuck you," Garrett snapped. "Don't tell him to kick my shoe."

"Don't worry," Julius said. "He can't kick for shit. Haven't you seen him out there after school trying to play soccer? He's a total fuckup."

"Major fuckup," Garrett said, stepping in front of me to block any hope I had of leaving.

Garrett was thin, but he was tall. He wore a green army coat every single day, no matter what the weather was, and had a tattoo of an eagle on his neck. The year before, he'd spent a few months in juvenile detention at Ferris because he beat up Angelo Puente so bad that by the end of it, Angelo had two broken arms and blood pouring out of his nose. There was no way I was going to mess with him.

But when the bell rang and the other kids started filing out into the gym, Garrett still didn't budge. The locker room was in the school basement and it was so quiet right then that I could hear water coursing through the pipes. There wasn't anywhere for me to go. Garrett took a step closer. I didn't know what he was going to do. And then Mr. Samuels, the gym teacher, poked his head into the room.

"You boys are supposed to be out in the gym," he said.

Garrett didn't move. Neither did I.

"Now!" he barked.

So that was one thing. The other thing, as Julius had pointed out, was soccer. The only reason I'd gone out for the team in the first place was because my dad had forced me into it. For him, the logic went something like: I was Latino and male and not a cripple, therefore I should play soccer. Soccer was for Latinos, basketball for blacks, and the whites could keep their tennis and golf as far as he was concerned. He'd applied the same reasoning to my brother, too, except that in Enrique's case, it had actually worked out. Enrique had been the first player in the history of our school to make varsity as a freshman, and when he got a full-ride soccer scholarship to Maryland, it was like my dad had been vindicated. "See?" he'd said, waving around the offer letter when it came in the mail. "You were meant to do this! The next Pelé! And this one," he'd said, pointing at me, "the next Maradona!"

Enrique might have been the next Pelé, but I wasn't even in

the same galaxy as Maradona. Two weeks into practice, I had bruised shins, a scabby knee, and a scraped elbow. Coach even pulled me aside once to ask whether I was wearing the right size cleats. I told him they were size seven, which was my size, and he patted my shoulder and said, "Okay, then. Maybe you should just sit it out for a while," and directed me to the sidelines.

In the past few days, a flock of girls had started coming to our practices, sitting in the empty stands and pointing at us while they texted and talked. Word got around that they were new freshmen. They didn't look like any freshmen I knew, in their skimpy tank tops and lacy black bras they wore underneath, but what I did know was that our team got a hell of a lot better after those girls showed up. Everyone was running faster and kicking harder than before. I felt like a loser, hanging around the sidelines all the time. Whenever the girls broke out in laughter, I was sure they were laughing at me. One day, I asked Coach if I could go back in, even if just for a few drills. When he looked ambivalent, I lied and said, "I've been practicing with my dad at home. Even he thinks I'm getting better." Coach worked his jaw from side to side like he was thinking about it. "Please?" I said. Finally he gave in. "Okay. Let's see what you got."

We set up a star drill where guys spread out into a circle and dribbled the ball a few paces into the middle before passing to a teammate who took the ball and repeated the sequence. Each time I ran through and got back in line, I looked up at the girls in the stands, who weren't laughing anymore, just watching. Maybe I got overconfident. Maybe there was a divot in the grass. The next time I ran into the middle to get the ball, my ankle turned. Ethan Weisberg was stepping toward me, waiting for me to pass to him. I was so eager to get the dribble going again that when

I went for the ball with my other foot, I rolled my cleat up over it instead. The ball was still spinning, and I stumbled again just as Ethan, impatient and frustrated, finally came at me and tried to spear his foot in to swipe the ball out for himself. When he did, I fell. His leg caught under mine. And before either of us knew it, I had taken him down, both of us landing on top of each other in the middle of the field. "What the fuck, Mayor!" Ethan yelled. My hip throbbed. Coach blew his whistle and jogged in to untangle us. The girls erupted in laughter.

# Rafael Toro

I was born in 1967 in a town called Los Santos in a little country by the name of Panamá. I was an only child. My father
moved us to Panamá City when I was five because he had politi-
cal ambitions. He read the newspaper every day to keep himself
informed. He had a small transistor radio that he listened to in
the morning while he was in the shower. My father used to walk
around the house in his socks and make speeches about everything. He made speeches about the dishes stacked in the sink or
about Gerald Ford or about the raspado vendor who'd gotten in
his way. He had a temper, too. He broke our teacups and one
time he broke the television set when he threw a vase through
the screen. Well, it broke the vase, too, but I was ten and I only
cared that he had broken the television set. I remember one
time he got so furious that he picked up a ham my mother had
prepared for dinner and heaved it into the front yard. My mother
ran out to retrieve it and when she brought it back inside, she
was crying and picking pebbles and dirt off the seared skin. My
cousins were over that night and I remember them all laughing
at her. I thought that was how a man behaved, so when I got
upset, even as a young boy, I would throw things or kick the
wall. I had a terrible temper. After my father died, when I was
thirteen, it only got worse. Because then I really had something
to be angry about. I missed him after he was gone. My mother
must have felt the same way, because in the years following his

death she often got sick. She went to doctors but they never knew what it was. She was depressed and tired. There were days she didn't get out of bed. I don't think she could function without my father. Then one morning I went to wake her and she didn't move. I remember her arm was cold when I shook it.

I spent a long time after that feeling like I didn't care about anything. The house went to the bank, and I lived with various friends for a few months at a time, sleeping on their couches or more often on the floor. I stopped going to school. I started drinking during the day. I got into fights at the bar or with guys on the street. I washed people's cars to earn enough money to get by.

My wife, Celia, saved my life. Who knows what would have become of me if I hadn't met her? I was playing a pickup baseball game with some friends on a beach by Casco Viejo. That beach is filthy now, but back then people used to go swimming there and sunbathe on the sand.

I was terrible at baseball. I was always trying to persuade the other guys to play soccer instead, but baseball was the big sport then, and one of the guys would bring cold beers in a cooler to the pickup games, so I used to go for that.

Celia was walking by with her girlfriends—they had on their bathing suits and the kind of platform sandals that were popular—and they stopped to watch the game for a few minutes, all of them laughing like nervous birds. I think one of them knew one of the guys. Celia didn't stand out to me right away. But after the game, she was still there with one of her friends—everyone else had left by then—and I remember she touched my shoulder. I must have said something funny, but I don't know what, and if you ask her, she'll claim I've never said a funny thing in my life. But she laughed and laid her hand on my shoulder, and I thought to myself, Who is this girl?

I was eighteen then. We started spending time together. I was still sleeping at friends' apartments with no place of my own, so Celia and I sat on park benches and drank bottles of beer or walked down Avenida Central or sat on the rocks by the bay, listening to the water slap below us. Her favorite was always that small Casco Viejo beach where we met. She could sit for hours with her toes in the sand, letting the sea foam come up to her ankles. I never saw her happier than when we would go there together.

She wasn't very demanding, Celia. She didn't care that I couldn't give her a lot of things. But *I* cared. Eventually I got a job at a restaurant, just so I could have enough money to buy her gifts and take her out once in a while to a movie. That's what the man is supposed to do. She was in university, studying to become a secretary, but I didn't want us to have to rely on the money she would be making one day. I wanted to be able to take care of her myself. And, I guess, all of a sudden I wanted to be able to take care of me.

I got my life straight after that. Instead of spending my paychecks on rum and beer like before, I saved enough to buy Celia a gold ring from Reprosa, and I asked her to marry me.

We got married in Iglesia del Carmen in front of about twelve guests. Her sister, Gloria, her parents, a few of our friends. One year later, we had our son Enrique. Then Mayor.

Both Celia and I miss certain things about Panamá. It was our home for so many years. It's hard to let go of that, even when you have a good reason for leaving. How can I describe what it was like during the invasion? We slept in a city bus one night because the bus was barricaded and when we and all the other passengers tried to get off, men from the Dignity Battalions were standing outside the door with guns pointed at us, telling us not to move. Celia was holding Enrique in her arms, pleading with them because we didn't have any food for him. And in the morning, when they were gone, we walked home listening to gunfire in the distance. No one was outside except people who were fighting. Well, and a few people who were looting. But most of the stores were closed and the owners had pulled the metal gates down over the front windows and doors, padlocking them shut. We went three weeks without leaving the house. We were eating toothpaste by the end of it. There was static on the television. We didn't know what was going to happen. Then one day we heard from a neighbor that Noriega was gone, and suddenly there were voices in the streets again. Everyone was wandering around, looking up at the sky, knocking on each other's doors, sharing stories about what it had been like, how scared we had been, the parts of the city that had been destroyed. But the stories were nothing compared to what we saw when we went out. El Chorrillo. San Miguelito. I didn't even know how to comprehend it. Burnt-out cars and the rubble of buildings. Broken glass and charred palm trees along the sides of the roads. It looked like a different place. It was just destruction and more destruction. I remember Celia burst into tears the first time she saw it all.

We tried to give it time, but three years later we made the decision to leave. We never felt safe there again. We felt as if our home had been stolen from us. And part of me felt embarrassed, I think, that my country hadn't been strong enough to resist what had happened to it. Maybe the way to say it is that I felt betrayed.

We're Americans now. I'm a line cook at a diner, and I make enough to provide for my family. Celia and I feel gratified when we see Enrique and Mayor doing well here. Maybe they wouldn't have done so well in Panamá. Maybe they wouldn't have had the same opportunities. So that makes coming here worth it. We're citizens, and if someone asks me where my home is, I say los Estados Unidos. I say it proudly.

Of course, we still miss Panamá. Celia is desperate to go back and visit. But I worry what it would be like after all this time. We thought it was unrecognizable when we left, but I have a feeling it would be even more unrecognizable now. Sometimes I think I would rather just remember it in my head, all those streets and places I loved. The way it smelled of car exhaust and sweet fruit. The thickness of the heat. The sound of dogs barking in alleyways. That's the Panamá I want to hold on to. Because a place can do many things against you, and if it's your home or if it was your home at one time, you still love it. That's how it works.

# Alma

Arturo started work a few days after we arrived. Before we came he had arranged a job at a mushroom farm, just over the state line in Pennsylvania. It was the only company near Maribel's school that had been willing to sponsor our visas.

"How was it?" I asked, running to meet him at the door when he came home. He had dirt under his fingernails and smelled like rotten vegetables.

I pinched my nose. "Maybe you should take a shower before you tell me."

But he didn't laugh. He walked past me and sat on one of the chairs by the table. "How was it?" he said. "Well, I stood in a warehouse for ten hours and picked mushrooms out of the dirt."

"So it was great."

Arturo pushed his chin to one side, cracking his neck.

"Sorry," I said, sitting across from him. He wanted to be serious, so I would be serious. "The mushrooms grow inside the building?"

He nodded. "In boxes. They're stacked on top of each other with just enough space in between for us to fit our hands in. Everything is controlled. The ventilation, the humidity. And they keep it dark."

"You work in the dark?"

"It doesn't matter to the mushrooms whether there's light."

"But don't you need to see what you're doing?"

"I can feel when I've found one. Then I have to snap the stem, brush off the dirt, and toss it in the collection bin. Pero tan rápido. We have quotas to make."

"But in the dark?" I asked again. I tried to imagine him standing in the dark all day. What kind of conditions were those?

"It's mindless," he said.

"Do they know about your experience? You could be a manager there."

"No, I couldn't."

"Tell them that in México you owned a construction business."

"They're not going to care about that."

"But you could do more than pull mushrooms in the dark."

"We knew this was going to be the job, Alma."

"Who knew? I didn't know."

"I told you."

"You told me you would be working at a mushroom farm, but I didn't think you'd be doing this."

"Well, this is what I'm doing."

"Why don't you want to tell them about your qualifications?"

"I'm not going to make waves, Alma. I'm happy just to have a job."

"I know, but—"

"Please!" Arturo snapped.

I felt my chest cave slightly, wounded by his tone.

"I'm sorry," he said. "I'm just tired."

"Let me get you a drink," I said, standing up, pulling a glass from the cabinet and filling it with water.

He took it greedily.

"When's the last time you drank something?" I asked.

"Before I left this morning."

"You didn't drink anything else all day?"

"There wasn't time."

"Did you eat?"

Arturo shook his head. "No one eats."

I was appalled, though I didn't want to say so. What kind of place required a man to work all day without being allowed to eat or drink? There had to be rules, didn't there? This was America, after all. I couldn't help but think of how in Pátzcuaro Arturo used to come home at midday and sit at the kitchen table, eating the lunch I had spent much of the morning preparing for him. Soft tortillas that I had ground from nixtamal, wrapped in a dish towel to keep them warm, a plate of shredded chicken or pork, bowls of cubed papaya and mango topped with coconut juice or cotija cheese. On Fridays, we would eat vanilla ice cream that I spooned into dishes the size of small, cupped hands or pan dulce that I baked. The sunlight melting through the windows. The smell of wood and warm air. And now this? This was where I had brought him? To a windowless building where he stood in one place all day sifting through dirt without eating or drinking or seeing the sun? The thought of it cut through me. And guilt once again reared its head.

"I'll make you something to eat," I said.

At my back, while I unwrapped a hot dog from its plastic package, Arturo asked, "How was she today? Did you hear from the school?"

"They didn't call," I said. I didn't need to look at him to know he was disappointed.

Both of us were waiting. We had done all the required things—submitted immunization reports, showed proof of residence, filled out forms—and now we were ready for the next step, word that Maribel had been approved to start school.

I dropped the hot dog into a pot of water. I could hear Arturo behind me, working through his thoughts, trying to box in his frustration. After all these years, I could interpret his various silences. I knew he didn't want to say any more about it. I didn't want him to, either.

Finally, "She's in the bedroom?" he asked.

"She's resting," I said. "The hot dog will be ready soon," I added, as if it were some sort of consolation.

But when Arturo didn't say anything, I felt acutely the meagerness of it, the insufficiency. We wanted more. We wanted what we had come here for.

AND THEN, five days later, it seemed like we would get it.

"I'm sorry it's taken us so long to get her enrolled," the translator from the district said when she called. Her name was Phyllis, but when I tried to repeat it, it came out, "Felix?"

"Phyllis," she said.

"Phyllis," I tried again, though the coordination between my tongue and teeth and lips felt clumsy and strange.

"Do you speak English?" she asked, and when I confessed with some embarrassment that I didn't, she went on in Spanish. "It's okay. That's the case with the majority of the families I work with. Which is why you get me. Think of me as your conduit to the school. Anytime you need to communicate with them, call me, and I'll get them the message, and if they need to communicate something to you, it's the same thing. I'll get you the message."

So this is the doorway, I thought, between us and the rest of this country. I was grateful to have it, but of course the limitations were clear: We couldn't walk through the door without someone to guide us to the other side.

Phyllis went on, explaining how A. I. duPont had a terrific

bilingual school psychologist, Adira Suarez, who would be calling us soon, too, but that she—

"Excuse me," I said. "What is A. I. duPont?"

"The school your daughter will be going to."

"She's supposed to go to the Evers School."

"Does she have an IEP?"

"A what?"

"An Individualized Education Plan. She needs one before she can be placed in a school like Evers. So first she'll go to A. I. duPont, where she'll be in an ELL program—"

"A what?"

"English Language Learners. Or does she already know English?"

"No."

"So we need to get her in that program to start. While she's there, they'll evaluate her to see if she's eligible for special education services."

"Eligible? But we have a letter from the doctor. We came all the way here so she could go to Evers."

"If they determine that she needs to be at Evers, that's where she'll go. Just not right away. They have to do an evaluation first."

Disappointment gathered around me like storm clouds. "How long will it take?" I asked.

"It usually takes one to two months."

"Two months!" I said.

"We'll try to get her situated as quickly as we can," Phyllis said. "I promise."

And what else could I do but say okay and wait, again?

ARTURO WASN'T HAPPY—neither of us was—but he was an optimist, and at least, he said, we were one step closer. At least, he said with his hands on my shoulders, the process was under way.

So on Maribel's first day of school in the United States, Arturo and I woke up early, filled with impossible expectation, and roused Maribel, watching her push her hair off her face.

Arturo said, "Today's the day, hija. You're starting school."

He had switched shifts at work to be able to stay home for the big send-off.

"What school?" she asked.

"A new school. Here in Delaware."

"You didn't tell me."

"Yes, we did."

"Where is my old school?"

"Your old school is in Pátzcuaro."

"I want to go there."

Arturo shot me a pained look.

"You're going to this new school now," I said.

"Where?"

"It's here in Delaware."

"What is?"

"Your new school, hija."

She stared at us, and I waited for some sign either that she had absorbed the information or that she was still confused. It was impossible to tell. Her expression never gave anything away anymore.

"Come on," I said, trying to mask my impatience. "The bus will be here soon. You need to get up and get dressed."

Maribel rose to her feet, like a filly finding her legs, and stretched. She chose a sweatshirt and jeans from the piles of clothes I had folded and placed on the floor along the wall.

"I can wear this," she said, holding up the top.

"You can wear whatever you want," Arturo said.

She slid the jeans up her legs and, when they were over her hips, I raised the zipper and snapped the button for her. She wrestled herself into the sweatshirt after that, pulling it on backwards, and though usually neither Arturo nor I would have pointed it out—we tried to make her feel capable when we could—I wanted her to look nice on her first day, so I started pulling her arms back through the sleeves to turn it around.

"What are you doing?" she asked.

"I'm fixing your shirt."

"I liked it how it was," she said.

"But it was backwards."

"I liked it how it was."

So I left it alone. I didn't comb her hair either, because any time I tried to, she complained that it hurt, that it pulled at the scar across her scalp. When Maribel was little, she used to get up early in the morning so I could plait her hair in two long braids down her back. She inspected them when I was finished, and if the braids weren't tight enough, she would undo them and make me start again. So stubborn. So sure of what she wanted. One thing that hadn't changed.

We ate eggs in the kitchen, and when it was time to go, I handed Maribel a backpack—the same one she had used in México—that I had packed with a pencil, her green notebook, a ruler that was part of a sewing kit my mother had given me for my quinceañera, a small wooden box filled with medicine tablets, a note for the nurse, and a tag with her name, address, and phone number written on it.

"Are you ready?" I asked.

"For what?"

"Maribel, you're starting school today. Remember?"

"What school?"

She stared at us with those wide, beautiful eyes. The way she used to stare at us when she was a baby. It had taken us so long to have her, so many years of trying and failing. So many doctors, so many prayers. But then I had gotten pregnant. At last. Our miracle de Dios. And after she had arrived, Our Everything.

"It's a new school," Arturo said. "I think you'll like it there."

Maribel studied his face. Arturo and I waited. So much of our life with her now was about waiting, something I wasn't very good at.

"Okay," she said.

There was no rhyme or reason to it. Sin pies ni cabeza. She resisted, she was confused, and then, suddenly, something would snap back into place and she was compliant, agreeable. Even a year after the accident, I was still unable to discern the pattern.

It was humid when we walked outside. The three of us stood in the weedy grass along the edge of the parking lot until a long yellow bus dragged itself up from the street. It stopped in front of us and the door folded open. The driver, a woman wearing a baseball cap, waved and yelled hello. That much I understood. But when she kept talking, I got lost. Arturo looked at me as if to ask whether I knew what she was saying. I shook my head, and thought, This is how it is for us here. This is how it will be. We simply had to trust that the bus driver would deliver Maribel safely to school and that her teacher would make sure she was in the right classroom and that all day long, people would take care of her the way she needed to be cared for. We had to push past trepidation and believe that by sending her off we were doing the right thing. What other choice did we have?

Standing next to each other, Arturo and I watched as Maribel climbed aboard the bus. Through the windows, I saw her sit in a seat near the front and push her sunglasses up.

We had been planning our life here for so long. Filling out papers, hoping, praying, waiting. We had all of our dreams pinned on this place, but the pin was thin and delicate and it was too soon to tell whether it was stronger than it looked or whether, in the end, it wasn't going to hold much of anything at all.

As if he had read my mind, Arturo said, "She'll be fine."

But I couldn't tell if he was only trying to convince himself that it was true.

"Say it again," I said.

"She'll be fine."

And because I wanted to believe him—because I wanted more than anything for her to be fine and fine and eventually better than fine, for her to transform again into the girl she used to be, for this past year to have been nothing but a strange, cruel detour that we could move beyond and never venture down again—I nodded and watched the bus heave away.

ARTURO LEFT FOR WORK not long after—he had his own bus to take, three of them, actually, all the way to the mushroom farm—which meant that I was alone in the apartment for the first time since we had arrived. I wasn't used to being alone, here or anywhere, and the silence felt like an invasion. Usually in Pátzcuaro someone—either my mother or else one of my friends—stopped by in the morning. I would make café con leche and we would talk, sometimes for only a few minutes, sometimes for hours. And even on the days when no one came over, through the open windows of our house I could hear the noise of our neighbors—a Juanes song from a nearby radio, a barking dog, the dull banging of a hammer, the ripple of voices, the hush of the breeze. Here, it was as if I was sealed into a noiseless box, and even when I opened a window, all I could hear was the rhythmic whisper of cars driving on the nearby road.

I turned on the television for company and studied people's mouths as they spoke in English, trying my best to replicate the sounds, even though I had no idea what they were saying. And they spoke so fast! I wasn't sure if I was mouthing individual words or bunches of them strung together like grapes.

After a while, I turned the television off and wandered into the kitchen. I pulled out my comal and thought, Maybe I'll make something. Something to remind me of home. But I didn't have any of the ingredients I needed, so I just stood there, staring at the flat cast-iron pan, feeling homesickness charge at me like a roaring wave, filling my nostrils and my ears, threatening to knock me down. I took a deep breath. I would do something else, then. I would go out. This was my life now, I told myself, and I was going to have to figure out how to spend my days. I had to learn how to outrun the wave. Or else I had to learn how to stand far enough inland that it would never approach me in the first place.

I showered and dressed, parted my hair down the center and combed it back into a low ponytail. I dabbed candelilla wax on my lips from the small tin pot I had brought with us. I inspected myself in the mirror, pinching my cheeks to flush them and baring my teeth to make sure they were clean. Then I picked up my purse and headed toward the door.

We needed more food, but the only place I knew where to get any was the gas station, and I didn't want to go there again, so I stood outside on the balcony, my hands around the metal railing, and tried to think of something else. I looked up at the clear sky and listened to the low roar of cars and semi-trucks headed to places I didn't know, driven by people I had never seen. I closed my eyes, feeling the warmth of the sun on my face. It's the same sun that shone on us at home, I told myself. The same sun.

Then, from below, I heard the rickety sound of wheels against the pavement. When I opened my eyes and looked down, I saw the boy from the gas station riding his skateboard, pushing himself up the slight incline to our parking lot where the gravel changed to asphalt. As quickly and as quietly as I could, I slipped back into the apartment. What was he doing here? I snuck over to the front window to watch him. He stopped in the middle of the lot and stomped his foot against the tail of the board, flipping it up into his hand. He stood like that, calmly, and stared at our apartment door. Had he seen me? Had he recognized me? Had he come here because he was looking for us? But how had he known where we lived? Had he followed us that day, after the gas station? I was breathing fast. Calm down, Alma, I told myself. Maybe it's only a coincidence. Maybe it's not even the same boy. But when I curled around the side of the window again to peer at him, I was sure. I could see the tattoo, the navy blue ink of it, winding up his neck.

He didn't move for at least five minutes. I kept expecting him to turn around, to look at the other apartments, but he only stood with his hand gripping the top of his skateboard and stared at our door. As if he were waiting for us. For Maribel.

At last, he spit on the ground and dropped the skateboard with a clatter. He turned around and pushed off, jumping the curb at the edge of the lot, and glided down to the gravel.

I took a deep breath. What had that been about? Was it only that he liked Maribel or was there something else?

When I was sure he was gone, I stepped back outside. At the end of the balcony, a man was standing with his arms crossed, looking grimly at the parking lot. As soon as he saw me, he raised his hand above his head and waved. I nodded, and he walked toward me.

"I was just coming to find you," he said. "I'm the landlord. Fito Angelino at your service. I have your mailbox key." He pulled a small brass key out of the chest pocket of his shirt and handed it to me.

"Thank you," I said quietly, dropping it into my purse.

"You are okay?" Fito asked. He was slender and sinewy with a pointy gray goatee.

"Yes," I said. "I just . . . I thought I saw someone."

"You mean that boy? On his skateboard just now?" Fito shook his head. "Just a local troublemaker. Un alborotador. He's always hanging around by the Shell station. The 7-Eleven, too. He lives in Capitol Oaks down the road." Fito looked over his shoulder in the direction the boy had gone. "I don't know what he was doing here." When Fito turned back to me, he said brightly, "But don't worry, Señora. He's nothing to worry about."

I nodded slowly, wanting to believe him.

"You're going somewhere?" Fito asked.

"I don't know," I said.

"You're coming from somewhere, then?"

"No."

"I see. You are confused." Fito chuckled. "Fortunately for you, this is not a confusing area. You have Main Street and all the university students. You have Hockessin with all the gringos. Downtown Wilmington is where most of the blacks live, and Greenville is where all the rich white people stay. Elsmere and Newport are for the lower class. It's all very simple."

"And here?" I asked.

"Here is us! Venezuela, Puerto Rico, Guatemala, Nicaragua, Colombia, México, Panamá, and Paraguay. We have it all."

"All in this building?"

"You'll fit right in," Fito said.

He was jumpy and quick, all sharp angles and sudden movements. I didn't know what to make of him. But there was a certain comfort that came with hearing someone speak Spanish, to understand and to be understood, to not have to wonder what I was missing.

"And don't give a second thought to that boy," he went on. "It's safe here. Very safe."

I realized that Fito was concerned that he'd scared me away and that if he had, he would lose out on the rent he would be getting from us.

"Nothing to worry about," he said again. "Yes?"

"Nothing to worry about," I said, testing the words on my tongue to see if they felt true.

# Mayor

I expected to run into the Rivera girl at school. Not right away, obviously. But sooner or later all the kids who moved into our part of town showed up at school. When Fernando Ramos walked into homeroom the first day of freshman year, he told the teacher to call him Adiós because that's what she'd be saying to him soon anyway. "We never stay anywhere for long," he explained. When Lucia Castillo got here, she spent the whole year as a mute, shuffling from class to class and eating the food her mom made her—pinto beans and rice and tamales—by herself in the corner of the cafeteria. And when Eddie Pabón arrived, he was so excited to be in the United States and out of Guatemala that he took the concept of educational opportunity to another level—another *planet*—and joined every single one of the fourteen clubs at our school, started playing the trumpet in the band, lettered in three sports, volunteered as a hall monitor during his free period, and cozied up to the teachers so much that by the end of the first marking period, he was having bagels with them in the morning in the lounge. People started calling him Lambón Pabón, a nickname he accepted like it was an honor to be called a suck-up.

"You have anyone new in your classes?" I asked my friend William one day.

We were sitting in chemistry lab, waiting to see what happened when we mixed silver nitrate and salt. Everyone had on goggles, and the girls had spent the beginning of class complaining that the elastic straps were messing up their hair. Mine didn't even have a strap, so I had to hold them against my face with my hand.

"There's always someone new," William said. "Can't keep track of them."

"A girl."

"Way to narrow it down."

"Her last name is Rivera," I said. "I think she's Mexican."

"No shit? 'Rivera' sounded Chinese to me." William grinned, and his braces glinted under the fluorescent lights. He was skinny, like me, but he was pale and his brown hair flopped down over his forehead.

"She moved into my building last week—"

"So?"

"—but I haven't seen her at school yet. *So,* I was wondering if you'd seen her."

William snickered. "Oh, I get it now. She must be hot."

"I hardly even saw her."

"Is she a hot taquito?"

"You're a jackass."

"A hot little taquito for little Mayorito." He cracked up at himself. "All warm and soft inside."

I crossed my arms. My goggles fell onto the table. "Forget I even asked," I muttered.

I HAD STOPPED going to soccer practice after the day I crashed and burned in the star drill. I just didn't have it in me to show my face there again. I also didn't have it in me to break the news to my dad, who'd been especially tense and moody lately because he was worried about losing his job at the diner where he worked as a line cook, so for now I was pretending like I was still on the team. Every morning I packed my gym bag and every night over dinner I told my parents about the drills Coach had us doing to gear up for our big games or about Jamal Blair's crazy bicycle kick near the end of a scrimmage or about whatever else I imagined was happening on the field without me. I probably didn't need to try so hard. My parents were so wrapped up in their own problems that they barely even registered me. My mom had decided that she should get a job, just in case my dad really did lose his, an idea that my dad found unacceptable. "I am the provider," he said over and over. "That's all there is to it."

My mom kept having phone conversations with my tía Gloria in Panamá, the two of them brainstorming about positions my mom might qualify for. I'd overhear my mom saying things like "I'm a very capable woman" and "Is it a crime that I should want to help my family?" and "Claro. My life is not only about fulfilling his life. But try getting him to see it that way." Once, after my dad caught an earful of their conversation, he rushed over to the phone base and stabbed the button down with his finger to disconnect the call. I was sitting at the kitchen table. My mom looked at him in shock. "Those phone calls cost a lot of money," he said. To which my mom, the receiver still in her hand, the coiled cord stretched across the room, said, "We could afford them if you would let me get a job." To which my dad thundered, "Ya. ¡Basta, Celia! I don't want to hear about it anymore!" Which sent my mom wailing, and him bellowing in return.

The day I finally met the Rivera girl, I'd broken free of my parents' latest argument to sit outside on the curb and play Tetris on my phone, when my mom stormed out.

"Ven," she said when she saw me.

"Where?"

"I can't be in that apartment anymore."

"But where are we going?"

"Anywhere," she said.

We ended up at the Dollar Tree, mostly because the day before, someone had stolen our entire load of laundry from the washing machine at the Laundromat. Along with a pair of my mom's pajama pants and a few pairs of my boxers, my dad's dingy white briefs and white undershirts had been in the load, too, but my mom, in her simmering anger toward him, told me on the bus on the way to the store that he could buy his own underwear if he wanted it. "He's so good at doing everything for himself, let him do that, too," she said.

We were walking through the aisles, me with an econo-pack of boxers under my arm like a pillow, when I caught sight of her. She was skinny and petite. Big, full lips and a long, thin Indian nose. Black hair that reached down her back in waves. Long-as-hell eyelashes.

I stopped and stared. She was standing in the aisle with all the cheap dinnerware, looking bored while her mom turned over a package of plastic silverware.

"What?" my mom said, glancing at me.

"Nothing," I mumbled, and made a move to keep walking.

But my mom backtracked to see what had snagged my attention. "Who is that?"

I tried to distance myself further. I would just talk to her another time, I thought, preferably one when my mom wasn't around.

"Are those our new neighbors?" my mom asked. And before I

knew it, she was marching toward them, her pocketbook bouncing against her thigh.

"Buenas," she said when she reached them.

The mother turned, surprised.

"I'm Celia Toro and this is my son Mayor," my mom said in Spanish. "You live in our apartment building, no? The Redwood Apartments?"

Sra. Rivera smiled. She was small and plump. Her wavy black hair was slicked back in a ponytail. "Ah! Sí. Redwood. I'm Alma Rivera. And this is Maribel."

Maribel, I said to myself. Forget about how she was dressed— white canvas sneakers straight out of another decade and a huge yellow sweater over leggings—and forget about the fact that her black hair was mussed like she'd just woken up and the fact that she wasn't wearing any makeup or jewelry or anything else that most of the girls in my school liked to pile on. Forget about all of that. She was fucking gorgeous.

My heart was jackhammering so hard I thought people from the next aisle were going to start complaining about the noise. Then I remembered the package of underwear I was carrying. In case there was any question, across the front of the plastic in big, black letters, it was labeled "Boxer Shorts. Size X-Small." I shuttled the package behind my back.

"I hope you're not looking for food," my mom said. "You won't find much of it in this store. There's a Mexican market nearby, though. Gigante. It probably has everything you're looking for."

"We bought food at the gas station," Sra. Rivera said.

"The gas station! Ay, no. And what have you been eating for dinner? Gasoline?"

This was my mom's attempt at a joke, and thankfully Sra.

Rivera laughed. "Almost as bad," she said. "Canned beans and hot dogs and something the Americans call salsa."

"Wait until you try the American tortillas," my mom said. "Horrible."

I was trying not to look at Maribel, or at least to pretend like I wasn't looking, but my gaze kept brushing over her, watching as she stood still, her hands folded in front of her. I thought I should probably say something to her, you know, just to be neighborly, but she was clearly so far out of my league that I was having trouble remembering how to work my mouth.

I put one hand in my pants pocket, trying to seem cool. She didn't even look at me. Whatever I said, it had to be good, something that would make her think I had game. Finally, I blurted out, "You just moved in."

Sra. Rivera glanced at me. Maribel barely looked up.

Great. I was an asshole. "You just moved in"? That's what I'd come up with?

"To our building," I went on. Jesus.

She stared at me, her face as blank as a wall.

"Yeah," I said, and looked at my feet in humiliation. What was wrong with me? I should just keep my mouth shut from now on. Which is exactly what I did after that. Our moms talked while I stared at my shoes—my brother's old black-and-white Adidas that I always thought looked cool and retro but at the moment just seemed stupid and old—and counted the minutes until we could get out of there. Then, through my fog of embarrassment, I heard her mom say something about the Evers School.

I looked up and saw my mom raise her eyebrows. "Did you say Evers?"

"Yes," Sra. Rivera said.

I looked at the girl again. Evers? That was the school for retards. We all called it the Turtle School.

My mom said, "Of course. Yes. That's a great school. She'll be very happy there," and smiled a little too big.

The girl pulled her arms all the way into the body of her yellow sweater so that the empty sleeves hung like banana peels, and I saw it was true. There *was* something wrong with her. I never would have guessed it. I mean, to look at her . . . it didn't seem possible.

My mom changed the subject after that, telling Sra. Rivera where to find the cheapest hair salon and the best Goodwill and how to get to the nearest Western Union. She told her to steer clear of the sandwich shop at the end of Main Street because Ynez Mercado, who lived in our building, had found a hair in the hoagie she'd bought there, and of course she told her about the horrors we'd just experienced with the Laundromat. Sra. Rivera repeated "Thank you" anytime my mom gave her an opening, and finally my mom wrapped up by telling her our unit number and encouraging them to stop by anytime. "I'm almost always home," she said. I guess she couldn't help herself, because she added pointedly, "My husband likes it that way."

# Benny Quinto

My name is Benny Quinto. I came from Nicaragua, baby. The Land of Lakes and Volcanoes. Been here eight years almost to the day.

Back in Nicaragua I was studying to be in the priesthood. I thought I heard God calling my name from up in the clouds somewhere, man, and I thought he was telling me I was the chosen one. This deep, booming voice. I wasn't even high. Drugs hadn't come into my life yet. But I think I must have been hallucinating or something, because I've had conversations with God since then and He's like, Nope, don't know what you're talking about, Benny. Never said all that about you being the one. Sorry to disappoint.

A few buddies of mine left Nicaragua to come make some real bones over here. Wasn't no money for pinoleros like us back home. Politically, you know, it wasn't so bad anymore. Somoza was long gone, the contras were nothing but a memory. But leaving the poverty of Nicaragua to go to the richest country in the world didn't take much convincing.

I left when I was twenty. Told a dude I would pay him two thousand dollars to bring me over, three hundred up front. Took me a while to scrape it together. Three hundred dollars! In Nicaragua you could live off that for a while. I'm ashamed to admit it, but I stole some of it from the church. Stuffed the offering envelopes up under my shirt one week when I was supposed to be doing my Eucharistic Minister duties and walked out with it. I was gonna do what I had to. I'm like that. Get something in my head and it's like some kind of block. No way to get around it. I just have to bulldoze through.

I got shunted into this house in Arizona until I could pay the rest of the money. I mean, they told us we were in Arizona. It was me and twelve other guys. But we coulda been in Russia for all we knew. We coulda still been in México, which is where we had to come up through to get over. It's like a funnel. Woulda been nice if Nicaragua bordered with the U.S. but it doesn't, so up through México I went.

That house in Arizona, that place was intense. I didn't see the sun for, like, weeks, and Arizona is one of those places that might as well be *on* the sun, that's how sunny it is, so it's nuts that we never saw it. The blinds were shut and there were heavy bed-spreads over all the windows. And me and those guys, we were like cockroaches, crawling over each other at all hours of the day. There was no room to move. Just sit tight, keep the faith. I don't even know why we had to pay so much money. I mean, it wasn't no Ritz-Carlton. Wasn't even no Ritz cracker box. But that's the thing. It's just extortion. Top to bottom.

I wanted to get the hell out of there, so I called an uncle I used to be close with—I mean he used to come to my birthday parties when I was a kid and he would take me to the beach sometimes and let me play in the water while he smoked and hit on girls—but he didn't have the funds. I didn't even bother to ask my mom and pop. Those two never had nothing. You know how the gringos say it? No dee-nair-oh moo-chah-choh. If that weren't the truth, I never would have left Nicaragua to begin with.

One of the guys in the house started dealing for the smugglers. He earned out his fee in two weeks. I didn't know how else I was gonna get out of there, so I signed up, too. Figured I'd burn through it, you know, just *get it done,* until I had enough to leave, and then I'd be on to bigger and better things. Problem is, you get a taste for that kind of money and it's hard to go back to anything else.

I was out on the streets in Phoenix. We had certain places we always hit up. White kids who wanted to score. Came with their parents' money rolled up in their fists, acting all sly as they handed it over, thinking they were so street, but the truth was you could name your price with those kids and whatever you told them, they would pay. They didn't know any better, most of them. There were some real junkies who came by, too. Some pretty hard dudes. I got tangled up with a few of them once— just a stupid fight—and the next thing I knew, I woke up one morning busted out of my mind, bleeding out my side. I'd been stabbed and didn't even know it. That's when I decided it had to end.

I hitched a ride out of Arizona with a guy who was driving to Baltimore. But the drug scene there was wicked. Ten times worse than in Arizona. I was trying so hard to be on the straight and narrow. I was talking to God about it all the time. I was like, Where's your deep voice now, God, when I really need help? And then I swear I heard it. He told me to split. To where? I asked Him. Funny thing about God, though. He doesn't always give you the answers, not right when you ask for them anyway. 'Cause I didn't hear nothing. But I knew. I gotta leave. So I went down to the Greyhound station and said, Here's how much money I have. Give me a ticket. And the bus brought me to

Delaware. It's not paradise, but at least here I can be at peace. It was never like that for me in Nicaragua. And not at my first few stops here neither. I flip burgers now at the King. Used to be at Wendy's but they gave me, oh, man, the worst shifts, so I switched it up. A person needs regular sleep, you know! I ain't getting any younger! But I feel settled here. I took a couple nasty turns, but I ended up all right.

# Alma

Maribel took achievement tests and cognitive tests. She went through evaluations with both a psychologist and an educational diagnostician. They gave her written exams in Spanish to see whether she could write a sentence, whether she could write a paragraph, whether she could do certain math problems. We had a meeting where the psychologist asked if there had been any complications while I was pregnant with Maribel. She asked if Maribel had met her developmental milestones as a child. When did she start to talk? When did she start to walk? Phyllis sat next to me, translating everything. Frustrated, I replied, "She wasn't born like this. It's all just because of the accident. Don't you see it in the reports?" And the psychologist said yes, yes, she saw it, but these were standard questions that she was required to ask.

And then, after everything, the district told us what we already knew: Maribel had a traumatic brain injury that was classified as mild, but it was severe enough that she was eligible for special education services. She would be transferred to Evers.

I nearly wept with joy when I heard the news. Now, I thought—finally!—we would move forward.

They sent a different bus to get her, one that was stumpy and brown. I saw her off the first day and was waiting for her when she came home that afternoon.

"How was it?" I asked.

"What?"

"How was school?"

"Fine."

"Is there anything else you want to tell me?"

"I'm tired," she said, and I nodded, deflated because I had expected more. I had expected her to come home full of energy, gushing about the other students and her teacher and how much she had learned. I had wanted the school to act like a switch, something that would turn her on again from the second she walked through the door.

"Give it time," Arturo told me later that night when he detected the disappointment in my voice. "You're always so impatient. It was only the first day."

Every afternoon Maribel brought home reports from the school that Phyllis translated into Spanish. They were formal and brief and said things like "Maribel is unresponsive and unengaged, even when she is directly addressed in Spanish." "She is withdrawn and rarely interacts with other students, even in activities that require no verbal communication." "Maribel has a limited attention span and often fiddles with her pencil or other desk supplies during class time."

Day after day I read the letters, hoping for better news, trying to believe that eventually it would come.

After school, I sat with Maribel at the kitchen table and helped her with her homework. In addition to everything else, she was expected to learn English, and one day the teacher sent home an English worksheet with nine boxes, each filled with a drawing of a face making a different expression. At the top of the sheet was a story in Spanish about a young Chinese boy, Yu Li.

"Do you know who this is?" I asked Maribel.

She shook her head.

"Can you read the story?"

"Okay."

I waited while she stared at the paper. Was she reading? I wondered. Or just looking at the words? I said, "Why don't you read it out loud?"

She did, although haltingly. I had to help her with any word longer than four letters. It was a story about how Yu Li came to the United States from China with his parents. He went to school one day and some of the kids taunted him and some of them were kind. But Yu Li didn't know English, so he was bewildered.

When Maribel was finished, I said, "Now you need to write down words that describe how Yu Li was feeling in the story." Maribel looked at me. There was an eyelash on her cheek. I picked it off and held it on the tip of my finger, then blew it away. "Do you remember what happened in the story? What was one emotion Yu Li felt?"

"I don't know."

"But you read the story to me."

"I don't remember."

"Do you need to read it again?"

"I already read it."

"I know. But you said you didn't remember anything."

"Okay."

"Maribel, how did Yu Li feel in the story?"

She shrugged.

"Do you remember when he went to school?"

"Yes."

"And what happened to him at school?"

"I don't know."

"Were the kids nice to him?"

"Yes."

"And how do you think that made Yu Li feel?"

"Who is Yu Li?"

I took a deep breath. It's okay, Alma, I told myself. It's only the beginning of the year. She's just getting started.

When Arturo came home later and kicked off his boots, he asked what we were working on.

"I don't know," Maribel said.

"Math?" he guessed.

"Yes," she said.

"We're working on English today," I said.

"¡Inglés!" Arturo beamed. "Once you learn English, you can teach it to me, too. Here, does this sound like something? Howdy dere, pardner." He made a clownish face, and I knew he was trying to get Maribel to laugh, trying to extract the tiniest hint of the girl she used to be. It was something we both did. We cast lines out again and again hoping to reel something in, anything to sustain us, but she never bit.

Arturo said, "Did you hear me?"

"Yes."

"Did that sound like English?"

"No."

"What?" he said, acting shocked.

"It sounded good to me," I said.

"Thank you," he said.

I wanted him to come to me, to take my hands and kiss my fingers, to run his thumb over my lips, but those weren't the sorts of things we did anymore.

He peeled off his socks and unbuttoned his shirt.

"Dinner will be ready soon," I said. "I made tacos de bistec."

He leaned his boots against the wall. "Okay."

I waited for more—I was desperate for more—but he only pushed his boot back with his toe when it started to slip and walked down the hall to shower.

DURING THE DAY, I kept myself busy by cleaning and watching television. I had found a Spanish-language channel that, if I angled the antenna just right, I could see through the static. I cooked lunch for myself—pork and beans, or chicken basted in onions and orange juice, or on days when I was feeling lazy, soup from a can—and sat at the table alone eating it. I got up afterwards and cleaned again. Once, I used the prepaid cell phone we had bought in a market in Pátzcuaro and called my parents, even though the phone was supposed to be reserved for emergencies only. We had called them just after we arrived to tell them we got here safely, but we hadn't spoken again since. My mother shrieked when she heard my voice and I laughed at hearing my father in the background dashing to my mother in alarm, asking what was wrong. They wanted to know how we were doing, what it was like here, how Maribel was adjusting. I imagined the two of them crowded around the receiver in their small kitchen, the kitchen I had grown up eating in with its half-moon window over the sink and the clay rooster my mother kept on the counter next to her bean pot and a jelly jar filled with flowers. How far away it seemed. My mother brought me up to date on the latest gossip from town—Reyna Ortega finally had her baby and they'd been invited to the bautismo, a new assistant chef had started at Mistongo, two hogs had gotten loose from the Cotima farm—but hearing it all only made me feel more disconnected from Pátzcuaro, oddly disappointed to hear that life was going on even without us there.

In the two weeks since we'd been in the apartment, many of the neighbors—mostly the women—had stopped by to introduce themselves. Quisqueya Solís arrived with a platter of coconut cookies in her arms—besitos de coco, she told me—and when I invited her in, she walked through the apartment slowly, letting her gaze sweep over our few pieces of furniture, and then refused to sit when I offered a chair, explaining as she patted her fiery red hair that she had errands to run. Nelia Zafón knocked on the door and clasped one of my hands between hers, apologizing for taking so long to stop by and assuring me that everyone was happy to have us here. Ynez Mercado stood in the doorway and told me if there was anything we needed not to hesitate to ask. I explained that we had acquired some things along the way, but when she heard that Arturo, Maribel, and I were sharing one mattress, she insisted on bringing over an old sleeping bag she and her husband had. "It's from José's navy days," she said. "It kept him safe, and it will keep whoever sleeps in it safe, too." I smiled and said, "Thank you. That sounds perfect for Maribel."

When no one came, I went out, determined to explore and acclimate myself to the town. A few times I went to the Laundromat—despite Celia's warning, it was still the nearest one—and sat with my hands in my lap while the load ran, watching the clothes spin in the portholed dryers lined up along the back wall. People walked in and out—a brown-skinned man chewing a toothpick, a motorcyclist wearing a leather vest, a woman with two children—their baskets hoisted up against their stomachs, their clothes spilling over the sides like seaweed. I yearned for them to talk to me, especially anyone who looked as though they might speak Spanish. I readied myself to say hola if anyone so much as glanced my way, but day after day people walked by without acknowledging me in the least.

I walked to Gigante some afternoons and pulled mangoes and chiles from wooden crates, holding them to my nose, inhaling the scents of home. In the back, I stared at the fish and the lobsters in their giant glass tank and when the man behind the meat counter asked in Spanish if there was something he could get me—everything was recién matada, fresh, he assured me—I told him no. "Too expensive," I said, smiling sheepishly. "We have a sale," he said. "It's only for beautiful women," and I laughed in spite of myself.

And sometimes I went to the small church we had found, St. Thomas More Oratory, with its water-stained drop ceiling and its folding chairs in place of pews, and sat alone in the empty sanctuary, reciting the same prayers over and over, imploring God to listen. I know I'm not very important, I told Him. I know You have other things to worry about. But please forgive me for all that I've done. Please give me the strength to fix it. Please let her get better. And please let Arturo forgive me, too. In Jesus' name. Amen.

ONE AFTERNOON I made chicharrones and carried them over to Celia's apartment.

She clapped her hands together in delight when she saw me and motioned for me to come inside.

"These are for you," I said, holding out a foil-covered plate.

She lifted a corner of the foil and sniffed. "Sabroso," she said.

I loved how full her home felt, embroidered pillows on the

couches, a curio stacked with milk glass bowls and recuerdos and folded tablecloths, red votives along the windowsills, spidery potted plants, woven rugs, unframed posters of Panamá beaches on the walls, a box of rinsed beer bottles on the floor, a small radio on top of the refrigerator, a plastic bag filled with garlic hanging from a doorknob, a collection of spices clustered on a platter on the counter. The great accumulation of things almost hid the cracks in the walls and the stains on the floor and the scratches that clouded the windows.

"Mi casa es tu casa," Celia joked as I looked around. "Isn't that what the Americans say?"

She poured cold, crackling Coca-Colas for both of us, and we sat on the couch, sipping them and taking small bites of the chicharrones. She looked just as she had the first time I met her: impeccably pulled together, with a face full of makeup, fuchsia lips, chestnut-brown chin-length hair curled at the ends and tucked neatly behind her ears, small gold earrings. So unlike most of my friends at home, who used nothing but soap on their faces and aloe on their hands and who kept their hair pulled into ponytails, like mine, or simply combed after it had been washed and left to air-dry.

Celia told me about the provisions we would need for winter— heavy coats and a stack of comforters and something called long underwear that made me laugh when she tried to describe it— and about a place called the Community House where they offered immigrant services if we needed them. She gossiped about people in the building, telling me that Nelia Zafón was in a relationship with a gringo half her age and that, when they first came here, Celia's husband, Rafael, thought José Mercado was gay. Celia said, "He and Ynez have been married for more than thirty years!" She laughed. She told me that Micho Alvarez, who she claimed always wore his camera around his neck, had a sensitive side, despite the fact that he might look big and burly, and that Benny Quinto, who was close friends with Micho, had studied to be a priest years ago. She said that Quisqueya dyed her hair, which was hardly news—I had assumed as much when I met her. "It's the most unnatural shade of red," Celia said. "Rafael says it looks like she dumped a pot of tomato sauce on her head." She chortled. "Quisqueya is a busybody, but it's only because she's so insecure. She doesn't know how to connect with people. Don't let her put you off."

Celia began telling me about when she and Rafael and her boys had come here from Panamá, fifteen years ago, after the invasion.

"So your son, he was born there?" I asked.

"I have two boys," she said. "Both of them were born there. Enrique, my oldest, is away at college on a soccer scholarship. And there's Mayor, who you met. He's nothing at all like his brother. Rafa thinks we might have taken the wrong baby home from the hospital." She forced a smile. "Just a joke, of course."

She stood and lifted a framed picture from the end table. "This is from last summer before Enrique went back to school," she said, handing it to me. "Micho took it for us."

In the photo were two boys: Mayor, whom I recognized from the store, small for his age with dark, buzzed hair and sparkling eyes, and Enrique, who stood next to his brother with his arms crossed, the faint shadow of a mustache above his lip.

"What about you?" Celia asked. "Do you have other children besides your daughter?"

"Only her," I said, glancing at my hands around the glass. The perspiration from the ice had left a ring of water on the thigh of my pants.

"And she's going . . ." Celia trailed off, as though she didn't want to say it out loud.

"To Evers."

Celia nodded. She looked like she didn't know what to say next, and I felt a mixture of embarrassment and indignation.

"It's temporary," I said. "She only has to go there for a year or two."

"You don't have to explain it to me."

"She's going to get better."

"I've heard it's a good school."

"I hope so. It's why we came."

Celia gazed at me for a long time before she said, "When we left Panamá, it was falling apart. Rafa and I thought it would be better for the boys to grow up here. Even though Panamá was where we had spent our whole lives. It's amazing, isn't it, what parents will do for their children?"

She put her hand on mine. A benediction. From then, we were friends.

I WAS TIRED of going to my usual places, so one rainy morning I went instead to the Community House, just to see what they offered.

I took the bus Celia told me to take and walked into a building filled with white tables and chairs. Beige computers sat on some of the tabletops and a row of beanbag chairs slouched along one wall like giant gumdrops. The receptionist asked me in Spanish, "Are you here for the English class?"

"English class?"

"I'm sorry. Our new session starts today, so I just assumed that's why you were here."

I was about to say no, but I stopped myself. Maybe it was luck that brought me here, or maybe it was providence. I envisioned myself in the school uniform I used to wear when I was a girl—the starched blue shirt and navy vest, the pleated skirt, the knee-high socks—and all of a sudden I liked the idea of being a student again. Maybe I would even learn enough to be able to help Maribel with her homework.

"Yes," I said. "I am."

The woman directed me to a room behind her.

A few people were already inside, seated at desks, and they glanced at me as I walked in. I smiled at them and sat with my purse on my lap, fiddling with the clasp until the teacher entered. She strode to the front and grinned at us with big horse teeth.

"Welcome, everybody," she said in English. "I'm your teacher, Mrs. Shields."

Of course, at the time I didn't understand what she was saying. I only learned it later. That first day, the words were merely sounds in the air, broken like shards of glass, beautiful from a certain angle and jagged from another. They didn't mean anything to me. Still, I liked the sound of them.

No one in the class said anything in return.

The teacher, in Spanish this time, said, "Hola a todos."

"Hola," a few people replied.

She put her hands on her hips. "We need to wake you people up," she said in Spanish. "¡Hola!" She cupped one hand to her ear.

More people responded this time.

"¡Hola!" she yelled once more.

"¡Hola!" I said.

Profesora Shields threw her hands together. "Terrific. For today," she explained, "I'm going to speak in Spanish, but as the class goes on, I'll speak it less and less. That will be okay, because you'll understand English more and more. You see? This is how it works." She used her hands to mimic a scale. "Less and less," she said, lowering her right hand. "More and more," she said, raising her left. "Now some people will tell you that English is a difficult language. But don't let them scare you. I congratulate you for being here at all and for having the courage to try. Bravo! Give yourself a round of applause."

We all looked at one another.

"Go on," she said.

We clapped lightly. Is this what Maribel was doing in her school? I wondered. Is this what school was like in the United States? It was like theater.

Profesora Shields called out greetings and had us repeat the words. Hello. Good-bye. My name is. What is your name? How are you? I'm fine, and you? Then she split us into groups of two and told us to practice. I was paired with a woman named Dulce, who was missing some of her teeth, so when she spoke she bowed her head self-consciously and directed the sounds at the floor. I asked her in Spanish, "Where are you from?"

"Chiapas," she said.

"¿Eres mexicana?" I asked.

She nodded.

"Hello," I said, in English, trying out the syllables on my tongue.

Profesora Shields had told us to pronounce the letter $h$, even at the beginning of words. "I know it won't sound natural to you," she said, "but you need to work to get it out. It's important."

I repeated the word. "Hello."

In Spanish, Dulce said, "My son lives here with his wife. They brought me here." She peeked at me. "Hello," she tried.

"I came from Michoacán," I said. "With my husband and our daughter."

"My son's wife just had a baby boy."

"¡Ah, felicitaciones!"

"That's why they brought me. To help take care of the baby."

"What's his name?"

"Jonathan. I wanted Carlos, but they said no, he's an American baby."

"Maybe Jonathan Carlos," I said.

Dulce smiled. "Hello," she said.

"Hello."

"How jou are?" she asked.

"Fine, and jou?"

English was such a dense, tight language. So many hard letters, like miniature walls. Not open with vowels the way Spanish was. Our throats open, our mouths open, our hearts open. In English, the sounds were closed. They thudded to the floor. And yet, there was something magnificent about it. Profesora Shields explained that in English there was no usted, no tu. There was only one word—you. It applied to all people. Everyone equal. No one higher or lower than anyone else. No one more distant or more familiar. You. They. Me. I. Us. We. There were no words that changed from feminine to masculine and back again depending on the speaker. A person was from New York. Not a woman from New York, not a man from New York. Simply a person.

I was still thinking about it as I got on the bus after class, mouthing the words while I sat, trying to accustom myself to the feel of them on my tongue, the shape of them as they escaped into the air. Profesora Shields had given us all pocket-sized Spanish/English dictionaries to carry with us so that we could look things up with ease. "Practice, practice, practice!" she urged. I turned the tissue-thin pages, reading words at random. To trade, cambiar. Blanket, cobija. To grow, crecer. Outside, a light rain had begun to fall, and after a few minutes I closed the dictionary and watched the drops of water skid diagonally across the window as I listened for the driver to announce "Kirkwood," which was my stop. But after a while—longer than it had taken on the way there—he still hadn't said it. I sat up in the seat and looked around. Were we on a different route? I rubbed my hand over the foggy window and peered out. But of course I didn't recognize anything. Relax, I told myself. The only reason you don't recognize anything is because you don't know anything here yet. I stayed put for a few more stops, fixing my gaze out the window while the bus rumbled along. I watched people get off, still more people get on. The driver shouted out other words, but never anything that sounded like "Kirkwood."

The man sitting next to me was wearing a watch that read 1:57 in small, glowing numbers. Maribel would be home at 2:15. I was supposed to be there to meet her when her bus dropped her off. Panic fluttered in my chest. What was I going to do? I must have gotten on the wrong bus. I had a feeling I was only getting farther and farther from the apartment now. I had to turn around.

I stood and tugged the cord that ran above the seats. The bell dinged. I squeezed past the man next to me and walked to the front of the bus, trying to stay calm. The driver pulled over and opened the doors.

Now what? I thought once I got off. I was standing on a deserted road in the rain. There were no houses or buildings as far as I could see, only wheat-colored fields patchy with dirt and cracked wooden telephone poles with drooping black wires strung between them. Dios, I said to myself. Where was I? Why had I decided to get off the bus in the middle of the country? I could be killed out here and no one would know the difference. I shivered. Then I forced myself to laugh. Who was going to kill me? The telephone pole?

Before long, I heard a sound and looked up to see a car approaching. I watched as it neared and got louder, then sliced by and faded into the distance again. I told myself, It's a good sign. If there was one car, there will be another. You just have to wait.

The rain was falling harder now—my hair and clothes were damp—and I crossed to the other side of the street and stood, clutching my purse. Maybe I could call the school and tell them not to let Maribel get off the bus if I wasn't there in time. The translator, Phyllis, had told me that for students Maribel's age the school didn't require that anyone be there to meet them. She was allowed to get off the bus whether I was there or not. But maybe if I explained that this was a special circumstance? Maybe the bus driver would wait?

I dialed the school and when a voice answered, I said in English, "Hello?"

"Hello?" the woman on the other end said.

I didn't know how to say, "I'm looking for my daughter," so I just blurted out her name. "Maribel Rivera," I said.

"Hello?" the woman said again.

"Is there someone there who can help me?" I asked in Spanish. There was silence from the other end.

I reached in my purse and pulled out the dictionary, flipping through the pages to find the English word for "help."

The woman on the other end said something I couldn't understand.

In Spanish I said, "My name is Alma Rivera. My daughter Maribel goes to your school. Is there someone who speaks Spanish?"

I waited for a response while I fumbled again with the dictionary, searching for any word that might make a difference.

"I need to speak to someone," I said. "I need the bus driver to wait."

The woman said something else that I couldn't understand and I nearly wept in frustration. They were only words. I had the sense that I should have been able to unpack them, that there was only a thin veneer separating me from their meaning, and yet the veneer was impenetrable.

A second later, I heard the clap of plastic against a hard surface, as if the woman had put the phone down. I waited to see if someone else was coming, someone who could help me, but what I heard next was the beeping of a disconnected line.

In a fit of defeat, I threw both my phone and the dictionary to the ground, watching them skid and spin across the wet pavement. Why hadn't I called Phyllis instead of the school? I was wasting time. But when I picked up the phone, the screen showed that there was no reception. I held it up like a torch and squinted. Still nothing. Even after walking a few steps in every direction, I couldn't get it back. Chingada madre! I should have known better. It was a cheap piece of plastic, but it was all we had been able to afford since Arturo had insisted that we buy two—one for each of us—to be able to use while we were here.

Rain pattered against the ground like the sound of applause.

The pebbles along the shoulder of the road where I stood were slick and glistening. Weeds bent toward the earth. I crossed my arms over my chest to cover my blouse, which was wet enough now that anyone could have seen through it to my bra, then uncrossed them again when I remembered there was no one here to see me.

What time was it? How long had I been out here? I imagined Maribel getting off the bus, standing in the middle of the parking lot, her backpack hitched high on her thin shoulders, confused because I wasn't there. Then I imagined the boy from the gas station skating up the way he had the other day, looking for her, and dread welled inside me.

Why hadn't I stopped that car earlier? I should have run into the middle of the street, waving my arms. I shouldn't have let it pass by.

Frantically, I scanned the road in both directions. I started walking, glancing over my shoulder every few seconds to see if perhaps another car was coming down the road behind me. I jogged for a while until I was out of breath. How late was it now? I checked the phone again, but there was still no reception. I punched all the buttons and held it to my ear, praying for a tone. But still nothing. I leaned my head back and screamed at the sky. A useless scream. No one could hear me out here. And then I started crying, my tears falling as dully as the rain.

I heard it before I saw it: the rumble and the whir. I stopped and turned around. A bus. It wasn't just a mirage, was it? Was it the same bus that had dropped me off before? It didn't matter. It was going the opposite direction now, the direction I needed to go, and it was coming toward me. I waved my arms and started crying harder. In Spanish I yelled, "Stop! Please stop for me!" I didn't care that the driver wouldn't understand what I was saying. He would see me and stop, wouldn't he? And when he did, I stood on the road and shouted up at him, "Kirkwood?" He nodded and I stepped up onto the bus.

TWENTY MINUTES LATER, I arrived, soaking wet and shivering, at my stop. I ran so fast to the apartment that my lungs burned.

"Maribel!" I yelled as I flew into the parking lot. "Mari!"

It must have been 2:45 by then, maybe later. I dashed up to our front door, but it was still locked. Through the window, I could see that the lights were off. I turned and shouted again. "Maribel!" I thought someone would hear me and open their door—Nelia or Ynez or Fito if he was home—but to my dismay, no one did. I stood on the balcony and scanned the apartments, wondering if Maribel was inside one of them. Maybe someone had seen her and brought her inside. Celia, I decided. I should try her first.

I hurried so fast down the wet metal staircase that I nearly slipped, but as I started toward the Toros' apartment, suddenly there she was. And right behind her, Mayor Toro.

I gasped and ran to her, lifting her sunglasses off, cupping her face in my hands, studying it for bruises, for anything that might seem amiss. She winced as I turned her head from side to side.

"She's okay," Mayor said.

"What were—?"

"I saw her when she got off the bus. I was just talking to her for a little while."

"Are you okay?" I asked Maribel.

She nodded and stared at me with her wide owl eyes.

I felt the punch of relief, swift and firm to my gut. She was okay. Maybe it should have bothered me more, the thought of Maribel out here alone with Mayor. But as boys went, Mayor struck me as the harmless sort. Besides, I was so overcome with gratitude in that moment that there wasn't room for much else. She was okay. I didn't even have the heart to ask whether she was sure because I didn't want to give her the chance to take it back. She had said she was okay and that was all I wanted.

# Mayor

The Riveras started going to the same Mass as us, and afterwards my mom usually invited them over for lunch at our house. They protested the first time—"No, no, it's too much, we don't want to impose"—but my mom, who was always eager to make new friends in this country, wore them down eventually, and the three of them got off the bus with us and walked straight to our apartment, laying their coats over the back of the couch, getting comfortable on the chairs my mom pulled in from the kitchen and arranged around the living room.

My mom made sure everyone had drinks and then she got busy, week after week, making her special party food—ham sandwiches on white bread with the crusts trimmed off. She cut them into triangles and speared them with plastic toothpicks, then carried them out on a ceramic platter that she passed around to everyone along with square white napkins that we used to catch the crumbs.

My dad, on the other hand, didn't let the presence of the Riveras interfere with his usual routine. He turned on the television, cracked open a can of beer, and put his socked feet up on the coffee table. He watched soccer if it was on, which inevitably led to him talking about Enrique and bragging about the latest goal my brother had scored against Georgetown or the assist he'd had in the big game against Virginia, which was Maryland's main rival, and how almost every week Enrique's name was in the paper under the sports stats that were listed for every high school and college within a hundred-mile radius of us. "Mayor plays soccer, too," he said. "But I haven't seen his name in the paper yet." He didn't say it to be mean. It was the truth, even though not for the reason he thought, and he looked at me with pity. "But he's getting better. Aren't you?" he asked. And I struggled to nod through the rush of guilt I felt about lying to him and the humiliation I felt about sucking so bad.

When soccer wasn't on, my dad turned to football. One week during an Eagles game when Sr. Rivera cheered Donovan McNabb on, my dad rode him, saying, "Arturo, it's no use. I've been watching this game since I got to this country, and yes, the Eagles are a bird, but let me tell you, they no can fly." He said the last part in English, to be funny, and even though I'm not sure Sr. Rivera understood him, he was nice enough to laugh.

In the beginning I ate the crustless sandwiches and opened a can of Coke, then excused myself to my bedroom to do homework or to listen to my iPod. My mom would track me down sometimes and give a disapproving look and try to convince me that it would be nice if I came out and talked to Maribel because she and I were basically the same age and because she was new here so she would probably appreciate me talking to her. "Don't you think that would be nice?" my mom asked. But I didn't think so. I mean, maybe it would have been nice for Maribel, but otherwise what was the point? Looking at her, sure. I could have looked at her all day. But actually having conversations with her? That was a different story.

Then one week I was walking home from my bus stop in the rain when, from behind, someone said, "Where you going?"

I turned around and saw Garrett Miller grinning at me, his skateboard under his arm.

"Home," I said.

"Back to Mexico?"

"I'm not from Mexico."

"My dad says all you people are from Mexico."

When I didn't respond, Garrett said, "What are you looking at?"

Garrett didn't have a single friend that I knew of. His older brother had gone to Iraq with the air force and had come back in a body bag. The rumor at school was that Garrett's mom had a breakdown after that. She just couldn't handle it, so she'd split and hadn't been back since. Supposedly Garrett's dad started drinking so much that he lost his job. They must have been living off benefits from the military or something. Or maybe they were on welfare by now. I didn't know.

I started walking away. I could hear Garrett trailing me, the shuffle of his sneakers on the pavement, the drag of his jeans. What was I supposed to do? Was he going to follow me all the way up to my door? What did he want? And then I heard another sound—the low rumble of an engine. I looked back and saw a bus, Maribel's bus, turning off the road. It drove past Garrett and me and pulled up in front of the building. I watched as Maribel got off, walking down the steps like a deer carefully picking its way down the side of a mountain. At the sight of her, I forgot about Garrett for a second. She might have been one of the Evers kids, but she was still the prettiest girl I had ever seen in real life.

After the bus bounced back onto the road, Maribel just stood in the middle of the parking lot in the drizzling rain. She didn't move.

"Hey," Garrett called.

Maribel turned.

"You remember me? I saw you a few weeks ago at the gas station."

Maribel stared at him.

"What's your name?" Garrett asked.

When she didn't answer, he said, "What's the matter? You don't speak English? ¿No inglés?"

She shook her head.

I watched as Garrett took a step back and surveyed Maribel from head to toe, nodding in appreciation. She didn't squirm, didn't shift, just stood there letting herself be ogled.

"Take off your sunglasses so I can see your eyes," Garrett said, but instead of waiting for her to do it, he pulled her sunglasses off her face himself. When Maribel reached for them, Garrett held them up in the air where she couldn't get them. Reflexively, Maribel put her hand over her eyes.

"What?" Garrett said. "Something wrong with your eyes?"

He pried her hand away and held on to it.

I cringed.

He snaked his head closer to study her face and then pulled back, looking confused. "Something wrong with you?" he said, dropping her hand like he'd just been burned. Then he whistled as if he'd put it together. "That's why you were on that bus, isn't it? You're some kind of retard. How do you say 'retard' in Spanish? Hey!" Garrett said, waving his arm in front of her blank face. "I'm talking to you. Can't you hear?"

I took a step, then stopped. What did I think I was going to do?

Garrett twirled her sunglasses around. "You need these back?"

When Maribel reached for them, Garrett tossed the sunglasses up in a high arc over her head and let them land on the wet pavement. Maribel bent down to get them, and Garrett crowded up behind her, settling his hands on her hips, drawing her against him.

"Hey!" I yelled.

Garrett whipped his head around like he'd forgotten that I was there.

"Leave her alone," I said.

"Fuck you."

"She hasn't done anything to you."

Garrett narrowed his eyes to slits and sauntered toward me, nudging his skateboard along with the toe of his shoe. My heart was thudding so hard it felt like it was taking up my whole chest, but at least I'd gotten him away from Maribel. Over his shoulder, I saw her stand and put her sunglasses back on, pushing them up the bridge of her nose with her finger.

"What are you? Her fucking fairy godmother?" Garrett said. He was right in front of me now, a head taller and at least thirty pounds heavier. I should've just stayed out of it, I thought. Why, why, why didn't I just stay out of it?

"No," I managed to say.

"You wanna be a hero?"

I shook my head.

"Because I was just talking to her," Garrett said. "That's all."

But that wasn't all, and both of us knew it. "I saw you," I said.

Garrett grabbed the collar of my shirt and twisted it into his fist, pulling me close. "Saw what, shitface?"

I didn't dare look in his eyes.

"Couldn't hear you," Garrett said, squeezing my collar until it felt like a noose around my neck.

"Nothing," I managed to get out.

It was probably only a matter of seconds, but it felt like a full minute passed, maybe more, before Garrett finally let me go, sending me stumbling back onto my ass.

"That's what I thought," he said. "Fucking none of your business."

He kicked a spray of pebbles in my direction, then turned around and looked at Maribel, who was still standing basically in the same place she'd been the whole time. "I'm not done with you," he called to her.

He picked up his skateboard and started walking out toward the road, through the gravel.

I brushed myself off and walked over to Maribel. "Are you okay?" I asked.

She nodded.

"Don't pay attention to him," I said. "He's a jerk."

And then we were just standing there, and the rain was still drizzling like static, and I didn't know what to do next.

"Are you going home now?" I finally asked after a traffic jam of silence.

"I'm waiting for my mom."

I looked up and down the length of the building, but besides Maribel and me, no one was around. "Where is she?" I asked.

"Who?"

"Your mom."

"She meets me at the bus."

"Do you think she's in your apartment?"

Maribel shook her head. "I'm meeting her here."

What was I supposed to do? I didn't really want to stand out in the rain with her for who knew how long. Maybe Micho or Benny would walk out and one of them could keep her company. After another minute, though, it was still just her and me, so I said, "Well, let's wait on the fire escape at least. It's covered, so we can get out of the rain."

As soon as we sat on the metal fire escape landing, Maribel slid her backpack off and pulled out a green notebook. She snapped the cap off a pen and started writing, hunched over the paper.

"What's that?" I asked.

"My notebook."

"You're doing homework now?"

"I'm writing."

"About what?"

She shrugged. "The doctors told me to write."

"Like, stories?"

She didn't answer.

"I just finished the new Percy Jackson book, *The Titan's Curse*. Have you heard of it?"

Again, nothing. I couldn't even tell if she was listening to me, but for some reason now I wanted her to. I wanted her to pay attention to me.

"I write sometimes," I went on. "Like, I might write, 'Note to self: Do not touch a habanero pepper, even if your best friend dares you to.'"

Unexpectedly, she smiled. "Habaneros are hot," she said. It was the kind of smile that could wreck a person.

"No kidding," I said. "I learned the hard way."

I couldn't see her eyes because of her sunglasses, but I had the feeling she was staring straight at me.

Then I heard a voice calling her name. Screaming it in panic.

"My mom," she said. She dropped her notebook in her bag and the two of us grabbed our things and walked out to see Sra. Rivera darting across the parking lot like a wild animal.

"Mari!" she said when she laid eyes on us. Her hair was falling out of its ponytail and her face was flushed. She ran to Maribel and put her hands on Maribel's cheeks, turning her head from side to side, examining her.

"She's okay," I said. "I saw her when she got off the bus. I was just talking to her for a little while." I figured there was no reason to tell her about Garrett. I had taken care of it, hadn't I? And she would only freak out if she knew. That's how parents were.

"Maribel?" Sra. Rivera said, looking for confirmation of my story. "You're okay?"

Maribel nodded, and even though Sra. Rivera looked skeptical, she took Maribel by the wrist, leading her up to their apartment while I stood there in the spitting rain and watched them go.

After that, something between Maribel and me changed. I felt this weird protectiveness over her, so on Sundays after church, instead of hiding away in my room like I used to, I made it a point to sit next to her on our brown couch, attempting to have quiet conversations with her and telling stupid jokes in an effort to make her smile again like I had that one time.

One Sunday, while our parents debated the meaning of Father Finnegan's homily that morning, the doorbell rang. When my mom got up to answer it, Quisqueya was standing at the door with a coffee cake in her hands. Ever since the Riveras had moved in, my mom hadn't shown as much interest in Quisqueya as she used to, preferring instead to spend her time with Sra. Rivera. I didn't blame her. I'd never understood why my mom hung out with Quisqueya at all, except that my mom craved friends—any friends—as a way to keep her from feeling lonely here.

"Oh," Quisqueya said, peeking inside, "I didn't know you had company."

"Did you tell me you were coming over?" my mom asked.

"No, but . . . Well, there was a time when I didn't have to make plans to see you."

"I didn't know if I'd forgotten."

"I see."

"Do you want to come in?"

Quisqueya peered into our living room. Sra. Rivera waved.

"No," Quisqueya said.

"Maybe tomorrow morning?" my mom offered. "I'll be here if you want to stop by."

Quisqueya shrank a little and twisted her lips. "Maybe," she said.

My mom was still standing with one hand on the doorknob. When neither Quisqueya nor my mom said anything else, my dad yelled, "Have a good day, Quisqueya!"

"Yes. Well," she said and walked away. I watched her pass by our front window on her way back to her apartment.

My mom closed the door and said to my dad, "You're so bad."

My dad said, "You're lucky I didn't ask her to leave the coffee cake!"

The conversation turned to politics after that, which was all anybody had been talking about lately. The elections had happened a few weeks earlier and everybody we knew had been pulling for Barack Obama. Since she'd become a citizen, my mom had voted in every election—local and federal. She never missed a single one. She would come home and say, "Well, I did my duty. May the best man win." This year, she'd been the first in line at her polling place. She'd worn her American flag sweater, and I'd seen her praying before she walked out the door that morning. "A little extra insurance can't hurt," she'd explained, crossing herself. "En el nombre del Padre, y del Hijo, y del Espíritu Santo. Amén." When she came home she said, "Well, I did my duty. May Obama win, because if it's McCain, I will shoot myself." And then she glued herself to the television all day long to watch the returns.

Even my dad, who, whenever politics came up, usually dismissed the entire topic with his patented line, "All politicians are equally corrupt," showed an interest this year. A few times I even caught him watching the news segments about Obama in the evenings, after he got home from work.

It seemed like everyone in our building was excited. I'd seen José Mercado totter outside one day and plant an Obama/Biden sign in the grass bordering the parking lot, and Fito, who usually had a thing against signs (he'd taken down Benny's Phillies banner at the start of last year's baseball season), let it stand. Micho made sure that all of us who were documented were registered to vote, talking about how important it was that Obama, a black man who looked like no other U.S. president and who had family that came from different places, could possibly lead our country. It meant that we, who also resembled no other U.S. president and who also had family from faraway places, could one day rise up and do the same thing.

"I don't think his ears are so big," my mom said.

"His ears?" Sra. Rivera asked.

"He keeps saying they're big, but I think he's very handsome."

"That's why you voted for him?" my dad said. "Because you think he's handsome?"

"Yes, Rafael. That's why I vote for one politician over another. Because he's handsome. Are you crazy?"

My dad glared at my mom for a second, then emphatically put his feet up on the coffee table, something that my mom hated. "We'll see," my dad said.

"We'll see what?" Sr. Rivera asked.

"We'll see what he does for us. I like him, okay? But I don't know if he's going to be who he said he would be. Politicians will say anything to get elected. For some reason with this guy, I believed what he said. I believed *he* believed what he said. But we'll see. The first thing he needs to do is get the economy out of the sewer. No one comes to the diner anymore. No one has money to eat out."

"And now there are pirates," my mom said.

"Pirates?" Sra. Rivera asked, alarmed.

"From Africa," my mom said. "Black pirates."

"That's awesome," I said.

"They're hijacking ships!" my mom said.

I pictured guys with beards and eye patches and peg legs. I still thought it was pretty awesome.

Sr. Rivera said, "But here? It's safe, no?"

"It's not as safe as it used to be," my dad said.

"But it's safe," Sr. Rivera pressed, like he wanted to be reassured.

"Yes," my dad said. "Compared to where any of us are from, it's safe."

I WAS LESS than a year old when my parents brought my brother and me to the United States. Enrique was four. He used to tell me things about Panamá that I couldn't possibly have remembered—like about the scorpions in our backyard and the cement utility sink where my mom used to give us baths.

He reminisced about walking down the street with my mom to the Super 99, the dust blowing up everywhere, the heat pounding down, and about looking for crabs between the rocks along the bay.

"It's in you," my dad assured me once. "You were born in Panamá. It's in your bones."

I spent a lot of time trying to find it in me, but usually I couldn't. I felt more American than anything, but even that was up for debate according to the kids at school who'd taunted me over the years, asking me if I was related to Noriega, telling me to go back through the canal. The truth was that I didn't know which I was. I wasn't allowed to claim the thing I felt and I didn't feel the thing I was supposed to claim.

The first time I heard my parents tell the story about leaving Panamá, my mom said, "Our hearts kept breaking each time we walked out the door." They tried to give it time. They assumed conditions would improve. But the country was so ravaged that their hearts never stopped breaking. Eventually they sold almost everything they owned and used the money to buy plane tickets to somewhere else, somewhere better, which to them had always meant the United States. A while after I was old enough to understand this story, I pointed out how backwards it was to have fled to the nation that had driven them out of theirs, but they never copped to the irony of it. They needed to believe they'd done the right thing and that it made sense. They were torn between wanting to look back and wanting to exist absolutely in the new life they'd created. At one point, they had planned to return. They'd thought that with enough time, Panamá would be rebuilt and that their hearts, I guess, would heal. But while they waited for that day, they started making friends. My dad got a job as a busboy and then, later on, as a dishwasher. Years passed. Enrique was in school, and I started, too. My dad was promoted to line cook. More years slid by. And before they knew it, we had a life here. They had left their lives once before. They didn't want to do it again.

So they applied for U.S. citizenship, sitting up at night reading the Constitution, a dictionary by their side, and studying for the exam. They contacted someone at the Panamanian consulate in Philadelphia who helped them navigate the paperwork. Then they woke up one morning, got dressed in their best clothes, caught a bus to the courthouse, and, while my mom held me in her arms and my dad rested his hand on Enrique's shoulder, took an oath along with a group of other men and women who had made living in the United States a dream. We became Americans.

We never went back to Panamá, not even for a visit. It would have taken us forever to save enough money for plane tickets. Besides, my dad never wanted to take time off from his job. He probably could've asked for a few days of vacation time, but even after years of being there, making omelets and flipping pancakes, he knew—we all knew—that he was on the low end of the food chain. He could be replaced in a heartbeat. He didn't want to risk it.

Because of that, we'd missed my tía Gloria's wedding, which she'd had on a hillside in Boquete. She told my mom that her new husband, Esteban, had gotten so drunk that she'd convinced him to dance and that therefore the whole event was a success. We had my aunt on speakerphone and my mom had said, "Take it from me, hermanita, they dance at the wedding and then they never do it again." My dad had said, "That's what you think?" and clutched my mom by the wrist, sending her into a small spin in the middle of the kitchen. She squealed with delight while he swayed with her for a few beats and then he broke out into some goofy merengue moves, kicking his leg up at the end and shouting "¡Olé!" My aunt started yelling through the phone, "Are you still there? Celia! Rafael!" And my parents laughed until my mom dabbed the corners of her eyes with the back of her hand. I'd never seen them so happy with each other, even though it was just for those few seconds.

We almost went back for my dad's high school reunion, which my dad somehow got into his head that he didn't want to miss. The reunion was on a Friday, so maybe, he told us, he could fix his work schedule so that he was off on Friday. We could fly there, go to the reunion, and then fly back Saturday night. He was usually off on Sundays, but if he took off Friday instead, he'd have to be back and work Sunday to make up for it. So one night would be the longest we could stay, but one night would be enough. He had decided. And it looked like we were going to try.

My mom was as excited about the trip as I don't know what. She went to Sears to buy a new dress and had giddy phone conversations with my aunt about seeing each other again and what they would be able to pack into our eighteen hours on the ground. She started laying out her clothes weeks in advance even though my dad kept telling her she only needed two outfits—one to go and one to come home. "And why the hell do you have ten pairs of shoes here?" he asked, pointing to the sandals and leather high heels my mom had lined up along the baseboard in the bedroom. "Ten!" my mom scoffed. "I don't even own ten pairs of shoes." My father counted them. "Fine. Seven. That's still six too many." He told her that he intended to take only a duffel bag for our things because that would make it easier to get through customs. My mom said, "I'll check my own bag, then." My dad kicked the row of shoes my mom had lined up and sent them flying into the wall. He walked right up to my mom and held his index finger in front of her face. "One bag, Celia. One! For all four of us. Don't talk to me about it again."

A few weeks before the reunion, my dad called the number on the invitation to RSVP. The guy who answered had been the class president. He and my dad joked around for a minute and then my dad told the guy we were coming. According to what my dad told us later, the guy said, "We'll roll out the red carpet, then." When my dad asked him what he meant by that, the guy said that my dad would have to forgive him if the party wasn't up to my dad's standards. "We didn't know the gringo royalty was coming. We'll have to get the place repainted before you arrive." When my dad asked again what the guy was talking about, the guy said he hoped my dad didn't expect them all to kiss his feet now and reminded my dad how humble Panamá was. It didn't take long for my dad to slam the phone down. He stormed over to my mom, who was washing dishes, and said, "We're not going. If that's what they think, then we're not going."

My mom said, "What?"

"They think we're Americans now. And maybe we are! Maybe we don't belong there anymore after all." My dad went out on the balcony to smoke a cigarette, which he did whenever he was really upset.

My mom stood in the kitchen, a soapy pot in her hand, and looked at me, baffled. "What just happened?" she asked.

When I told her everything I'd been able to gather, she walked out to the balcony and closed the door behind her. At the commotion, Enrique came out of his room.

"We're not going anymore," I told him.

"Huh?"

"On the trip."

"Are you serious?" Enrique asked.

My brother and I huddled together, listening through the front door. I heard my mom say, "Please, Rafa. He doesn't know anything about us. We can still go. You'll see. Once we get there . . . All your friends . . . And everyone will love you." I imagined her reaching out to touch his shoulder, the way she did sometimes when she was asking for something. "Don't you miss it?" she asked. "Can't you imagine landing there, being there again? You know how it smells? The air there. And seeing everyone again. Please, Rafa."

But my dad wasn't swayed.

The following year, we talked about going back, too. My dad's anger over being cast as a holier-than-thou gringo had finally simmered down, and my mom, who couldn't bring herself to return the new dress she'd bought and who hadn't gotten over the disappointment of not being able to see her sister after all, had been dropping hints ever since that she would still like to go even if the trip was only for one night again. She'd become a genius at turning any and every little thing into a way to talk about Panamá. She would get a mosquito bite on her ankle and point out the welt to us, reminiscing about the bites she used to get in Panamá and wondering aloud "what the mosquitoes there looked like now," as if they were old friends. She would make rice and start talking about the gallo pinto at El Trapiche, which was her favorite restaurant, saying things like "I wonder how Cristóbal—wasn't that the owner's name?—is doing. Wouldn't it be nice to find out?" We would drive over a bridge and suddenly she was talking about the Bridge of the Americas near the canal. "Do you remember, Enrique? That time we took the ferry back from Taboga at night and it was all lit up? It was so beautiful. Mayor, I wish you could have seen it." She sighed. "Maybe one day." And my dad would sometimes shake his head at her melodrama and other times would just stay quiet, like he'd fallen into the haze of a particular memory himself.

My mom's birthday was September 22, so my dad finally gave in and made plans for us to go to Panamá. The Toro Family! One night only! Put it in lights! My mom worked herself into a froth all over again, conferring with my tía Gloria on the phone. My aunt apparently said she wanted to take my mom to the new mall and for a drive through Costa del Este, which used to be a garbage dump but now had been transformed into an up-and-coming area of the city, and out for sushi on the causeway, and afterwards they could hit the clubs along Calle Uruguay and yes, she realized they weren't twenty anymore but it would be so much fun! Besides, she and my tío Esteban weren't doing so well, she told my mom. He was never home. He spent the night at friends' apartments. So she could use some distraction and someone to talk to. "Not a divorce!" my mom gasped. To her, there could be nothing worse. "No," my aunt assured her. "Just problems."

Then, less than two weeks before we were scheduled to go, two planes flew into the World Trade Center in New York City and another one into the Pentagon in Washington, D.C. The country went into shock and we went right along with it. My dad called my mom from the diner, where, on the television above the counter, he had just seen the second plane hit the second tower. "They're blowing it up!" he apparently told her. "It's just like El Chorrillo. They're destroying it!" And my mom, in her nightgown, rushed to the set and stood in front of it, watching with her hand over her mouth. I had been eating cereal in the kitchen. I carried my bowl over and stood next to her and kept eating, which, when I thought about it later, seemed kind of messed up, but at the time we didn't know what was happening. The world hadn't stopped—just stopped—like it would later that day and for days after. Everything was still just unfolding in front of our eyes and we had no idea what to make of it.

It didn't take long before everyone in our building was knocking on each other's doors and convening out on the balcony, standing around stunned and shaking with fear. Nelia Zafón just kept repeating, "What is happening? What is happening? What the hell is happening?" I heard my mom say to someone, "We moved here because it was supposed to be safer! Where can we go after this?" All day long she kept herself no more than an arm's length from me and my brother, hugging us against her and then letting us go, like she wanted to assure herself that we were still there and that we were okay. Enrique, who was old enough by then that he usually squirmed away from my mom's embraces, must have known the situation was serious, because he let her do it. I let her, too, even though every time she did, instead of comforting me, it only made me more scared.

By evening, everyone's front doors were open and people were roaming in and out of each other's units, watching each other's televisions as if a different set would deliver different news, checking to see if anyone had heard anything new, getting tedious translations. Benny Quinto led prayer circles in his living room and offered to smoke with anyone who needed to calm their nerves. "Weed," Enrique told me when he heard Benny talking about it. "Nice." Micho Alvarez paced up and down the balcony, talking on his cell phone and jotting things in his notebook. Gustavo Milhojas, who was half-Mexican and half-Guatemalan, wrote a letter to the army telling them that as of that day he was 100 percent American and that he was ready to serve the country and kill the cowards who had murdered his fellow paisanos. At the end he wrote, "And here is a list of people who are willing to join me." He drew a few blank lines and spent the afternoon trying to recruit everyone in the building. When my mom saw what it was, she said, "More killing? That's what you want? *More?*" And Gustavo said, "Not killing. Justice."

That year around the holidays we were all miserable. Holidays were always bad—my mom in particular got homesick sometimes like it was a genuine illness—but that Christmas was the worst. We were depressed and on edge, still shaken up about September 11, and then re-shaken when someone tried to blow up another plane by hiding a bomb in his shoes two days before Christmas Eve.

My aunt called, which cheered my mom up for a while, but once that wore off, she was more down than ever, shuffling around the house in her slippers, no makeup, her hair a disaster. She carried tissues in the pocket of her bathrobe and made a big show of dabbing her nose with them every so often. Eventually, my dad came up with an idea. "You want Panamá?" he said. "A beach is the closest thing you're going to get." He hustled us out the door and down the street, where we took a chain of buses for an hour and a half to Cape Henlopen in southern Delaware. It was snowing when we arrived—Enrique kept complaining that the snow was going to mess up his beloved Adidas sneakers—and everything was so colorless and barren that it looked like the moon. I had to hand it to my dad, though. With the water and the sand, my mom said it almost *was* like a little piece of Panamá. The waves roared in toward us and then silently pulled back again, slipping over the shore. Even with the falling snow, the air had the sting of salt water, and we crunched broken seashells under our shoes. But one beach isn't every beach. And one home isn't every home. And I think we all sensed, standing there, just how far we were from where we had come, in ways both good and bad. "It's beautiful," my mom said, staring out at the ocean. She sighed and shook her head. "This country."

# Gustavo Milhojas

My name is Gustavo Milhojas. I was born in Chinique, El Quiché, Guatemala, in 1960, the year hell came to that country. I arrived in the United States on November 14, 2000. Before that, I resided in México.

My mother is of Guatemalan descent, while my father's bloodlines run through México. However, my father was not part of my life. My mother raised my three brothers and me by herself in Guatemala. She did her best, working two jobs and attempting to teach us right from wrong, but there were forces beyond her control.

The military in Guatemala at that time became too powerful, and the people revolted. The army began kidnapping citizens who they suspected were against them. They were burying people alive. They were raping women thirty times a day. They were laying babies on the ground and crushing their skulls with their boots. How could a baby be against them? Perhaps it was a way to torture the parents.

I couldn't take it anymore. When I was twenty, I decided to leave. I attempted to persuade my mother and my brothers to go to México. I made the argument that because of my father, we had a claim to it. But my mother was stubborn. She said if I didn't like the way things were, I shouldn't run away. I should stay there and commit myself to fixing them. But that's what the guerrillas had been trying to do for decades and I saw no progress. "No," I told her. "I need to go somewhere else."

I went to México on my own. I believed it would be easy for me to make a new home there, but no one in México wanted anything to do with a Guatemalan. The Mexicans look down on us. They believe Guatemalans are stupid. To tell them I was half-Mexican only made things worse. They were offended to think that any Mexican man would have stooped so low as to be with a Guatemalan woman to create me.

I was living in Córdoba. Things were terrible for me there— I couldn't find a job unless I was willing to let myself be taken advantage of, working sometimes for only a few pesos a day— until I met a woman named Isabel, who changed everything for me. She was Mexican, from Veracruz, and her parents disapproved of me. But we fell in love and decided we would be together no matter what anybody said.

We married in 1982 and had two children—first a boy and then a girl. We were so happy. I was still treated poorly sometimes, but I had gained a different sort of confidence since being with Isabel, and the poor treatment didn't bother me as much.

Seventeen years after we married, Isabel passed away. She had cancer of the breast. Here, I find that everyone knows about this cancer. Last fall, there were pink ribbons in the movie theaters and in all the stores, and someone told me it was for this type of cancer. But at that time we lived in a small village called Tehuipango where the medical care was very basic. We found a doctor who told us what she had, but he could not tell us how to fix it. He said, "She needs to rest. She will die soon." I did my best to take care of her. By the time we found out, she was already very weak. I put bags of ice on her chest to help numb the pain. I gave her aspirin to ease the aches. Nothing helped. Three months later, she was gone.

The children were very upset. They were both in high school

at that time. Isabel and I were so proud of them. They studied hard. They wanted to go to college. My son wants to become a businessman and my daughter wants to become a nurse.

After Isabel died I didn't know how I would make this happen. Isabel was a cook. She made desserts for everyone in our village—dulce de camote con piña, empanadas de guayaba, palanquetas de cacahuate. When someone wanted a birthday cake, they came to her. When someone was throwing a party, they came to her. Every day, she sold fresh soups straight out of the pots on our stove. I worked, too, harvesting maize and fava beans. But the money she made from cooking helped support us. Without it, we didn't have much.

I came to the United States to earn more money for my children. They are living with a family friend now while I'm here. I did not think of it so much as a choice as an obligation. It is my obligation to provide a good life for them. My son is in college now, and my daughter will start college next year at Universidad Veracruzana in Orizaba. This makes me happy because I believe it means they will both get to do what they want to do. There are not many people who can say that.

I thought it would be very difficult to cross. It was after September 11 and the security was supposed to be high. I crowded with a group of men into the back of a van with tinted windows. We were all on the floor, under a heavy black burlap blanket and, on top of that, a lot of empty cardboard boxes that were meant to look like freight. We drove right up to the checkpoint. A guard examined the driver's papers, which were legitimate. The guard did not know we were in the back of the van. He did not even look. The driver simply told him he was transporting construction supplies for a job in El Paso. There was a long pause. All of us in the back held our breath, waiting to be discovered. And then the guard let the driver through. That was it. It was almost unbelievable to me.

I found a job as soon as I could and began sending money back to my children. I started off in a mattress warehouse, dragging mattresses down metal ramps at the back of the store and loading them onto delivery trucks. When a mattress was defective, sometimes one of the employees kept it. The bed I have today is from that job.

For a while, I worked at a canning factory where we packaged chiles and salsa. It wasn't very clean. There were maggots everywhere. The owners blamed the conditions on the workers. Besides that, I didn't like standing in one place for ten hours. We got only one break for fifteen minutes.

Now I have two jobs. Five mornings a week I work at the Newark Shopping Center movie theater, cleaning the bathrooms and the theaters. I make sure there's toilet paper in the stalls. I mop the floors. I have a wire brush I use to clean the sinks. In the evenings I work at the Movies 10 movie theater in Stanton. That job is harder because there are so many theaters. If too many movies finish all at once, it's a challenge to clean the theaters before the next group of people comes in. I have been reprimanded for leaving an empty cup in the seat arm. Usually I don't have time to go home between my shifts, so many times I eat popcorn and soda for dinner.

But I am very grateful for these jobs. They allow me to send money to my children to pay for their schooling. When both of them graduate, I would like to go back to México to be with them. My wish is that they'll do something worthwhile with their lives, something more important than sweeping popcorn. I have done what I can for them. I would like to see them give something back.

# Alma

Arturo came home from work each day tired and hungry, the crevices of his skin caked with dirt. He went straight to the shower and stood under the spray of the warm water until I knocked on the door and told him that dinner was ready. When we started seeing each other, one of the traits that had attracted me to Arturo was how serious he could be, the way that he furrowed his eyebrows when I used to watch him on a job, the intensity of focus and the pride he took in doing the job well. I was stubborn, but I had never been as solemn as him, and I admired the strength that his solemnity seemed to represent. Of course, in time I learned his soft spots, like bruises on a piece of fruit. He was compassionate and kind, and hearing of others' hardships affected him so much that usually he couldn't stop himself from doing something to help. Once, when a young girl in our town lost her sight after a propane tank exploded in her face, Arturo built a birdhouse and put it on a stake in the girl's backyard so that when she opened her bedroom window, she would hear the songs of warblers and mockingbirds. But he could also be uncompromising and hard on himself. And since the accident, those traits that I loved had given way to something darker—seriousness had become gravity, sensitivity had transformed into melancholy. I didn't always see it. Arturo fought to preserve his better nature. But occasionally his despair came through.

I found him one Sunday morning in the kitchen on his hands

and knees, his head inside a cabinet. I had just gotten dressed, and I went up behind him and kicked him lightly. "Hey!" he shouted, curling his head out.

"What are you doing?" I asked.

"I'm looking for a bowl."

"Why?"

"Maribel wanted pineapple."

"I would have gotten it for her."

"I thought we had a glass bowl," he said.

"We didn't bring it with us."

"Why not?"

"We have a metal bowl." I started toward the cabinet where I'd stored it.

"I don't want a metal bowl," he said.

"It's a perfectly good bowl."

"When I eat something out of a metal bowl, it tastes different afterwards."

"What are you talking about?"

"It tastes like I mixed in a handful of coins."

I smiled.

"You know what I'm saying, don't you?"

"Yes, I know what you're saying."

"I wish we had brought that glass bowl," he said.

I looked at him and understood that we weren't just talking about bowls anymore. I smoothed my hand over his thick hair, cupping the back of his neck. Arturo wrapped his arms around my legs like a child.

"We'll see it again," I said.

And I imagined it, that glass bowl with the flat bottom and the broad rim, nestled in the lower kitchen cabinet whose door creaked when it opened, nestled among the pots and pans, in the room nestled among other rooms—the bathroom where Maribel had hung a calendar to mark when to expect her next period, the bedroom where the nightgowns and socks and collared shirts that we had left behind were piled on top of the quilt my mother had sewn and given to us as a wedding gift, the sala with the bone-inlaid picture frames housing black-and-white photographs of our grandparents, who had passed, and of our great-grandparents, whom we had never known—all of which were nestled between the backyard with our old rope hammock and the stone half wall that was crumbling at one corner and the front yard, which was hardly a yard at all, just pebbles and aloe plants and a space where Arturo parked the pickup truck that he and I used to sit in together while we looked up at the stars. And all of that nestled in the town where the three of us had been born and had grown up, the town where my parents still lived and where Arturo's parents had died, the town where we'd shared meals and drinks and late nights filled with laughter with our lifelong friends. All of it waiting so patiently. All of it so far away.

FOR A WHILE I made the meals we used to eat in Pátzcuaro—sopa tarasca and huachinango and corundas con churipo—but eating foods from home in a place that wasn't our home only made things worse. Besides, the imported chiles and guajillo were expensive, and already we were living on so little. We had some money saved, but Arturo and I had both agreed not to touch it unless there was an emergency, which meant unless we had to take Maribel to a doctor or rush her to the hospital. For now we were getting by on Arturo's paycheck week to week, which was just enough to cover rent and bus fare and food.

Eventually I stopped shopping at Gigante because it drove

me crazy to see all the things we couldn't afford to buy. All those crates of nopalitos and epazote and tender corn, all those shelves of pickled red onions and tequesquite and coriander taunting me. I started buying food at the Dollar Tree instead. Food in cans, food in boxes. Add water and heat.

One morning, I saw a Mexican woman there taking three drumlike containers off a shelf.

"What is that?" I asked her, pointing.

"Avena," she said. "Oatmeal."

"Like atole?"

My mother used to make me atole de grano when I was a girl, the dense corn kernels buried in the anicillo broth. But I hadn't eaten it in a long time. The idea that this might be something similar piqued my interest.

"This is the American version," the woman said. "It's not the same. But it's cheap. One can will feed you for a week. And it's hot. Good for the winter."

"Thank you," I told her, and started loading containers of oatmeal into my basket until I cleared the shelf of it.

I made it that afternoon. The instructions on the back were in English, but there were drawings, too—a faucet pouring water into a measuring cup, a hand holding a spoon and stirring—and there were numbers that I could read. I followed it all, heated it on the stove, and before I knew it, I had made a pot of pale gray mush. I dipped a finger in. It tasted like paper. Maybe the slightest hint of nuttiness somewhere at the edges. The woman had been right. It wasn't good. Not at all like the atole I remembered. But I had barely made a dent in the oats and I had cooked a whole pot of them. It was enough to feed all three of us. Maybe, I thought, I could sprinkle some cocoa powder on it, or stir in some honey, just to liven the flavor.

Maribel and Arturo looked skeptical when I set out the bowls that night.

"What is it?" Maribel asked, poking at it with her spoon.

I had made it too early. I didn't know that the longer it sat, the more it hardened. By the time I put it out for dinner that night, it was like rubber.

"Oatmeal," I said, pronouncing the word in English. "The Americans love it." I pointed to one of the cardboard cans on the counter. "You see that man? He makes it on his farm."

Maribel touched the surface with her finger. "It feels . . . weird."

"You're not supposed to use your fingers to eat it. Use your spoon and put some in your mouth. Come on. Which one of you is going to try it first? Arturo?"

But I could tell Arturo had his own reservations. He just stared at the bowl with his spoon poised in his hand.

"Maribel?" I asked.

"What's it called again?" Arturo said.

"Oatmeal."

Arturo tried to stifle a laugh in his nose that escaped anyway. The sound of it—the tinkle of joy in the midst of our bleak American winter—was startling. "What are you laughing at?" I asked.

"Say it again," Arturo said.

"What? 'Oatmeal'?"

His face cracked into a smile beneath his mustache. I loved seeing that smile. So rare these days. I would have said the word for the next hundred years if it made him smile like that.

"Oatmeal," I repeated.

Arturo started laughing. "Oatmeal!" he said, and I laughed, too. In English, it sounded funny to us, as mushy and formless as the cereal itself. And then, the sound of angels: Maribel laughed, too. Light and crystalline. Thin glass bubbles of laughter.

Arturo looked at me in astonishment. She was laughing. Laughing! She had smiled once in Pátzcuaro when the three of us were eating ice cream in the square and Arturo's had fallen and splattered on the sidewalk, and she had cried at no longer being able to do simple things like hold a fork or write her name or wash her own hair, although of course in time she had relearned all of that. But laughter? It was the first time in over a year that we had heard it. Just like her old laugh. Just like our old Maribel.

"Oatmeal!" I bellowed.

"Oatmeal," Arturo said with tears in his eyes. He jammed his spoon into the bowl and dug out a mouthful. "Delicious!" he declared, rubbing his belly after he had swallowed, making a show of it, and the three of us broke out in helpless, gorgeous laughter once again.

I LAY IN BED most nights, long after Arturo and Maribel had fallen asleep, and stared at the ceiling. Sleep was like wealth, elusive and for other people. I lay rigid on the mattress, remembering what it used to be like, before all of this. Maribel running at the hammock, flipping it over her head, laughing wildly. Maribel darting across the street ahead of us, looking back and tapping her toes in mock impatience. Maribel swimming in the lake with her friends, coming home with her hair dripping wet, her clothes clinging to her thin frame. Arturo and I looked at her sometimes in awe. It had been difficult for us to conceive a child. We had tried for nearly three years, visiting doctors and curanderas. My mother had said prayers and begged for an audience with the priest. Every month, we waited to see if perhaps it had happened at last. Every month, suffering the disappointment that it hadn't. And then, after we had said enough with the doctors and with the discussion, just as we started to believe that having a child simply wasn't going to be part of our lives, that being parents was a distinction we weren't meant to have, when we had hardened ourselves to the pain of seeing everyone around us carrying and feeding their babies, those downy heads and wet lips, I missed my period. We had a hiccup of hope. Could it be? we thought. Nine months later we were holding her in our arms. Tiny starfish hands, ribs pushing up against her skin like piano keys. She wriggled and croaked. Our Maribel. "You won't ever have another one," the doctor told us. But that didn't matter. We had her.

Maribel was fourteen when the accident happened. Arturo was leading the construction of an outbuilding for a rancher who had bought more livestock than he had room to house, and Maribel had circled around me that morning like a gnat, begging me to let her go to the job site with her father. Ever since she was young she had clung to Arturo, interested in everything he did, every move he made. That day I told her, "I don't know. Your father's going to be busy." She said, "But I won't get in his way!" And I had glanced at Arturo, who was across the room pulling his boots on, asking him with my eyes what he wanted me to tell her.

He stood and said, "You could come with us, too, Alma. If you're worried about it."

"Yes!" Maribel said. "You come, too."

"It will be like the old days. Remember when you used to come? Sitting there in your dresses."

"You wore dresses?" Maribel asked, surprised.

"She used to try to look nice for me," Arturo said. "She was almost as pretty as you are now."

"Almost?" I said, and when he laughed, at last I gave in.

The building was simple—walls built from mud bricks and straw, a roof made of wood beams and clay. There were plans for a swinging, louvered door at the front that the men hadn't yet installed. The roof was nearly complete, although Arturo pointed out a few areas where sunlight filtered through, which needed to be patched. That's what he was working on that day.

He climbed a ladder that was leaning against the overhang and settled himself onto the roof with a bucket of clay and a trowel he used to spread it. Maribel hurried around, handing things to the men when they asked for something, smiling at me giddily as she trotted from spot to spot. She hammered a row of nails into a board. She sanded around the latch on the door. She rinsed out the towels in plastic buckets of water. I stood off to the side, watching her and Arturo, and, when I thought it wouldn't distract them, speaking occasionally to the men on the crew, some of whom had been at our wedding and some of whom had been at the hospital the day Maribel was born.

The air was still damp from rain the night before, but the sun had burned through the haze of the morning and shone brilliantly in the sky. One of the workers—a husky man named Luis—gave Maribel his hat when he saw that she didn't have one. She laughed. "It's too big on me," she said, letting the brim fall to her cheeks. "Oh, come on. You look preciosa," Luis told her.

Arturo was on his knees on the roof. He was pulling clay out of the bucket with his hands and slapping it into the crevices between slats of wood. He was smoothing it with his iron trowel. And then he ran low on clay. Maribel was just below him, talking with Luis.

"Luis," Arturo yelled, "I'm going to need another bucket of clay soon."

Luis nodded and Arturo turned back to what he was doing.

"I'll get it," Maribel told Luis.

"Do you know where it is?" Luis asked.

"Of course," Maribel said, and ran off to find another bucket. When she returned, Luis offered to take it from her.

"It's so heavy," he protested.

Maribel grinned. "I'm so strong," she replied.

"Do you have it?" Arturo yelled down.

"I got it, Papi," Maribel said.

"It's heavy," Arturo said.

"She's strong," Luis yelled up, and Maribel and I laughed.

"Let Luis bring it up," Arturo said, and turned his back again, smoothing clay.

Maribel pouted.

Her whole life, I had watched her climb trees and scale stone walls in the courtyards in town with ease. Arturo usually frowned when she did those things—they didn't fit the Mexican conception of what girls could and should do—but I loved that about Maribel. The ways she was unconcerned with trying to be like everyone else. She and Arturo were similar in that, although he didn't seem to recognize it.

"Can I take it up?" Maribel asked me.

"Let me," Luis said, reaching for the bucket.

But Maribel moved it away from him. She looked at me again with her big, expectant eyes. I never could resist her.

"Go ahead," I said.

I stood at the bottom to hold the ladder secure.

"Cuidado," Luis cautioned as she started climbing.

When she reached the top, Maribel shoved the bucket onto the roof. "Here you go," she said.

Arturo turned. "I thought I told you to let Luis bring it up."

"Mamá said I could do it."

"Alma!" Arturo shouted down. "She shouldn't be up here."

"She wanted to surprise you," I shouted back.

Arturo walked like a crab over to the bucket, careful to keep his footing on the slanted roof.

"I'm stronger than you think, Papi," Maribel said. From the ground, I watched her hold one arm out and make a muscle. Such a small muscle. Like a torta roll.

Finally, Arturo softened and laughed. "Superwoman," he said.

"Come back down now, hija," I said.

"Are you holding the ladder?" Arturo shouted.

"I've got it."

"Go on down," I heard Arturo say.

And so she started. One rung. Two. Then, a noise. Something clattered off to the side. I startled and turned. I must have jerked the ladder. It slid in the mud on the ground from the rain the night before. And when I turned back again, it was as if the world was unspooling in slow motion. I saw Maribel's body tilt backwards. She let out a sharp scream. She reached her hand for the ladder, but her fingertips only grazed the rung. Arturo yelled. Maribel dropped two stories to the ground below. Her body smacked against the mud, sending it splattering into the air, all over me, all over Luis. Her neck snapped back. Her eyes closed.

Luis got to her first. Arturo scrambled down the ladder, jump-ing off when he was halfway down. "Maribel!" he was shouting. "Maribel!"

I stood in shock, blood frozen in my veins.

"Don't touch her," Luis said, but Arturo didn't listen. He held his hand under Maribel's nose to make sure she was breathing, then picked her up, her body limp as a rag doll, her head rolled back over one of his arms, her legs hung over the other, and said her name, over and over and over again, as if it was the only word he knew. She didn't wake up.

The other men on the site started running over, asking what had happened, offering to help. Without a word, Arturo cut through them all, cradling Maribel, trying to keep her still, walk-ing quickly toward the truck while I hurried behind them, afraid to look, afraid to know what I already knew.

There was no discussion. Luis got in the driver's side while Arturo climbed in the back with Maribel, holding her across his lap. I sat in the front, staring out the window, my eyes unfo-cused, my palms sweaty, my breath catching in my throat.

At the hospital, Luis jumped out of the truck and came back not a minute later with a nurse, who took one look at Maribel and called for a gurney.

"We have to take her away now," the nurse said. She was stocky and firm.

"We'll go with her," I said.

The nurse shook her head, and when someone else arrived with the gurney, Arturo laid Maribel down on it. As they started to wheel her away, I tried to follow.

Arturo put his hand on my arm. "Let them do what they need to do," he said.

We sat in the waiting area, a small room with a cluster of wooden chairs. Arturo had sent Luis back to the job site. I trained my gaze on the floor, squeezing my hands. Once, I dared to look at Arturo. He had a wild, frantic look in his eyes. He saw me looking at him.

"What happened?" he asked.

"I don't know," I said. "She fell."

"But what happened to the ladder, Alma?"

"I don't know. I—"

"You were supposed to be holding it."

"I was!"

"Then how did she fall?"

"It must have slipped."

"You were supposed to be holding it," Arturo repeated.

"I turned around. Just for a second."

"Why did you even let her go up there? It wasn't safe."

"I thought she would be fine."

"But I *told* you!"

"I know."

"And now she's not fine!"

"I'm sorry," I murmured, the combined weight of horror and reproach pressing against my chest.

Arturo leaned forward, propping his elbows on his knees, burying his face in his hands. I stared at the curve of his back and tried to remember: I'd had my hands around the ladder, and I had turned. Had I really let it slip? Was it my fault? Arturo had said as much, hadn't he? My fault, I thought. My fault. Repeating it in my head again and again.

We waited. And waited. Until finally the doctor emerged from the bowels of the hospital and told us: A bruised tailbone. Two broken ribs. Minor injuries except for one. Her brain. Because of the way her head snapped back against the ground, the way it had snapped back up again and down one more time, her brain had been shaken inside her skull. "The brain is very tender," the doctor said. "When it shakes like that, it can tear against a small piece of bone in the skull that acts as a ridge. It's called shearing. That's what happened here. And now her brain is swelling. We can't let it keep swelling. There's only so much room inside the human head. If it swells too much, well—" He looked at us both. He was an old man with a bushy mustache. "She might not survive," he said. At the moment those words came out, someone— some spirit somewhere—snatched the air from my lungs. The doctor went on: "She's intubated and on a ventilator. We gave her drugs to relieve the pressure, but they haven't helped in the way we hoped they would. So now what we need to do—what I need your permission to do—is remove a small piece of her skull to make room for the swelling and to keep the pressure from building too much." He stopped and looked at us again. "If it builds too much, she could die. And the longer we wait to relieve it, the more damage she'll likely experience." Neither Arturo nor I said anything. We were holding hands. Gripping each other's fingers as if strength could be found there. "It's the only option," the doctor said.

They opened her head. They removed a piece of our daughter. And when it was over we realized that in that piece had been everything. Until then, I had believed that a person inhabited his or her whole body. I had believed that a person's essence was spread throughout them. Who could think that a person's entire being is housed in a finger or in a hip bone or in a small piece of a skull, and that the rest of the body exists for appearances only?

But Maribel changed so completely after the surgery, what else could I believe? Of course, I knew better. Medically, scientifically, they had explained everything to us. It wasn't the surgery that stole her from us. It was the accident. The moment her head snapped and bounced up and fell back again, her brain, like a mass of Jell-O, slid inside her skull. Forward and back, and it tore against bone. And when it tore, it destroyed some of the connections between neurons, which was a word the doctor had to explain to us. And then there was the swelling, which second by second was only making everything worse. No, the surgery wasn't the thing that took her from us. It was the thing that supposedly saved her.

Maribel stayed in the hospital for weeks. She regained consciousness shortly after the surgery and woke agitated and confused. With the tube in her throat, she couldn't speak. She looked hysterically at us, asking with her eyes where she was and what had happened. We explained everything. We explained it and told her we loved her until she calmed down.

Most nights we slept on a blanket on the floor of her hospital room. When we slept at home, we trembled and huddled against each other in our bed in the dark. Many times, we cried. My parents came over and cried with us. Our friends came and wrapped their arms around us. I woke up every morning and knelt on the floor, praying to God to heal her. I might have questioned God, I suppose, about how He could have allowed such a thing to happen, except that it didn't just happen. It wasn't an earthquake or a gust of wind that knocked her to the ground. It was me. I believed that completely by then. So I prayed for forgiveness and for God to bring her back to us. I wanted Maribel to grow up and get married and have children and friends and find meaning in her life. I wanted to see her graduate from high school, and I wanted to see how shy she would become when she introduced us to the man she had fallen in love with, the man that one day Arturo and I would welcome to our family. I wanted to sew yellow, blue, and red ribbons into her wedding lingerie for good luck. I wanted to see her grow round with a child and hold that child in her arms. I wanted her to stop by the house for meals and laugh at the television and rub her eyes when she was tired after a long day and hug me when it was time to leave again, her husband waiting in the car, her child's hand in hers. I wanted her to have the full, long life that every parent promises his or her child by the simple act of bringing that child into the world. The implicit promise, I thought. I said every prayer I knew.

After the surgery, a therapist came to Maribel's room and administered tests, to make sure she could move, to make sure she could understand basic instructions, to make sure that her brain could still tell the rest of her body what to do. The doctor was pleased. She had a brain injury, but it could have been much, much worse. We began to hope. Would she come back to us? Our Maribel? The Maribel we had known for nearly fifteen years? They said perhaps. In time. But more likely, there would be something about her that remained permanently changed. They couldn't say for sure. Every brain injury patient was different. We heard that too often. It began to sound like an excuse for ignorance. It made me want to scream, "What *do* you know?" After weeks of rehabilitation, after working with a psychologist and a speech language pathologist and the doctor, all they could tell us was things like: She struggles with finding the right words sometimes, and that will likely persist. Her short-term memory is erratic at best. Her emotional affect is flat, which may or may not change. She has trouble organizing her thoughts and her actions. She gets easily fatigued. She might be more prone to depression, even long-term. But she's young, which gives her a better chance at recovery. "Besides," they all said, "the brain is a remarkable organ. With the right attention and exercise, it can heal."

Neither Arturo nor I knew what that meant. We thought, We'll be gentle with her. We'll be patient. And when she was released from the hospital we sent her back to school with the idea that a learning environment was exactly what she needed. Get her using her mind again, we both thought. That would be good.

But day after day Maribel came home frustrated and depressed. The teachers talked too fast, she said. She spent hours in the nurse's office, complaining of headaches. Even when the teachers tried to be accommodating—giving her extra time to take tests, repeating things for her benefit—it was of little help.

After two weeks, we went back to the doctor at the hospital and asked for advice. He told us that if we could find her the right kind of school, a school with a strong special education program, it would help immensely. There were a few in México City, he said. But the best were in the United States, if we were willing to go. He gave us a list of schools that he knew, schools with good reputations. Which one we chose was just a matter of where Arturo could find work.

I said, "Well, why didn't they tell us that earlier!"

"The United States?" Arturo said.

"You can get a job there, can't you?" I was energized now that a solution was within sight.

"But this is our home," Arturo said. "It's always been our home."

"It would only be temporary."

He furrowed his brow in his particular way. "Why are you so sure she can't get what she needs here?"

"¡Qué vergüenza, Arturo! I'll take her there myself if you won't go."

"It's just ... So much has changed already. We've been through so much."

"So it's just one more thing."

"I don't know if she can handle one more thing."

"Well, she can't stay here, doing this. Don't you want her to get better?"

"Of course."

"Then ... ?"

He nodded. But when I looked at him, I understood. He was the one who wasn't sure he could handle one more thing.

"We have to do this," I said. "All I need is for you to say yes, and I promise I'll take care of everything after that. You won't have to worry about anything."

"I want to do what's best for her," Arturo said.

"I know. This is it."

And finally Arturo agreed, and the decision was made.

# Mayor

What can I say? She grew on me. Those Sundays after church, instead of sitting on the couch with our parents, Maribel and I started hanging out in the kitchen by ourselves. She wasn't always good at keeping up a conversation—she lost her train of thought sometimes, and she talked slow in order to find the right words as she went along, and sometimes she forgot that we'd already discussed something, so I had to repeat myself—but a lot of the things she said were smart. Besides, I had learned that she was listening even when it seemed like she wasn't. When I had met her in the Dollar Tree, before I knew anything about her, she had seemed intimidating and aloof. But now that I knew better, I understood not to take it personally. She would trace her fingernails along the top of the kitchen table or look at the ceiling sometimes, but when I stopped talking, she would respond in a way that proved she'd been paying attention all along and, even better, that she was actually interested in what I'd said. Which was more than I could say for most people and definitely more than I could say for any girl I'd ever known.

My dad didn't like it. "Why can't you talk to normal girls?" he asked me once after the Riveras left.

"What is that supposed to mean?" my mom said.

But we all knew what he meant: Why couldn't I talk to a girl that wasn't brain-damaged? I did talk to the so-called normal girls, of course. I mean, I asked them to pass me a paper in class or I mumbled an apology when I bumped into one of them in the hall. But it was never easy for me, at least not the way it was easy for me with Maribel, maybe *because* she was brain-damaged, maybe because she didn't seem so intimidating because of that. In another life, one before whatever had happened to her had happened, I was pretty sure she would have been just another girl I was scared of. And I was pretty sure, too, that she wouldn't have given me the time of day. I had a feeling she'd been one of the popular girls, the one all the guys lusted over. But this was a different life, one where I was getting a chance with her. Maybe it was terrible to think of it like that, but I wasn't going to pass it up.

"Do you remember that girl Enrique used to date?" my dad went on. "What was her name? Sandra? The one who wore headbands. You can't find someone like that?"

"I don't want someone like that," I said.

"Leave him alone," my mom chimed. "Maribel's a nice girl."

"Maybe," my dad conceded. "But not for Mayor."

My dad's narrow-mindedness only made me feel more connected to Maribel, though. Like maybe I was the only one who understood her, the only one who was willing to give her a chance.

I started stopping by her apartment sometimes after school. Her mom wouldn't let Maribel actually go anywhere with me, so she and I just sat on the floor in the bedroom she shared with her parents and talked. They had clothes folded in piles along the wall and a mattress wedged into the corner. Maribel had a sleeping bag that she rolled up during the day and set under the window. But the atmosphere was uninspiring, to say the least, and I found myself wishing that I could take her somewhere, even just to Dunkin' Donuts down the street, where I knew we could score free doughnuts if they were about to throw them out anyway, or maybe to the movie theater, where I could show her how to sneak in the side door, which William and I had been doing forever. I thought she deserved it, you know, getting out into the world. As far as I knew, she only went to school and came straight home, which made her seem a little like a caged bird who no one trusted to fly. But her mom wouldn't budge. The rule was that if I wanted to see Maribel, it had to be at either her apartment or mine—no going outside, no taking a walk, no nothing.

Most of the time I found her sitting on the bedroom floor, writing in her notebook or standing and staring out the back window. I'd ask her what she was looking at or what she was writing about. Sometimes she told me. Other times she didn't. Either way, it didn't matter much to me. I was aware that my original reason for talking to Maribel, which had been fueled by a sense of responsibility, had been replaced by something else: I just wanted to be around her. I still wanted to take care of her in certain ways, but it was more than that now. I liked her. I liked her more than I'd ever liked anyone.

We talked about nothing mostly, like what she was doing in school and about music and our parents. I would tell her the most random things—"Did you know that the average person drinks sixteen thousand gallons of water by the time they die?" or about the time I saw Vicente Fox on TV—and she would smile sometimes, which was always my goal.

We talked about the weather because now that it was getting colder she was waiting for it to snow, to see what it was like.

"I guess there's no snow in México, huh?" I said.

"Yes."

" 'Yes' there's no snow or 'yes' there is snow?"

"There is snow."

"In México? No way."

"In the north, yes," she said.

"You know there's different kinds of snow, right? There's wet snow, which can get crusty and freeze. And then there's really light snow, which is soft. And don't even get me started on snowflakes. There are four classes of those: columns, dendrites, needles, and rimed snow."

She pulled out her notebook. "Say it again."

I did, and she wrote it down.

"You liked that?" I asked.

She nodded.

"Can I see?" I held out my hand.

Without hesitation, she gave me her notebook. On the page that was open, she'd written, "Wet snow is hard. Light snow is soft." Her handwriting was small and tight, and she pushed down so hard with the black pen she was using that she made indents on the paper. Everything was centered—one line at a time—down the middle of the page. At the top, way up in the margin, she had written her name and address. I kept reading.

Close the door behind you.

Mrs. Pacer is room 310.

My room is 312.

How much does the bus ride cost?

What is the name of the bus driver?

Look at the bus driver's badge.

Crystal.

The school bus is free.

The city bus is not free.

I flipped back a few pages and read:

This is Newark, Delaware.
Delaware is 3,333 kilometers from home.
I feel the same today as I did yesterday.

I handed the notebook back to her. "What happened?" I asked.

"What?"

"Was it a car accident?"

"When?"

"Sorry. I mean, what happened to you?"

"I fell. I was on—" She stopped. "It's long."

"It's a long story?"

She shook her head. "A long thing. Of wood."

I racked my brain. "A bat?" I hated it when I didn't know what she was getting at. I wanted to show her that I could follow her. I wanted to be the one person that it was easy for her to talk to.

"A ladder," she said finally.

"Oh, a long thing made out of wood. Right. You were up on a ladder?"

"I broke two"—she held up two fingers—"of my ribs."

"And you hit your head?"

She lifted a flap of hair and showed me a scar, pink and waxy like a gummy worm, behind her ear.

"Does it still hurt now? Like, can you sleep on it?"

"I get headaches."

"So that's what the sunglasses are for."

"Yes."

"Do you even remember it?"

"I was on the . . ."

"Ladder," I filled in.

She nodded. "And then I was in the hospital. I don't know where I went in between."

"Well, someone must have taken you to the hospital."

"I mean . . . I lost myself. In between."

"Oh," I said, and then I just sat there, because something about that idea—that you could be one person in one moment and then wake up and be completely different—punched me in the gut.

"You don't ask me how I'm feeling," Maribel said. "I hate it when people . . . ask me that."

She'd told me that before, but I didn't point it out. I just said, "It probably gets old, huh?"

"I want to be like everybody else."

"Yeah," I said, because I knew just what she meant. I'd spent my whole life feeling like that. Like everybody else was onto something that I couldn't seem to find, that I didn't even know *existed*. I wanted to figure it out, the secret to having the easy life that everyone else seemed to have, where they fit in and were good at everything they tried. Year after year, I waited for it all to fall into place—every September I told myself, This year will be different—but year after year, it was all just the same.

I didn't say anything in response to Maribel that day. We moved on to another topic. But later that night, when I was lying in bed, I realized what I should have said, because for her at least it would have been the truth: "You shouldn't want to be like everybody else. Then you wouldn't be like you."

ONE DAY I walked back from her place to find my dad sitting on the couch, watching television. He had his sweat-socked feet up on the coffee table and a bottle of beer in his hand. Usually he didn't get home until later, so both of us were surprised to see each other.

"What are you doing here?" I asked.

He sat up, startled. "The diner closed early today. Not enough customers in the afternoons anymore. Aren't you supposed to be at soccer?"

I tensed. "I was," I said.

"You're not wearing your soccer clothes."

"Yeah." I scrambled through excuses in my head. "My clothes were dirty, so I borrowed someone else's stuff."

"This is someone else's? This? What you're wearing?"

"Well, I had to give it back after practice, so I changed into my regular clothes again."

"You gave dirty clothes back to someone?"

I nodded.

"Who?"

I said the first name I could think of. "Jamal Blair."

My dad pushed out his lips. He was sitting on the couch, twisted to look at me. "I never heard that name."

"He's good. He's a midfielder."

My dad squinted like he was studying me with X-ray vision. I tried to stand as still as possible.

"When's the next game?" he asked, like he was testing me.

"I need to check," I said.

"You don't know?"

I didn't say anything.

"You don't know?" my dad asked again, his voice booming this time.

This was how things went with him. One minute you were having a conversation and the next minute he was blowing up.

There had been one other time that my dad had mentioned wanting to go to a game, but the fact that his work schedule wouldn't allow it had saved me. It was basically the only thing that had been saving me all along. By the time he came home each day, I just said I'd been at soccer and he didn't know the difference.

But it was over now, I thought. He'd finally seen through me.

My dad raised his beer bottle and angled it toward the light. "Gone," he muttered. He held the bottle over the back of the couch. "Get me another." From where I stood, I could see four empties lined up next to the sink in the kitchen.

I took the bottle, and my dad slumped back down in the couch cushions.

Was that it? Were we done now?

Then from the couch my dad yelled, "Celia!"

I heard my mom's footsteps move through their bedroom and down the hall. "Are you calling me?"

"You can't keep up with the laundry?"

She walked into the living room, shaking her head. "What are you talking about?"

"Mayor's soccer clothes. He says they're in the laundry."

My mom looked at me, confused. I just stared at her, trying to look as innocent as possible. But then her face changed, and for a split second I thought that maybe she had figured it out. But if she had, she didn't give me away.

Instead she said, "Sorry. I'll do laundry today."

"¡Carajo!" my dad said, and that was the end of that.

# Quisqueya Solís

Where should I begin? Venezuela is where I was born and where I lived until I was twelve years old. I was a very beautiful child, happy in every way. But when I was twelve, my mother fell in love with a man from California. He asked her to marry him, so we moved to his home in Long Beach. It was an enormous house with a pool in the courtyard. I believe a famous architect had designed it. Hollywood studios called us sometimes to see about using the house in a movie or for a commercial shoot. It was very glamorous.

I was content there for a while. My mother's new husband had a son, Scott, from a previous marriage who was two years older than me. Scott paid no attention to me in the beginning, but soon enough, as my body began to change and I grew into womanhood, he took another look. He was always walking in on me in the shower, claiming he didn't know I was there, or I would catch him watching me while I tanned by the pool. I tried to ignore him when I could. I kept the door to my room locked.

Scott and I were at the house one night. I was sixteen. It was a rainy evening. My mother and his father were out at dinner. I was in the kitchen getting a soda from the refrigerator when he came up from behind and kissed me. I remember very clearly he said, "It's okay. We're not really brother and sister, so it's fine." But it wasn't fine with me. I tried to push him off, but he was stronger than me. I wasn't a prude. I had kissed boys before. But this was not what I wanted. He came at me again. He knocked me to the floor and climbed on top of me.

He did unspeakable things, all against my will. I don't know why, but he thought he could do whatever he wanted. That's how boys are.

Later, I told my mother what he had done to me, but she didn't believe it. She accused me of trying to ruin things for her. She said, "Look at this life they've given us." She warned me not to be ungrateful. Of course, I was only more upset after that. And I felt I couldn't stay there, in such proximity to Scott. I knew it was only a matter of time before he came for me again. I told my mother I was moving out. She didn't fight it. She didn't offer to go with me. I don't think she had ever even wanted a child. She had me as a result of a one-night stand. I was less important than the things she had now—a nice house and diamond jewelry, an expensive car and a big refrigerator. It was the life she had always dreamed of—we were even citizens now—and in the United States no less.

I went to a shelter and told them that I was on my own. I lied and said that my parents were both dead and that I had been fending for myself. I stayed with a girlfriend for a little while, too. I lived in her pool house for months, and her parents never even knew I was there. I missed my mother, but the truth was that I had missed her even when we were together, so it was nothing new.

As soon as I got my high school diploma, I left California. The girlfriend I had stayed with was going to college in New Jersey. Her parents had given her a car for graduation, so she was going to fill it with her belongings and drive across the country to her new school. She offered to take me with her. I stayed with her in her dorm for a while until I found a job waiting tables and saved enough money to live on my own.

I met a certain man while I had that job. He used to sit at the counter and order blueberry pie. He used to flirt with me sometimes. I tried to resist him. I was suspicious of men by then. I wanted nothing to do with them. But he was persistent and he was kind and he made me laugh. He started staying after the restaurant had closed, talking to me while I cleaned up. He used to walk me home when it was dark. He didn't know what he was getting into with me, though. He never did anything wrong, but it was a struggle for me to be truly close to him. It was difficult, because of my past, to trust him. I pushed him away—every time he came back to me, I pushed again—until finally he left.

But he's the father of my two boys, and I've gone out of my way to make sure that they turn out to be good and respectful. When they were in my house, they never laid a hand on a girl, never a kiss, nothing. I was very watchful. It's possible they're the only good boys in the world. With the help of scholarships and financial aid, they're able to attend university. They're studying hard there.

Now I receive money every month as part of my divorce settlement. So financially I'm secure, but I also choose to volunteer my time on Mondays and Wednesdays at the hospital because I feel I should do something positive with my time, something to help people. It's the least I can do. I have enough money that maybe I could live somewhere else, but my friends are here. Besides my boys, my friends are all I have.

Almost no one in my life now knows what I've been through, nor do I want them to know. Some things should be private. That's what I always say. Besides, I don't need anyone's pity. My life has been what it has been. It's not a wonderful story, but it's mine.

# Alma

The days that December were long and cold. We had been keeping our thermostat at eighty degrees but then our first heating bill arrived in the amount of $304.52, which made me cry when I saw it and made Arturo shred the paper into bits the size of confetti. Neither of us needed to say out loud that we couldn't pay it.

We turned the heat down to sixty after that and huddled by the radiators for warmth. We wrapped blankets around our shoulders, pinching them closed in our fists, and wore extra pairs of socks. I tied a scarf over my head, even though Arturo said it made me look like a terrorist. The wind sliced through the edges of the old, loose windows and shuttled cold air into our bedroom. Arturo tried to smooth caulk into the crevices, but the caulk cracked when it dried. He taped rags around the window casings, but it was little help.

"My body isn't made for this weather!" I told Arturo, who laughed the first time I said it and frowned when I repeated myself again a few days later.

"We shouldn't complain," he said.

So I did my best to focus on the positive. Maribel had laughed twice since that first time, and it seemed to me that she was able to remember more on her own now, too. She still relied on her notebook, but during Mass, for example, she knew when to kneel and when to stand, when to go up for communion and how to find her way back to our seat afterwards. The reports from school were encouraging, too. The most recent one had said: "Maribel speaks with increasing frequency, both to the teacher and to the aide, although only in Spanish. She has begun to respond to questions, although at times her response is inconsistent with the question asked. Both in voluntary speech and in reply, she has begun to modulate her voice to be more expressive."

Even so, I was a worrier by nature and I couldn't escape the feeling that anything could happen to her at any time. As if because something terrible had happened to her once, there was more of a possibility that something terrible would happen to her again. Or maybe it was merely that I understood how vulnerable she was in a way I hadn't before. I understood how easily and how quickly things could be snatched away.

Every school morning, I stood outside and waited for the bus with her. Every afternoon, I met her again in the same spot. Maribel had developed a sort of friendship with Mayor Toro, which seemed like one more way that she was making progress—he was her first friend since the accident—but I told her that she and Mayor were only allowed to spend time together under supervision, either at our apartment or at the Toros'. About that I was firm. The Toros' front door was no more than ten meters from ours, down on the first floor, but I stood outside and watched Maribel walk the distance, waiting for her to go inside before I did. When it was time for her to come home, I watched for her again.

I was making enchiladas de carne one day with some near-expired brisket I had found on clearance at the meat market. I was humming to myself, a song my mother used to sing me when I was a girl. I washed the black pasilla chiles off my hands, patting them dry against my pants, and glimpsed the clock, which read just past five. My heart leapt. How had it gotten so late? Maribel should have been home by then. Quickly, I walked to the door and opened it, expecting to see her mounting the stairs, walking toward me, but all I saw was the cracked asphalt and the faded white paint lines in the empty parking lot. Where was she? Was she still at the Toros'?

I closed the door behind me, stepped outside, and started toward the Toros' apartment. When I got to the bottom of the staircase, I heard laughter. Not Maribel's, but someone's. Coming from around the side of the building. And then I heard a boy's voice.

I crept toward it. "Maribel?" I called. No one answered. "Maribel?" I said louder, inching my way forward.

I kicked something and looked down to see Maribel's sunglasses on the ground. Unease rose beneath my breastbone. I picked up the sunglasses and kept walking, listening for her, but everything was quiet now.

And then, as I turned the corner, I saw her. Her back was against the cinder-block wall, and her hands were up over her head. A boy—the boy from the gas station, I recognized him instantly—was holding her wrists in place, staring at her. Her shirt was bunched under her armpits, exposing her white cotton bra, and her head was turned to the side, her eyes squeezed shut.

I screamed. The boy startled and spun his head around.

"Get away from her!" I yelled.

I raced to wedge myself between them, yanking Maribel's shirt down, shielding her with my body. The boy said something in English, something unintelligible to me, but I could hear the indignation in his tone, and without thinking, I turned and spat in his face. He grabbed my arm, digging his nails into my skin.

"Go, Maribel," I shrieked. "Go to the apartment!"

But she didn't move. She was mute and immobile, a tree rooted in place.

"Go!" I said again, tearing myself away from the boy. And then I ran, dragging Maribel with me to the front of the building, back up the staircase and into the apartment, where I locked the door behind us, gasping and trying to blink away the blinding white light of panic.

"WHAT'S WRONG?" Arturo asked that night while we sat at the kitchen table—that ridiculous stolen kitchen table—drinking manzanilla tea, as we did most nights after Maribel went to bed.

I looked at him, startled, as if he had woken me from a dream. "What do you mean?"

"You're so quiet," he said.

"I was thinking."

"About what?"

I hadn't told him what had happened. I wasn't going to tell him. I didn't want him to know that I had failed Maribel again. Besides, she was okay. I had asked her what the boy had done— if he had kissed her, if he had touched her, if he had hurt her—and she shook her head no. He had pushed her against the wall. He was *going* to do something. That was clear. But I had gotten there in time. And when I inspected her, examining every visible part of her body, there were no scratches, no marks of any kind. She's okay, I told myself, with a certain, strange relief. I tried to focus on that instead of on the other part of me that chimed, "This time."

"Alma?" Arturo prodded.

"I was thinking about Maribel," I said. It felt like a way of telling the truth.

At the sound of her name, he softened. "She's doing better, no? The reports from school—"

"Yes."

"But you're worried?" Arturo asked.

I attempted a smile. "No."

"You're worried about something."

I stared at him and shook my head lightly.

"Yes, you are. You worry about everything. You're a true mexicana. A fatalist."

"As if you don't worry about things."

"Of course. But I've been thinking. What if God wants us to be happy? What if there's nothing else around the bend? What if all our unhappiness is in the past and from here on out we get an uncomplicated life? Some people get that, you know. Why shouldn't it be us?"

I flattened my hand against the table, spreading my fingers out. It was a lovely thought, but hearing Arturo's optimism bubble to the surface, hearing the rawness of it, was excruciating.

"You have to think like a gringa now," Arturo said. "You have to believe that you're entitled to happiness."

I took a small sip of tea, feeling the warmth of it bloom in my mouth. Outside, the wind howled and sent the tops of the leafless trees casting back and forth in the night. Soon it would be Christmas, and all at once I wished that we were back in Pátzcuaro, where Christmases were warm and thick with the scent of cinnamon, where piñatas filled with oranges and sugar canes hung from the rafters, and where children paraded through the streets carrying paper farolitos in their small hands. I wished we were anywhere but here—geographically, emotionally. I wished our life was different, that it was what it used to be.

Two years ago, only six months before the accident, my parents had come over for Christmas Eve dinner, bringing Maribel a dress from Diseño y Artesanía that my mother insisted they wanted to give her.

Maribel had made the buñuelos that year because, at fourteen, she wanted to prove her independence and her capabilities. She first claimed she wanted to make the tamales and revoltijo de romeritos, but I argued they were too complicated. Besides, they were the main part of the meal. I thought, If they don't turn out, what will we eat? I told her, "Maybe you can make the buñuelos." Buñuelos had what? Flour, sugar, salt, eggs, milk, butter, baking powder, cinnamon. No more, no less. How bad could they be?

Early in the morning, she got out a bowl and fork.

"What are you doing?" I asked.

"I'm making my buñuelos."

"Already? They don't take more than half an hour to prepare."

"I know."

"Do you also know that it's eight thirty in the morning?"

"Yep."

"But we're not eating them until tonight."

"Mami," she said, putting her hand on her hip.

"Maribel," I said, putting my hand on my hip the same way.

She rolled her eyes.

"Come back around six," I said, shooing her out of the kitchen. "I'll be finished by then and you can have the kitchen to yourself."

At six on the dot, she came back and announced, "Buñuelo time!"

I was wiping down the counter. My food was ready, heaped into bowls that I'd covered with foil and put in the refrigerator. "Do you want my help?" I asked.

"You told me I could make them."

"You can. I'm just asking if you want help."

I knew the answer, though, when she pulled out a bowl, set it on the counter, and lined up her ingredients next to it.

"So you know where everything is?" I asked, before I left her alone.

"Mami," she said, "I live here. I've lived here all my life."

"That doesn't help your father," I said. "Try asking him where anything is."

Maribel dipped a finger in the sugar and licked it.

"Okay," I said. "Call if you need anything."

From the next room I could hear her humming as she measured and poured and stirred. I heard drawers opening and closing, and the clank of spoons against the inside of bowls. I heard the dough hit the counter and her little grunts as she kneaded it and rolled it out. I was sewing a button onto one of Arturo's work shirts when she walked out with flour on her chin.

"Are they done?" I asked.

She sat next to me and laid her floured hand on top of my knee. "It's going well," she said solemnly, as if she were a doctor who had emerged from the operating room to deliver an update.

She disappeared again, and I heard the crackle of the oil as it heated and the sighing sizzle as she dropped the flattened discs of dough in one by one. She's doing it, I thought. My girl.

My parents came over for dinner that night and we ate, flush with the merriment of the season. After everyone was finished, Maribel hurried into the kitchen, where her buñuelos waited on an oval platter covered by a dish towel. She brought them out proudly and, like a perfect hostess, carried the plate around, holding it over each person's shoulder while they helped themselves to the desserts. The buñuelos were golden brown, and the cinnamon Maribel had sprinkled on the top of each while they were still warm had melted into the dough like tiny amber crystals.

"You made these?" Arturo asked in disbelief.

"All by myself," Maribel said.

Arturo looked at me.

"She did," I confirmed.

"They look wonderful," my mother said.

And I saw Maribel, looking over all of us, her face ripe with pride. I saw her growing up before me. I saw the family she would have one day and the food she would make for them. I saw her entire life in front of her, waiting.

# Mayor

I hadn't had a run-in with Garrett since I'd stood up to him that day with Maribel. I'd seen him around, hanging out alone behind the school, scratching at the sidewalk with a rock, flicking pebbles at the tires of the buses as they lined up to take everyone home. I'd seen him slouched in the hall, his hands in his coat pockets, staring at his scuffed boots. And I'd seen him during gym even though he never got changed anymore. He showed up in his regular clothes, and Mr. Samuels would say, "You don't get dressed, you don't participate," and Garrett would shrug and plant himself on the wood bleachers and close his eyes for the next forty-five minutes while we ran around shooting basketballs and learning badminton.

Then one day, just before the winter break, I was digging a notebook out of my locker when I heard someone say, "How's birdbrain?"

I turned around.

"How's your girlfriend?" Garrett asked. "Retard girl."

"Don't call her that," I said.

"What? 'Girlfriend' or 'retard'?"

"I told you to leave her alone," I said.

"You did?" He screwed his face into an exaggerated look of confusion.

I put the notebook in my backpack, shut my locker, and started walking.

"Hey!" Garrett called. He trotted up beside me and grabbed my arm, yanking me so that I was facing him again. "I was still talking to you."

"I need to go," I said, trying to pull my arm free.

"She a good lay? I bet she is. I bet you can do whatever you want to a girl like that."

"Stop it."

"I've been thinking about all the things I could do to her. Tell her to take her clothes off—"

"Stop."

"Have her suck my dick—"

And that's when I punched him. I'd never punched anyone in my life, but before I knew it, I squeezed my hand shut, drew back my elbow, and punched Garrett right in the side of the neck. I'd been aiming for his face, but I missed.

"Jesus!" he shouted, falling back.

Then he ran at me, throwing his arms around my waist, ramming his head into my stomach, tackling me to the floor.

"Get off me!" I yelled.

Garrett socked me so hard I could taste blood in my mouth. All his weight was on top of me, pinning me to the floor. Very dimly, I was aware of a small crowd forming around us.

Garrett nailed me a few more times, in the chest and the ribs, before Mr. Baker, the driver's ed instructor, broke it up. "That's enough," he said, prying us apart. "Up on your feet, boys."

Garrett shook Mr. Baker off and paced in a tight circle. Mr. Baker snatched Garrett's coat sleeve. "Settle down," he said.

I put my hand to my mouth and felt my bloodied lip, split right down the center. What had just happened? Had I really punched him? But instead of feeling pain or any kind of remorse, I felt exhilarated.

"Principal's office for both of you," Mr. Baker said, still working to corral Garrett. "And then we're calling both of your parents."

Garrett spat out a laugh.

"Something funny, Mr. Miller?"

"Good luck with that."

"With what?"

"Listen, you talk to my dad, do me a favor and ask him where the fuck he's been. I haven't seen him in three days."

Mr. Baker took a deep breath. "Come on," he said. "We're going to sort this all out."

THE SCHOOL WANTED my parents to come in for a conference.

"What is this about?" my dad asked when my mom mentioned it that afternoon. She had intercepted him at the door when he got home from work.

"We need to go meet with his teachers," my mom explained.

"All of his teachers?"

"I don't know. Maybe just the guidance counselor. But I told them we would come in as soon as you got home. Someone's there waiting for us."

I was standing by my bedroom door, out of view, but I could hear everything my parents were saying. I had gone straight to my room when I came home, holding my phone over my mouth as I walked through the apartment, trying to hide my swollen, cracked lip from my mom, and I hadn't come out since. The school nurse had wanted to clean off the blood, but I'd begged her to leave it alone, and now I kept looking at it, dried and crusty, in the mirror, in amazement.

"Now?" my dad said.

"They want to see us as soon as possible."

My dad sighed. "Is he in there?"

"He's in his room. But he won't tell me anything. We can talk to him when we get home. Come on, let's go."

"Don't push me."

"We need to go."

I knew my mom was trying to guide my dad out the door, probably thumping him on the leg with her purse.

My dad shouted into the apartment, "What did you do, Mayor?" before I heard the door click shut.

An hour and a half later I was sitting on my bed, awaiting my fate, when my dad stomped down the hallway and swung open the door to my room. He wasn't a huge guy, but he was breathing in a way that seemed to inflate him, and he stood there staring at me, his neck bent over, his arms down at his sides. I swallowed hard. In the time that he and my mom had been gone, I'd talked myself into the idea that maybe my dad would be proud of me— just a little bit—when he found out I'd gotten into a fight. Maybe it proved I had a little bit of machismo in me after all. Plus, it was something that not even Enrique had ever done, at least not that I knew of. But now, seeing my dad's face, I could tell that idea was out the window. Silence festered in the room. I swallowed again, trying to get down the saliva that had collected in my mouth.

My dad closed the door behind him. He paced in front of me, breathing like a bull. I sat on my hands and stared at my knees.

After what must have been five full minutes, I said, "What?"

My dad stopped pacing and looked at me like I had just broken the first rule of engagement. Like I should have known that I wasn't supposed to talk first.

"What?" my dad repeated incredulously. "What? I'll tell you what. You punched someone."

"He deserved it!"

My dad started pacing again and suddenly, somehow, I knew that the fight wasn't the thing that was bothering him.

After another long stretch of silence, he said, "Your counselor told us your grades are slipping."

I hung my head. So that's what this was about. I'd been spending so much time with Maribel lately that I hadn't really been focused on things like homework.

But then my dad said, "I asked her if it was because you were spending too much time at soccer."

Something dropped through me like a runaway elevator. Shit, I thought. Shit, shit, shit. My dad was still pacing. I tried to steel myself for whatever was coming next. There was a distinct possibility, I thought, that he was going to hit me. Not that he'd ever done it before—he'd thrown things and kicked things—but I sometimes had the sense when he got angry that he was only about an inch away from getting physical, as if so far over the years, even though the thought might have crossed his mind, he'd been able to control himself, but that if he were pushed too far into the fire, there would be no stopping him.

"You lied," he said.

I nodded.

"This whole time."

I nodded again.

My dad worked his jaw from side to side. "This whole time!"

"I'm sorry," I said.

"You made me look like a fool tonight! Is that what you think I am? A fool?"

"No," I squeaked.

"I thought you were out there, every day, playing, part of the team. But what have you been doing instead? Drugs? Drinking?"

"No!"

"How can I know?"

"I'm not, Papi."

"This whole time!" he screamed, and he lunged toward me, squeezing my shoulders between his hands like a vise, lifting me to my feet.

His nostrils flared and he looked me right in the eyes. "Goddamn it, Mayor!" He dug his fingertips into my skin like he was trying to carve his way down to my bone.

I didn't want to cry, but I could feel my eyes burning.

My dad brought his face close to mine, close enough so that the tips of our noses almost touched. "You're done," he said.

CHRISTMAS THAT YEAR was both the best and the worst we'd had in a while. There was this kind of pall over everything, heavy and sticky like a film we couldn't get out from under. It hadn't taken long to deduce that "You're done" meant I was grounded until further notice. No Maribel, no William, no allowance, no nothing but school and home until my dad decided otherwise. And on top of that, my dad announced the next night, no Christmas presents this year, either. "Wait until you see the pile of gifts we're getting Enrique," my dad said. "A mountain of gifts! That will teach you not to lie to me again." My mom argued that my dad was being hard on me, but he didn't want to hear it. Which meant that what to do with me became just one more source of tension between them.

On Christmas Eve, the three of us took a bus to the Wilmington train station to meet Enrique, who was coming home for a few days for the holidays. My mom had begged him to stay longer, but he claimed he needed to be back on campus for some obscure reason he never disclosed. Even so, a few days was better than nothing—I needed any buffer I could get—and my mom was busting at the seams in anticipation of seeing her baby boy again, as she kept saying.

"He's a grown man now," my dad told her.

"He's still my baby," my mom insisted.

When Enrique came down the steps into the train vestibule, he was wearing a hooded sweatshirt that said MARYLAND across the front and black athletic pants. He was unshaven, carrying a duffel bag in his hand. Honestly, he looked homeless.

"Kiko!" my mom shouted, running to him, wrapping her arms around his neck.

"Hey, Ma," I heard him say.

When my mom and Enrique walked over to us, my dad took my brother's bag out of his hands and patted him on the back. "Here he is!" my dad said. "My good son."

I shrank a little. My mom looked at me with pity.

"How was the train?" my dad asked.

"Decent," Enrique said, then punched me in the shoulder.

"Hey," I said.

"What's up, kid?"

We caught the bus back home, and when we arrived, my mom started preparations for Enrique's favorite meal, which was pork tamales. She reminded him that we were going to church that night, but he begged off, saying he was tired and needed to catch up on sleep. I couldn't believe it when my dad didn't put up a fight. Instead, he just said, "Is the coach working you hard up there?"

"Yeah, Pop," Enrique said.

You could count on my mom, though. "But it's Christmas," she argued. "One time a year, God would like to see your face. One time!"

"He doesn't see it every day?" Enrique asked.

"In church," my mom clarified. "He would like to see your face in church. And so would I."

Enrique looked at my dad like, She can't be serious, can she?

"He's tired, Celia," my dad said.

"He can be tired later."

Enrique looked at my dad again, but this time my dad seemed resigned to the fact that there was no way he and Enrique would win this battle; my mom would wear them down eventually. "I tried," he said halfheartedly.

Later, as I was getting dressed for Mass, Enrique knocked on my door.

"Why are you getting ready so early?" he asked when he saw me.

I didn't tell him it was because I was eager to see Maribel, who I knew would be there. I had a feeling she wouldn't measure up to my brother's standards. I mean, if all he did was look at her, she would have made the grade, no problem. But if he knew the whole story . . .

"Nothing better to do," I said.

He laughed. "Yeah. I heard about that. What did you do anyway? How did the angel child get grounded?"

My lip had pretty much healed by then—there was just a faint, kind of purplish line where the split had been—but I pointed it out to him anyway.

"I got in a fight."

Enrique's eyes widened. "You mean by accident?"

"Nope. I started it. I punched someone."

"Man," Enrique said. "You turned into a tough guy while I was gone."

He sat on my bed and looked around like he was trying to

figure out if anything had changed since the summer, which was the last time he'd been home.

"There's no way I could live here again," he said. "This place is so depressing. Every time I come back, it seems shittier."

"It's not that bad."

Enrique chuckled. "That's just because you don't know any better."

I got my clip-on tie out of the drawer and started to hook it to my collar.

"See, that's what I'm talking about," Enrique said. "All these rules. Like God cares whether or not you're wearing a tie."

"You used to wear a tie to church, too," I said.

"Exactly. Used to. But I wouldn't be caught dead in that thing now."

"It's not a big deal."

My brother shook his head. "One day you'll get out of here and you'll see."

I tried to imagine it, going off to college in a few years, walking into a life that was all my own, one where I didn't have to wear a tie to church, one where I didn't even have to *go* to church, where no one could ground me, and where I could do whatever I wanted.

I pulled the tie off and tossed it on the bed. "Fuck that," I said, a little too loudly.

Enrique laughed. "That's what I'm talking about!"

We rode the bus to midnight Mass with the Riveras, although Enrique sat all the way in the back, plugged in to his iPod, so it was basically like he wasn't even there. The bus driver tuned the radio to the all-Christmas-music station, and when "Feliz Navidad" came on, I guess since we were the only people on the bus, he raised the volume and shouted back at us, "Here you go! A little piece of home for you!"

Under his breath, my dad said, "Every year the same thing. If it's in Spanish, it's a piece of home. Well, I never heard this song until I came to the United States."

"And every year, you complain," my mom said.

"You like this song?"

"No."

"It's like how everyone thinks I like tacos. We don't even eat tacos in Panamá!" my dad said.

"That's right. We eat chicken and rice," my mom said.

"And seafood. Corvina as fresh as God makes it."

"Yes."

This was one of the few things that could unite my parents, the thread that mended them: their conviction that no one else here understood Panamá the way they did.

I was sitting in front of them with my feet up on the seat, my dress socks pulled halfway up my calves. I had my coat zipped to my chin so that my mom wouldn't see that I wasn't wearing my tie. The Riveras were across the aisle from us.

"I like tacos," I offered.

My mom sighed. "Why would you say such a thing?"

"What about you, Maribel?" I asked. "Do you like tacos?"

When she didn't answer, I repeated the question, louder.

She was pressing the pad of her thumb against her incisors. She said, "My teeth are really sharp."

"So you could eat a crunchy taco?" I asked.

"Okay," she said.

My mom swatted my shoulder. "Leave her alone," she said.

"I was just asking if she liked tacos."

"I don't know what that means," my mom said.

"Tacos? It means tacos."

"I don't know if you mean something else by it now. All this taco talk."

That made me laugh. Taco talk. And as soon as I laughed, I realized I hadn't done it in a long time—too long—and I remembered how good it felt, how it made my muscles warm and filled me up with the kind of lightness that was usually missing in my life, the kind of lightness that was buried under my parents' bickering and under my awkwardness at school. I stared out the window into the dark, at the illuminated trail of streetlights streaking through the air, and laughed while everyone else on the bus stayed quiet.

THE NEXT MORNING, my mom brewed a pot of Café Ruiz— our annual treat—and brought out the rosca bread with almonds that she'd made the night before. Our apartment was decked out with the same tired decorations she displayed every year—angel figurines on the end tables, a crocheted snowman cozy that slid over the extra roll of toilet paper in the bathroom, a dried wreath with a red velvet bow that she hung over the kitchen doorway, a porcelain nativity scene on the floor. We hadn't gotten a tree and, as threatened, I didn't get any presents. Enrique didn't exactly get a mountain of stuff either, unless a four-pack of deodorant and a new Gillette razor along with a bunch of replacement blades counted. "I'm not really into shaving anymore," Enrique said when he opened them, and when I offered to take them he laughed and said, "Oh yeah. You can use them on that nonexistent hair above your lip." Besides him, the only person who got a gift was my mom, and it was nothing more than a lousy set of shampoo and conditioner that my dad swore he bought at the salon even though anyone could see from the sticker on the back that he'd gotten it from the clearance shelf at Kohl's. My mom placed the set on the coffee table. None of us mentioned the sticker.

My mom called my tía Gloria, only to learn that my aunt had finally decided to file for a divorce from my tío Esteban, news that sent my mom into a low-level state of shock, not because she hadn't seen it coming but because of her adamant objection to divorce. Anyone's divorce. But by the time the receiver was back on the latch, my mom was on a high from talking to her sister at all, which always cheered her at least for the short term until the cheer was displaced by missing her again.

Late in the morning, the radiators died, and my dad did what he always did—kick them and curse—until he gave up and plopped down on the couch. Not long after, the telephone rang. It was Sra. Rivera, calling my mom to tell her that the heat was out and to ask what they were supposed to do. My mom told her just to wait, that it would come back on eventually.

"The Riveras?" my dad asked from the couch when my mom hung up the phone. "I bet they're freezing their asses off. They never thought they would leave México for this, I'm sure."

"We should invite them over," I said.

"Why?" my mom asked.

I seized up. Why? It wasn't like we had heat either. What was I going to say? Just because I wanted to see Maribel? Because I'd bought her a present about a month ago, a red scarf that had cost me basically all of my allowance and that I'd wrapped in tissue paper and had been keeping under my bed for her, and now that I was grounded, I didn't know how I was going to get it to her?

"We should invite everyone over," I said. "The whole building. More body heat will warm everyone up."

"Genius," Enrique said sarcastically.

"It's true," I said. "It's thermodynamics and radiation. They've proved it."

But when Sra. Rivera called again at noon, concerned because the apartment was getting colder by the minute, my mom told them to stop by. Then she hung up and dialed Nelia and Quisqueya and told them to spread the word. She pulled out every candle we owned and lit match after match until the wicks were all burning with tiny flames. "It's pretty like this, don't you think?" she said, and I had to admit, it did look nice. Before she could brew another pot of coffee, people were knocking on our door, wishing us Merry Christmas and gripping bottles of rum in their gloved hands.

Everyone kept their coats and hats on. Quisqueya was wearing her fur hat on her head, which I always thought made her look Russian. Micho brought his camera, roaming around the apartment snapping pictures of everyone who was already there—Benny flashing the peace sign; Nelia sitting cross-legged on the couch, nursing a beer that my dad had given her; Quisqueya sitting next to her, pretending like she wasn't interested in having her photo taken. When the Riveras showed up, Micho bunched the three of them together in front of our door and made them pose while he snapped a shot. Maribel stared right at the camera, but she didn't smile, so I went up behind Micho, waving my arms and making goofy faces to see if she would react. When she cracked a grin, Micho said, "There we go! That was a good one."

Not long after, José Mercado and his wife, Ynez, showed up, her gripping his elbow while he hobbled with his walker.

"Gustavo had to work," Benny told my dad, even though my dad hadn't asked. "Movie theater might be the only place that's open on Christmas Day."

"Hollywood doesn't believe in God," my dad said.

Benny laughed. "But God sure believes in Hollywood. Have you seen those women? Megan Fox? And the mouth on Angelina Jolie? God is in the details, man!"

My dad raised his beer. "¡Salud!"

"Despicable," Quisqueya said.

Even our landlord, Fito Mosquito (that's what I called him), stopped by long enough to poke his head in the front door and announce that Delmarva, the energy company, was on their way to fix the heat. "Don't blame me!" he said.

"Don't worry," Micho shouted. "We won't blame you. We'll just deduct it from our rent checks this month!"

Fito wagged his finger, and a few people laughed.

Micho said, "We're just teasing you, man. Come on inside."

The radiators didn't kick back on until late that night, but with all the people packed into our apartment that afternoon, it started to feel a little more like Christmas. Everyone shivering and laughing and drinking and talking. When we ran out of coffee, my mom mixed up huge pots of hot cocoa that she made from heavy cream and some chocolate bars she'd found in the back of a cabinet and melted down. Sr. Rivera asked if she had cinnamon sticks to put in the cups to make it Mexican style, and my mom found a jar of powdered cinnamon in a cabinet that she sprinkled into the pot.

"Are you happy now?" she joked. "It always has to be the Mexican way. México, México. As if the rest of us don't exist."

"¡Viva México!" Micho shouted from the corner of the room.

"¡México!" Arturo said.

"¡Panamá!" my dad said.

"¡Presente!" my mom said, and everyone laughed.

"¡Nicaragua!" Benny shouted. "¡Presente!"

"¡Puerto Rico!" José said.

"¡Presente!" Ynez and Nelia chimed at the same time.

"¡Venezuela!" shouted Quisqueya. "¡Presente!"

"¡Paraguay!" said Fito. "¡Presente!"

Then "Feliz Navidad" came on the radio.

"This goddamn song again!" my dad said.

"Oh, come on!" my mom said. She started singing along and swishing her hips while my dad eyed her skeptically.

"What?" she said. "You don't want to dance with me? Fine. Benny, ven."

And Benny took my mom by the hand, spinning her around.

Ynez and José joined in, José leaning on his walker while he rocked back and forth, and Micho pulled Nelia up off the couch into a twirl. Almost everyone in the room started singing along and eventually my dad put his drink down and cut in on Benny and my mom, sliding his arm around her waist.

"Now this is more like it!" my dad yelled above the noise. "This is like the Christmases I knew!"

I took the dancing as the opening I'd been waiting for and stole Maribel away so that I could give her my present. We sat at the end of the hallway outside my bedroom where no one could see us, and I handed her the square lumpy package I had wrapped.

"You can open it," I said. "It's for you." I felt nervous all of a sudden, like maybe it was too much or maybe she wouldn't like it.

"It's light," she said, and I nodded, anxious for her to get on with it.

She pried off a piece of tape and folded open the tissue paper at one end. She held it up at eye level and squinted inside.

"It's a scarf," I said before she'd even pulled it out all the way. "It's alpaca."

She unfolded the whole thing and laced her fingers through the yarn fringe at the ends.

"Do you like it?" I asked.

"Yes."

"I picked out a red one so that it would match your sunglasses."

"It's so soft."

"It's alpaca," I said again, like I was suddenly some kind of alpaca salesman or something.

She wrapped the scarf around her neck.

"I'm sorry I haven't seen you," I said. "My dad grounded me."

"What is that?" she asked.

"It means he's not letting me go anywhere besides school. Whatever. It's not a big deal. I just wanted you to know why I haven't been around."

She nodded.

"I wanted you to know that it isn't that I don't *want* to see you."

"Okay."

Then, there in the shadows of the hallway, I kissed her. This strange electricity shot through my body. My first real kiss. Her skin was warm, and she smelled like laundry detergent and frost, as fresh as the winter air. She pulled away first, but she peeked at me and smiled. All I wanted was to do it again—to kiss her, to inhale her, to feel her mouth against mine. I was fuzzy with the thought of it, like I'd somehow slipped underwater. But then, from the living room, my dad started singing along in English: "I want to wish you a Merry Christmas from the bottom of my heart," warbling like a yodeler on "heart," and Maribel giggled and the moment passed.

# Adolfo "Fito" Angelino

I came here in 1972 because I wanted to be a boxer like the great Juan Carlos Giménez, who was from Paraguay. Like me. There was a trainer in Washington, D.C., who was good, who was very good, legendary, and who specialized in flyweight fighters. Which is what I was. Skinny but strong. I wrote the trainer a letter. Sully Samuelson. What a name! And he wrote me back. A letter signed with his name. He told me he wasn't taking on new fighters but that if I was ever in D.C. I should look him up. Maybe he assumed that because I was all the way over in Paraguay, the chances weren't good I would ever be in D.C. Maybe it was just a bluff, is what I'm saying. But I thought if I could just get a meeting with him, if I could show him what I was capable of, that I was going to be the next Giménez, there was no way he wouldn't want to work with me. So I went to his gym, and every day I bounced around, pow pow pow, light as air on my feet, and then, boom! a hook you never saw coming. I wore red satin shorts and the best pair of boxing shoes I could afford. I was waiting for Sully to take notice, to see me and recognize that I was a champion. But after a few days, nothing. And when I finally asked one of the other guys about him, I found out that Sully had moved to Vermont, which was a place I'd never heard of back then. Vermont? What is that?

I thought I would go. ¡Vermont, jaha! But I only made it as far as Delaware. I ran out of money on the way, so I got off here and found a job laying blacktop for a few days, trying to earn enough for another bus ticket. It was supposed to be temporary, but I was sealcoating the parking lot of this building and the landlord, he used to stand out on the balcony, smoking a cigar while I worked. Name was Oscar. Turned out he was heading back to Montevideo, where he was from, and the guy who owned the building back then wanted him to find a replacement to manage the property. For some reason he thought I could do the job. "No way," I told him. "I'm gonna be a boxer!" He took one look at me and laughed. "You?" he said. I challenged him to an arm wrestling match. I said if I beat him, he had to give me the money for the ticket to Vermont, but if he beat me, I'd take the building manager job instead.

Well, here I am. No shame in it.

Who comes to the United States and ends up in Delaware? I for one never thought I'd be here. But I've been surprised. It's popular with the Latinos. And all because of the mushroom farms over in Pennsylvania. Half the mushrooms in the country are grown there. Back in the seventies, they used to hire Puerto Ricans to harvest everything, but now it's the Mexicans. And they used to set up the workers with housing, too. Shitty housing with rats as big as rabbits, boarded-up windows, no hot water. After Reagan's amnesty deal, the workers started bringing their families up from México. They didn't put their wives and children up in that shitty housing, though. They found other places to live. Places like Delaware. It's cheaper than Pennsylvania. And no sales tax. We have all the Spanish supermarkets now, and the school district started those English programs. I know some people here think we're trying to take over, but we just want to be a part of it. We want to have our stake. This is our home, too.

I like it here. I started off as the manager, but now I own this building. Bought it out almost ten years ago after working jobs on the side, saving up. I got a good deal. The area is changing, though. A clash of cultures. I try to make this building like an island for all of us washed-ashore refugees. A safe harbor. I don't let anyone mess with me. If people want to tell me to go home, I just turn to them and smile politely and say, "I'm already there."

# Alma

I hadn't uttered a word to anyone about finding the boy with Maribel, but ever since it happened, I hadn't been able to stop thinking about it, either. I was suffocating under the weight of it, and I was furious at myself for letting him get to her, for creating an opening just big enough for him to slip through and find her.

So finally, just after the new year, I did what I should have done in the beginning—I went to the police. In México the police were corrupt and often powerless. No one trusted them. But maybe here, I thought, they would be different.

The police station was a brick and glass building with an American flag cemented in the ground out front. Inside, it smelled of cleaning solvents. I strode up to a window behind a black counter where a woman in uniform sat, turning the pages of a magazine.

"Me llamo Alma Rivera," I said when I got to the counter, shouting so she could hear me through the glass.

The woman held up one finger, got off her stool, and disappeared into another room. When she came back, a male officer with a chiseled face and a cleft in his chin accompanied her. He stood behind the glass and said in Spanish, "I'm Officer Mora. Can we help you with something?"

"I'm Alma Rivera," I shouted again in Spanish.

"I can hear you fine. How can we help you?"

I took a deep breath. "I'm here about a boy."

Officer Mora nodded. I waited for him to invite me behind the glass so we could talk in private, but he simply stood, waiting for me to continue. There was no one else in the lobby, so I went on. "I came home one day and a boy was with my daughter."

"How old is your daughter?"

"Fifteen."

"And the boy?"

"He's her age, I think."

"So a teenage boy was with your teenage daughter?" Officer Mora said.

"He had her against the wall of our building."

"Did he assault her?" Officer Mora asked.

"He had her against the wall," I said again.

"Did you see him punch her or kick or physically harm her in any way?"

"No. But the only reason he didn't was because I got there."

"Did he say something that made you think that?"

"No, but he came for my daughter," I said again, frustration burning my throat.

"Maybe she's friends with him."

"No."

"In our experience parents don't always know what their teen-aged children are up to."

"You don't understand . . . ," I started. I had the urge to tell him about her brain injury, but I didn't want his pity. I only wanted his help.

Officer Mora planted his hands on the counter behind the window. "What I'm hearing is that you came home and found your daughter with a boy her age. That's all you know. Is she a pretty girl?"

"He looked at us when we went to the gas station," I said.

"Who? The boy?"

"He was staring at my daughter."

"Staring at her? Señora Rivera, that's not criminal."

"He had her shirt up," I said. Shame had kept me from revealing it sooner. I didn't want anyone, not even the police, to envision Maribel that way.

Officer Mora's expression changed. "When?"

"When I found them the other day."

"You saw him pull her shirt up?"

"No, but—"

"So she might have done that herself?"

"She's not like that!"

Officer Mora rubbed the back of his neck, rolled his head around once, and took a deep breath. "Señora," he said through the glass, "this is a police station. We don't deal with teenage relationships here. Unless he assaulted her in some way, or unless he made some kind of verbal threat, there's nothing we can do."

I stared at him in disbelief. "I thought you would help her."

Officer Mora sighed, as if it were a great exertion to have to deal with me any longer. He said, "We can't protect her from a boy who, honestly, probably just has a crush on her. That's your job."

In English, he said something to the woman officer, who shook her head before flipping another page of her magazine. I was a fool, I realized, to believe that they would care about any of this. I tightened my lips and straightened my purse strap on my shoulder with all the righteousness that I could muster. Neither Officer Mora nor the woman seemed to notice.

"Gracias," I said sarcastically.

"De nada," Officer Mora said in earnest, as if he believed he had done his job.

I SHOULD HAVE gone home. But anger roiled in my belly, and after I boarded the bus back to the apartment that day I was seized by another idea. Fito had said the name of the neighborhood where the boy lived once. Capitol Oaks, wasn't it? If the police weren't going to help me, I thought, I would go over there myself.

I walked up the aisle and tapped the bus driver on the shoulder. In my best English I said, "Capitol Oaks?" He nodded and said something I didn't understand, but I waited behind him, hoping that when we got to the right stop, he would signal for me to get off.

As the bus drove on, I pulled my dictionary from my purse to look up the words I wanted. I hadn't learned them yet in my English class—I had been to a few more since the first time—so I would have to teach them to myself. I looked up dejar. Leave. Sola. Alone. Leave alone. Leave alone, I said in my head. I practiced the words, mouthing them silently, until the driver stopped the bus and fluttered his hand over his shoulder at me. "Capitol Oaks," he said.

As soon as I got off the bus and turned around, I saw it: a neighborhood that was probably only two kilometers from us, a place I must have passed a dozen times and never noticed. Capitol Oaks, with a sign screwed into a low brick wall at the entrance, half covered by weeds.

I crossed myself and whispered, "Dios me lleve," then clutched my purse and walked past the sign to the rows and rows of ranch-style houses. The yards were dry and overgrown, and lighted reindeer and inflated snow globes from Christmas still littered some of the front lawns. In México, Arturo had built our house before we married. He and some friends had dug a plot of earth with shovels and pickaxes. For weeks, they had poured cement and laid rebar. They had stood in a line that stretched from a pile of cinder blocks to the foundation, heaving each block from one man to the next until Arturo, who was nearest to the house, laid it. Until they had laid enough blocks that they rose high enough to call them walls. Into the hollows of one of the cinder blocks, the one centered just above the front door, Arturo placed a print of San Martín Caballero encased in a plastic bag, to bring us luck. Here, on the house fronts, the paint was peeling and the porches sagged. Pickup trucks and two-door cars were parked in the driveways. I could feel, like some sort of mist that hung in the air, that I was unwelcome.

I walked for ten minutes, maybe more. There was no sign of the boy nor of anyone. Just a chill in the air, an arc of gray sky overhead. This wasn't going to work. There was no one here but me. And how did I think I was going to find him anyway without an address? I was heading back toward the entrance when behind me I heard a sound.

I turned. And there, walking down the driveway of a brown clapboard ranch-style house with rusted gutters and a storm door askew on its hinges, I saw him—the boy—dragging a trash can down the cracked driveway.

He had seen me, I realized. He'd been watching me wander down the street. He came out here on purpose.

The two of us stood maybe ten meters apart, fixed in place, for a long time. Finally the boy stood the trash can upright. He walked closer, and I felt the world constrict, my heart pulsing against my ribs. When we were only an arm's length apart, he stopped.

I squeezed my hands around the lining of my pockets and whispered, "Leave alone."

He stared at me from under the hood of his navy sweatshirt.

From somewhere in my depths, somewhere beyond where I knew I could reach, I summoned enough courage to say it again, louder this time. "Leave alone."

The boy locked his eyes on me and said something I didn't hear. He repeated it, and the second time I understood.

"Go home," he said.

I knew those words, and I knew by the way he said them that he didn't mean I should go back to the apartment.

Then he lifted one hand and pointed at my face. He took a step forward and touched his fingertip to my cheek, to the bone that curved just under my left eye. He twisted his hand forty-five degrees and cocked it like a gun, three fingers drawn back, his thumb up in the air, and let a burst of air explode from his lips, his warm breath like a ball of fire against my face.

"¿Comprende?" he said.

I felt light-headed. I didn't know what to do. I wanted to leave. I wanted to run out of there and never see the boy again. But my feet were like dead weight. Move, I told myself in my head. Go, Alma.

I turned around and forced myself to start walking, listening for the sound of his footsteps, bracing myself for him to run up and shove me from behind or knock me down or do whatever he was going to do. But there was only the swish of my jeans as my legs scissored past each other until I got to the main road.

• • •

I WAS ON EDGE the rest of the day, the encounter with the boy sticking to me like burs pricking at my skin. I couldn't shake it off. When Arturo and I sat together at the kitchen table that night, I was quiet and preoccupied, staring into my cup of tea, the only sound the knocking of the radiator. I could feel Arturo looking at me—I knew he could tell something was wrong—but unlike last time, he didn't ask what it was.

I ran my fingers around the rim of the mug. Arturo cleared his throat and took another sip of tea. I lifted my eyes enough to watch him raise it to his mouth, to see his hands around the lacquered clay—those rough hands, the onion-thin peels of skin around his thumbnails where he'd bitten them, the scrapes on his knuckles where they rubbed against the top of the crate when he pulled mushrooms out from the soil inside. I saw the drooping neckline of the Baltimore Orioles sweatshirt we had bought from the Goodwill store and that he wore around the house, the field of dark stubble along his jaw. I knew every inch of him, it seemed, and yet, in the last year, we'd had such trouble finding our way to each other. Before the accident, we had been the happiest people I knew. "No one else," Arturo used to say to me, "has ever been in love like we are. No one else even understands what that word means." We believed we were special. We believed we were indestructible. But after the accident, under the gathering clouds of fate, something changed. We still loved each other as much as we ever had, but it was as if neither of us knew what to do with that love anymore. It was as if our sorrow was so consuming that there was no room for anything else. When we did fall into bed together or into each other's arms, pressing our bodies together skin to skin, it was out of desperation, a longing to somehow rediscover what was familiar and what was good. But what used to feel like a communion only emphasized our grief and eventually we had stopped trying altogether.

Looking at him now, though, a fire roared up inside me. I was tired suddenly of feeling so bereft, so unmoored by sadness. I wanted to smother that feeling, to clear it from our lives like cobwebs from a dusty corner. I wanted to erase the anguish and the distance, the remorse and the blame, and replace it with something new. I wanted to figure out how to grope our way back to each other. Even now, even after the day I'd had. Especially now.

I lifted my foot under the table and rubbed it against Arturo's leg.

He looked at me, startled. "What?" he asked.

I pushed back from the table and walked to him.

"What are you doing?" he asked.

I put my hand on the back of his neck and leaned down, kissing his skin, breathing in the scent of his hair.

"Alma," he said, curling away.

I lifted his hand from the mug. "What is all this?" I asked, touching the frayed skin around his thumbnail. I raised his hand to my lips, closing my mouth around his thumb, waiting to see if he would protest. I sucked each of his fingers one by one while he watched.

And then I climbed on top of him, straddled his lap. "I miss you," I murmured.

Arturo put his hands on my hips and pulled me toward him. "I'm here," he said.

"Closer," I said.

He shimmied me closer and buried his face in my neck. I

spread my fingers through his hair, feeling the warmth of his scalp, the faint scratch of his mustache against my skin. And by the time he pushed himself inside me I believed that even after everything, even after the accident, and having traveled so far, leaving behind the landscape that we had woken up to every morning our whole lives—cedar mountains and citrus groves, a blue lake and mango trees—no matter what else happened, we would be fine as long as we had each other. Contigo la milpa es rancho y el atole champurrado. And then, the rush. It was as if the whole world sighed. As if every human and every creature and every gas and liquid and speck of dirt and granule of sand and gust of air settled all at once, and all was right in the universe. If only for that moment.

# Mayor

Not long after New Year's, my tía Gloria called my mom to say that her divorce had gone through.

"Esteban is no longer part of my life," she said.

My mom burst into tears.

"Why are you crying?" my aunt asked. "It's good news. And listen to this—he has to pay me!"

"What do you mean?" my mom asked, sniffling.

"I'm getting eighty thousand dollars from the settlement!"

My mom's tears dried up immediately. Her voice turned serious. "How much?"

"It's from that summer house he had. The one his father gave him that we never went to. He has to liquidate it and I'm getting the money!"

"And," my mom told us over dinner that night, "she's giving some of it to us." She was pink in the face, barely able to contain herself.

My dad wiped his mouth with a napkin. "How much is she giving us? Fifty dollars?" He smirked.

"Well, that was nasty," my mom said. "You're going to feel bad when I tell you the real number."

I peeked at my dad, who was waiting with the napkin clutched in his hand. My mom started eating again, delicately picking the capers off the rice with the tines of her fork.

She took at least four bites before my dad finally said, "Well? Don't keep it a secret."

A grin played on my mom's lips.

"Never mind, then," my dad said.

"You don't want to know?"

"Why would she be giving us money anyway?"

"Because we need it."

"Who needs it? Not us. We're fine."

"We're fine? Now we're fine? For months you've been talking about how you might lose your job, but now you're telling me we're fine?"

"Yes."

"Unbelievable."

My dad shoveled rice into his mouth, probably to stop himself from saying anything else.

But my mom couldn't let it go. "I'm only saying we could use the money."

My dad dropped his fork onto his plate with a clatter. "Jesus, Celia! I told you we don't need it! What's she giving us? A hundred dollars? Two hundred dollars? We don't need it!"

"If you don't want to take it, you don't have to! I'll just keep it for myself, then."

"What is that supposed to mean?"

"What I said."

"You want to leave?"

"Who said anything about leaving?"

"You take this, I take that. Is that what you're doing? Just like Gloria?"

My mom rolled her eyes.

But my dad was in a groove. He lifted his plate from the table and slammed it down, scattering rice and capers and peppers and chicken across the floor. "Goddamn it, Celia! How many times do I have to tell you that I will take care of this family?

What do you think I'm doing out there every day? You think I'm working my ass off for fun?" He stood, toppling his chair.

My mom pursed her lips and stared at her plate.

He reached across the table and seized both of her wrists. "Look at me when I'm talking to you!"

But as soon as she did, my dad threw her wrists back at her in disgust.

"I don't know how many times . . . ," he muttered, shaking his head. Then he turned, using his leg to sweep aside the chair, which was on its back on the floor, stepped over the food, and walked out of the kitchen.

The clock on the wall ticked faintly. The glass bottles of vinegar and hot sauce that my mom kept on the shelves inside the refrigerator door rattled. I felt embarrassed for my mom, who sat across from me screwing up her face like she was determined not to cry, but I stayed absolutely silent, waiting to see what would happen next.

Finally my mom said quietly, "Mayor, finish your chicken."

TWO DAYS LATER, my dad and I learned the news: Tía Gloria was giving us ten thousand dollars. After the heat between my parents died down, my mom blurted out the number during dinner. My dad nearly choked on his food.

"I can't believe it," my mom kept saying.

"Well, we've probably given her almost as much money over the years," my dad said once he'd recovered from the shock.

"Ten thousand dollars, Rafa? Come on."

"We did what we could," my dad said.

"Of course we did. And now she's doing the same. It's just that she can afford to do more. Ten thousand dollars! I can't believe it."

It didn't take my dad quite as long to wrap his head around the idea. The morning the money landed in my parents' bank account, my dad said, "I think we should buy a car."

"A what?" my mom sputtered as she snapped a piece of bacon and popped it in her mouth.

"Nothing fancy," my dad said. "I'm not talking about an Alfa Romeo here. But a car. Something that runs."

He was happy, I could tell, at the mere thought.

"A car?" my mom asked, dumbfounded.

"Yes. You've heard of it? Four wheels. Takes gasoline."

It was no secret that since he was a boy, my dad had lusted after cars, and the pinnacle of his obsession would have been to own one. Once, he bought an issue of *Autoweek* at the Newark Newsstand, and for the past few years he'd consoled himself by flipping through it while he lay on the couch, licking his thumb before he turned each thin, glossy page, staring for what seemed like hours at a sleek black Maserati or a balloonish blue Bugatti. Enrique and I used to make fun of him about it, but even when the pages eventually started falling out, my dad just taped them together and flipped through it again.

"But what will we do with a car?" my mom asked. She looked at my dad now with mild amusement, as if he had just suggested they buy an elephant.

"What do you think?" my dad said. "We'll drive it."

"Where?"

"Anywhere. You could drive to the Pathmark."

"I don't know how to drive."

"You'll learn."

"Can I drive it?" I asked.

"You don't have a license yet," my dad said.

"But when I get one, I mean."

"Rafa, be serious," my mom went on. "We don't need a car. We could go to Panamá ten times with that money."

My dad rubbed his chin. He looked at the two of us, sitting there, eating breakfast. I could tell, and I'm sure my mom could, too, that he had made up his mind.

"We're getting a car," he said.

THE AUTO DEALERSHIPS in our town were on Cleveland Avenue. Cars waxed and gleaming, plastic pennant flags criss-crossed over the lots. But of course, because my dad was always looking for a bargain, Cleveland Avenue wasn't where we went.

We took a bus instead to a used-car lot that my dad had found through an ad in the newspaper. It was in the middle of nowhere, and the winter sun shone over the acres and acres of land that surrounded it. The hard grass crunched under our feet as we walked and the wind squealed, tearing holes through the air.

My mom grimaced and pulled the collar of her coat up around her face. "Is it supposed to snow today?" she asked.

My dad was already way ahead of us.

"It's supposed to snow?" I said, excited by the prospect.

"I don't know. I'm just asking. I can't believe it's January and we haven't even had flurries yet."

I looked up at the sky. Even though the air was frigid, it seemed to me like the sun was too bright for snow, but maybe I was wrong. I hoped I was wrong.

The only reason I'd come was because my dad thought he might need a translator. I told him, "You use English every day." But my dad had argued that he didn't know the language of cars. To him, everything had its own language—the language of breakfast, the language of business, the language of politics, and on and on. In Spanish he knew all the languages, but for as long as he'd been speaking English, he believed he knew it only in certain realms. He never talked about cars with anyone in English, he said. Therefore, he didn't know the language. It was no use explaining to him that I didn't exactly spend my days talking about cars with people, either. To him, I knew all the languages of English the way he did those of Spanish. And as proud as he was that I was so good at one, I think he was also ashamed that I wasn't better at the other.

The cars were in a big cluster, parked at odd angles, some with their tires in a rut, some without tires at all. My dad walked through the maze of them, his hands in his pockets, and examined them silently.

After a few minutes, a small, gray-haired man in a plaid jacket came out to greet us.

"G'morning," he said, shaking my dad's hand. "How can I help you folks today?"

"We want to buy a car," my dad said.

The man nodded. "We've got a few. D'jda have something in particular in mind? A sedan or a wagon? A truck maybe?"

"I like something fast," my dad said.

"A sports car?" the man asked.

My mom tugged my dad's sleeve like some kind of warning that he'd better not get too carried away. Predictably, my dad ignored her.

"Do you have anything Italian?" my dad asked, as if he hadn't just seen everything on the lot.

"An Italian sports car?" The man's eyes widened. "'Fraid not. What we've got here is mostly American or Japanese. There's a few Volkswagens in the bunch. But Volkswagen's about as European as you're gonna get. I have one, about fifteen years old, that still runs about as good as Secretariat when she was in her prime. Transmission's manual, so you could probably crank it up, get her going pretty speedy. You wanna take a look?"

I doubted my dad understood everything the man said, but he followed as the man led us to the back corner of the field where a small car, brown like cocoa powder, sat in the sun.

"Here she is," the man said. "Just got her last week from a fellow down in Bear. Not much wrong with her as far as I can tell. There's a dent in the hood and the seat belts are a little slack, but the lights work, gearshift is smooth as silk, and it's got power steering. Only thirty-two thousand miles. Little bit of rust around the wheel wells, as you can see, but the radio works. AC still gets cold. Not that you need it this time of year." He chuckled. "She'll probably last you another ten years. A real beauty if you ask me."

I wouldn't have gone that far. The car was small and unspectacular. But compared to the rest of the inventory, it might as well have been a Lamborghini, and I could tell by the way my dad was eyeing it that he was hooked.

"How much?" he asked.

"We run the Kelley Blue Book values on all these, so our prices are fair."

"How much?" my dad asked again.

"Twenty-three hundred," the man said.

My mom made a noise.

"You got that?" the man asked.

My dad, suddenly a master negotiator, shrugged. "We were just looking," he said.

"You aren't gonna find much better than this," the man said, patting the car's hood.

My dad peeked in the passenger-side window.

"Twenty-two hundred," the man offered. "Times are tough. I'll give you folks a break."

My dad wandered around to the other side of the car and checked out the view through the driver's-side window after smudging some frost away with the heel of his hand.

My mom shivered against the wind. "Rafa," she said.

The old man glanced at her, apparently interpreting this as my mom's way of telling my dad that it was time to go, because he said, "Okay. Two thousand even. That's the best I can do. And you can drive her off the lot today."

My dad took one more lap around the car, the sunlight bouncing off its rear windshield. Then he asked, "Do you take a check?"

WE DROVE HOME, two thousand dollars poorer, in our new Volkswagen Rabbit. In that big field, the old man, whose name we learned after we agreed to buy the car was Ralph Mason, gave my dad a quick lesson in the vagaries of manual transmission. My mom and I sat in the backseat as Mr. Mason, from the passenger side, took my dad through the gears, telling him when to depress the clutch and when to let it go. "Take her up!" Mr. Mason would shout. "Give her gas!" And my dad would obey the best he could. He was a mess at first, and each time the car twitched my mom would exclaim, "Ay!" but he took to the basic coordination of it surprisingly easily. After ten minutes, Mr. Mason declared my dad a natural. "Best student I've ever had," he said, clapping my dad on the shoulder, and my dad beamed. In the backseat, my mom rolled her eyes.

My dad didn't stall once on the drive home. Of course, he never made it above thirty miles per hour, either, even when we got on the stretch of Route 141 between I-95 and Kirkwood Highway. He crept onto 141 cautiously, like a beetle onto the tip of a branch, and kept a steady pace even though all the other cars in existence were flying past us at warp speed, honking as they swerved by.

"What are you doing?" my mom asked, buckled into her seat belt in the front.

My dad, focused on the road ahead, said nothing.

"Everyone's passing us!"

"Let them," he said, gripping the steering wheel with both hands now that we were in gear.

"No, this is not good, Rafa. You have to keep up."

"The speed limit is fifty," I said, trying to be helpful.

My mom peered at the speedometer. "You're only going twenty-five!"

Again, my dad said nothing. He offered no explanation, no defense. He just focused on the road ahead and on steering the car.

A semi-truck roared by, sounding a long honk as it did. From on high, the driver gave us the finger.

"I can't look," my mom said, putting her hand over her eyes. "This is awful."

"Give it gas!" I said, affecting the voice of Mr. Mason.

"Both of you," my dad said. "I know what I'm doing."

"I hope we don't see anyone we know," my mom said.

"We're on the highway, Celia, not at a party."

"This is so embarrassing!"

"No one we know even has a car," my dad pointed out.

"We're not going to have one for much longer either if you don't go faster."

"I know what I'm doing."

"It's dangerous, Rafa! Everyone has to go around us."

I had been glancing out the back window every now and then, watching people switch lanes and flash their headlights at us. At that moment, I saw a car that had been coming up behind us in our lane swerve out to the side just before it reached us. The driver hadn't realized until too late how slow we were going, or else he had miscalculated how fast he would catch up to us. He skidded onto the shoulder as my dad, totally unaware, kept moving us forward. The driver righted the car, put on his turn signal, and shot back into the traffic at the first opening. He careened around us and, as he passed by, yelled out his open window, "Learn how to fucking drive!"

My mom slumped in her seat. "Ay Dios," she said.

"It's a good thing Enrique's not here," I said.

"We would never hear the end of it," my mom agreed.

"We're almost there," my dad said.

"Where?" my mom asked.

"The exit."

And when we pulled off, two and a half miles later, my dad expertly brought the gears down to first, to idle at a red light. My mom sat up.

"You don't understand," my dad said. "They stop you."

"Who? What are you talking about?" my mom asked.

"That's why I was being cautious."

"Who stops you?"

"The police. If you're white, or maybe Oriental, they let you drive however you want. But if you're not, they stop you."

"Who told you that?"

"The guys at the diner. That's what they say. If you're black or if you're brown, they automatically think you've done something wrong."

"Rafa, that's ridiculous. We've lived here for fifteen years. We're citizens."

"The police don't know that by looking at us. They see a brown face through the windshield and boom! Sirens!"

My mom shook her head. "That's what that was about?"

"I didn't want to give them reason to stop me."

"You were driving like a blind man, Rafa. *That* will give them reason to stop you."

"Everybody else just has to obey the law. We have to obey it twice as well."

"But that doesn't mean you have to go twice as slow as everybody else!"

The light turned green and my dad brought the car out of first. We cruised under the overpass, a shadow draping over the car like a blanket.

"Next time, just try to blend in with everyone else and you'll be fine," my mom offered.

"The way of the world," my dad said.

"What?" my mom asked as we emerged back into the sunlight.

"Just trying to blend in. That's the way of the world."

"Well, that's the way of America, at least," my mom said.

EVEN THOUGH the general mood in our house had lifted, I was still grounded, which meant that I hadn't seen Maribel since Christmas. I had told her back then that it was going to be a while before I could come over again. She'd been getting better about remembering things—I didn't have to repeat myself as often anymore and sometimes she even referenced things we'd talked about days before—but I wasn't sure if she remembered this thing, and I hoped she didn't think I was just ignoring her or that I'd lost interest. If anything, the grounding just gave me time to miss her, and I'd sit at home most afternoons depressed, staring out the window through the frost creeping in around the edges, hoping to catch a glimpse of her getting off her bus. And then I would walk away, because I knew if I saw her, it would be torture. And then I would go back, because not seeing her was torture. And then I would try to steer clear of the window for a while and make myself do something else like take a shower or read or play a game on my phone, but it was no use. I just paced around in anguish, not knowing where to look, not knowing where to go, and feeling like I was about to lose my mind.

At school, things were no better. I sat at my desk, drawing hats and mustaches on the people in my textbooks while I thought about Maribel. I wondered what she was doing, if she was as miserable as I was, what her hair looked like that day, what she was wearing. Anytime a teacher called on me, I had no idea where we were in the lesson. I'd just say "Huh?" and usually, after getting a disappointed look or even more often, a surprised one, I'd slump down in my seat and feel like crap. I went to the nurse's office and complained that I had a stomachache or that I had a headache or that I was pretty sure I had the swine flu so I needed to go home. The nurse would take my temperature and send me back to class every time.

Sometimes when I got home from school, one of my mom's friends would be in our living room, sipping freshly brewed coffee out of the Café Duran mugs my mom liberated from the cabinet only for guests. Occasionally, I was greeted by the sight of Sra. Rivera, whose company my mom coveted, and anytime she was there, I would linger in the hallway outside the kitchen and eavesdrop, waiting for her to say something about Maribel. Once, my mom mentioned my name and after a pause Sra. Rivera said, "He seems to like Maribel, no?"

"Mayor?"

"He's been good for her, I think. She's different when he's around. More like herself."

"Really?" My mom sounded genuinely surprised.

"Did something happen, though?" Sra. Rivera asked. "He hasn't come over in a while."

"Didn't I tell you? Rafa grounded him. Mayor got into a scuffle at school, and Rafa flew off the handle as usual. Él es tan rabioso."

"It was serious?" Sra. Rivera asked. "What he did at school?"

"No, no. It was nothing. Trust me, Mayor is a good boy."

Sra. Rivera didn't say anything to that, and I wondered whether she believed my mom or whether knowing that I'd been grounded had somehow ruined her image of me.

One day I came home from school to find Quisqueya sitting next to my mom on our couch with her legs crossed. She used to be a regular fixture in our house, but lately I hadn't seen her as much. Her furry snow boots were by the door and her white fur hat was in the center of the coffee table like a cake.

"How was your day?" my mom asked, after I walked in and dropped my backpack on the floor.

"Okay."

"Anything interesting?"

"Nope."

My mom said to Quisqueya, "He's a man of few words these days."

"Like all men," Quisqueya said. "Except for my sons, of course. They call every night from the university to talk to me."

"Tell me again, what university are they in?" my mom asked, feigning ignorance.

"Your memory is so short, Celia. They're at Notre Dame."

"Oh, right! Notre Dame. I don't know why that never seems to stick with me."

Quisqueya twisted herself to look at me. "I notice you've been spending a lot of time with the Rivera girl," she said.

My mom tsked. "Not lately. Mayor is grounded."

Quisqueya gasped. "Grounded!"

My mom shook her head like she was sorry she'd mentioned it. "It was nothing," she said.

"Well, before. He used to spend a lot of time with her before."

Quisqueya twisted herself to me again. "It's a shame about her, isn't it? But when I see you with her, the two of you seem to be having actual conversations. Like real people."

"You don't know anything about her," I said, my cheeks burning, my voice flat as a wall.

"Not as much as you, certainly," Quisqueya said.

"They're just friends," my mom said.

Quisqueya replied, "Of course. That's how it starts."

"Mayor, go to your room and start your homework," my mom ordered.

"I don't have any homework."

"It's a good idea to do your homework," Quisqueya said. "Hard work is what got my boys where they are." She faced my mom again. "Did I tell you they're both majoring in computer science? You should hear them talk about their assignments. All these technical terms! They love it. But I have to tell them, Please! I'm just your little mom!" She smiled. "I don't understand any of it."

"Maybe that's because there's something wrong with *your* brain," I said.

"Mayor!" my mom snapped.

"What did he say?" Quisqueya asked my mom.

"I'm sorry," my mom said. "I don't know what's gotten into him lately."

"I said maybe you don't understand any of it because there's something wrong with your brain."

Quisqueya blanched.

"Ya, Mayor! To your room!" my mom said, leaping up from the couch and pointing. When I didn't move, she growled, "Now."

IT WAS ALL just bullshit. Quisqueya and Garrett and my dad and every other person on earth could say what they wanted, but Maribel and I were meant for each other. I knew it.

So the next day, instead of going straight home after school, when I got to our building, I walked to her apartment. My legs were shaking for fear that my mom, or worse, my dad, would catch me, so as soon as Sra. Rivera cracked open the door, peering over the tarnished gold chain latch, I said, "Can I come in?"

"Are you supposed to be here?" she asked.

"Is Maribel around?"

"Aren't you grounded, Mayor?"

"I *was* grounded, yeah. But I'm not anymore."

I could see the hesitation on her face.

"My dad called it off," I added, and finally she let me in. I found Maribel in the bedroom, standing by the window. She was wearing the red scarf I'd given her at Christmas and it was everything I could do not to walk over and kiss her right on the spot.

"Hey," I said.

She turned around and gave me a puzzled look.

"I wanted to see you," I said.

Maribel stared at me, blinking with her long eyelashes. "You got a car," she said at last.

"You heard about that? Yeah. It's not, like, a nice car or anything. And it's not mine, you know. It's my dad's."

"Where is it?"

"Out in the parking lot. My dad hasn't driven it since we brought it home."

"So the car is sad."

"It's sad?"

"It's lonely."

"If you say so."

"Should we visit it?"

"The car?" Then I realized what she was trying to do. See, she was smart. She was way smarter than anyone gave her credit for. I smiled. "I mean, sure, if you want to."

We told her mom we were going over to my apartment, and I promised, as I always did, that I wouldn't leave Maribel's side the whole thirty-step journey from her unit to mine.

"Don't say anything," I told Maribel as we squeezed in the door to my apartment. As quietly as I could, I lifted my dad's car keys from the windowsill, clutching them in my fist so they didn't jingle. Then I slipped back out and motioned for Maribel to follow me. The two of us were outside again before my mom even knew the difference.

I opened the car door and let Maribel climb in, then hurried around to the driver's side and got in beside her. The car was freezing inside and it smelled coppery and wet, like snow. I saw that someone—my mom, I assumed—had hung a rosary over the stem of the rearview mirror.

Maribel skimmed her hand across the bumpy, faded leather on the dash.

"My dad always wanted a car," I said. "Since he was a kid. But he had a donkey instead."

"A donkey?"

"He named it Carro."

Maribel laughed.

"Yeah, I know. A donkey named Car. How dumb."

"Your dad is funny."

"Not really," I said. I slid my hands around the steering wheel. When my foot accidentally rubbed the brake, the sole of my sneaker squeaked against the ridges of the pedal.

"Do you know how to drive?" Maribel asked.

"Pretty much," I said. "I took driver's ed last marking period, so I have my permit, but I haven't done the exam for my actual license yet. My friend William did it, though, and he passed it no problem, so it can't be that hard. The only thing I'm worried about is parallel parking, but I probably won't ever have to parallel park unless I go to Philly or D.C. or something. I don't know. The driver's ed teacher, Mr. Baker, always made us drive by his house so he could feed his dog. Every year on mischief night, his house gets egged and he complains to the principal about it, but it's like, duh, if you didn't take kids to your house all the time, no one would know where you lived and it wouldn't happen. He's kind of stupid."

"You talked for a long time."

"I did?"

"It was like hours."

"No way. Not even close."

"I don't mind," she said.

"What? You don't mind me?" I wanted to see what she'd say, but she just blushed.

"I like this car," she said. "It's very cool."

She grazed her fingertips across the center console, her nails scraping the hard plastic. I watched the delicate round bone at her wrist twist back and forth and felt blood pounding in my ears.

I took a quick look out the windows and in the rearview mirror to see if anyone was watching. Earlier, I thought I'd heard a door shut, but when I looked now, the coast was clear. I didn't know how much time I would have before either her mom or my mom came storming out, looking for us. I was getting all heated up even though it was cold as hell in that car. I unzipped my coat.

"Mayor?" Maribel said.

"Yeah?" I held my breath.

"I feel like you're the only person who . . . sees . . . me."

"Maybe everyone else just needs glasses," I said, attempting a joke, but it fell flat, and I squeezed my hands around the steering wheel until my skin pulled so tight I thought it would flare off at my knuckles.

I turned to her. Ever since the first time, kissing her again was all I'd wanted to do. Be chill, I told myself. It's nothing. It's just—

I closed my eyes and leaned across the console until my mouth found hers. I put one hand on her shoulder, on her rubbery coat, gripping the fabric in my fist. Her nose brushed my cheek, and the wool from her scarf tickled my chin. After a few seconds, I slid my tongue into her mouth, shocked by the feel of her seashell teeth and then by the wetness of her tongue as it touched mine. I moved my hand to her neck, her skin hot and soft, and holding her like that, my heart raced. Forget it: my heart was doing laps and hurdles and high jumps and I swear the fucking pole vault. My pants got tight. I could sense it, but I didn't care. We just kept kissing, my hand under her scarf. And then my pants were damp and warm. I pulled back. I threw my hands over my crotch and angled my body away from her.

"What's wrong?" she asked.

"Nothing," I said.

And, man, if that wasn't the truth.

# Nelia Zafón

I am Boricua loud and proud, born and raised in Puerto Rico until I told my mami in 1964, the year I turned seventeen, that I wanted to live in New York City and dance on Broadway. My mami put up one hell of a fight. You are only seventeen! You don't have any money! ¡Estás más perdido que un juey bizco! All of that. But I had a dream that I was going to be the next Rita Moreno. I was going to be a star. I told my mami, You can look for me in the movies! And I left.

I didn't know a soul when I got to New York. I slept on the floor of Grand Central Terminal for the first three nights, watching everyone's feet walk past, men in loafers, women in patent leather heels. Click click click. Everyone with somewhere to go except for me. I had gotten to my destination and now what? A dream isn't the same thing as a plan. I started feeling like I wanted to return home, but the way I left—all that youthful righteousness and conviction that I threw at my mami como un tornado—I would have been embarrassed to go back so soon. My mami would have said, "You see, nena! You're just a little girl after all." No. I had planted a stake and now I had something to prove, to my mami and to myself, to everyone from my neighborhood. I had to prove that I could make it.

I got lucky, though. In the train station, I met a girl, this chica de compañia named Josie, who had gotten kicked out of her parents' house for smoking dope. She had a friend, a guy in Queens, who was going over for the war and she was going to stay in his apartment until he got back. I'll never forget, she said, "I have to water his plants for him so they don't die." Later, when he didn't come home, when they couldn't even find enough pieces of his body to put together to send back, she cried so much and for so long that I knew: She was in love with him. She had been waiting for him, every day pouring cupfuls of water into the pots that held his plants, turning them in the sunlight, taking care of them because she thought it was a way of taking care of him.

I lived in that apartment for one year. I had gotten a job as a waitress, but Josie never charged me rent. Her friend's parents were paying for the apartment, she said. It was covered. Instead I put all my money toward dance classes and acting classes that I took in the mornings at a little studio in Elmhurst. For food, I ate leftovers off diners' plates at the restaurant. I scraped whatever people didn't eat into cardboard take-out containers and saved it for later. Hash browns, toast crusts, noodles, creamed corn, todo eso. The boss didn't really care.

I went to auditions when I heard about them. I remember there was an open call for *Man of La Mancha* at a small theater in Greenwich Village. I tried out for the role of the housekeeper. When I got there, a man was lining up all the girls. I remember I asked him whether it was okay that I wasn't Spanish. Because of course it was a Spanish play. He said, "What are you?" I told him, "Puertorriqueña," and he said, "What's the difference?"

I didn't get that role or any role after that. Not a single one. For years I tried. After the news of Josie's friend, I had left the apartment in Queens because it didn't feel right for me to stay there. Josie refused to leave. She took over the lease. She kept watering the plants. Maybe it was denial, but maybe it was her only way of holding on to someone she had loved. Maybe we should all be so passionate.

Once I was on my own again, I found a place in the cellar under a corner grocery store. Really a cellar. It had damp stone walls and one window no bigger than a squinted eye. I danced all day and took trains and buses all over the city to auditions, and at night I carried around trays of food and flirted with the men for bigger tips. On my walk home sometimes, and as I stepped back down into that cellar apartment, my eyes heavy from exhaustion, I would think, Is this what it is? This country? My life? Is this *all*?

But even when I thought that, I was always aware of some other part of me saying, there is more. And you will find it.

Oh, I didn't find it, though. I worked like crazy. I practiced dancing until my feet bled and my knees felt like water balloons. I rubbed Vicks into my cracked heels and took so many hot baths I lost count. I went to a voice coach and sang until my throat was raw. I killed myself, but it never happened for me. The world already had its Rita Moreno, I guess, and there was only room for one Boricua at a time. That's how it works. Americans can handle one person from anywhere. They had Desi Arnaz from Cuba. And Tin Tan from México. And Rita Moreno from Puerto Rico. But as soon as there are too many of us, they throw up their hands. No, no, no! We were only just *curious*. We are not actually *interested* in you people.

But I'm a fighter. You get me against the ropes and I will swing so hard—bam! So I thought, well, if I'm not going to find it, then there's only one other option: I will create it.

I researched and found out that taxes for new businesses were lowest in Delaware, so I saved money for a while—I stopped taking classes and signed up for extra shifts at the restaurant—

and said good-bye to New York. I came to Wilmington to try to start a theater company of my own. I got a job as a waitress again, only at nights, at a bar this time, and during the day I worked on getting the theater going. It was a different time then. The society was different. Free love, fellowship, turn on, tune in, drop out. There were communities of artists, people who didn't want to work for the big corporations, people who were willing to help a girl like me, and many times they worked for free. I met a guy who helped me build sets and put up some lights. I did all the painting myself. I got a whole truck full of wooden pews from a church that was being renovated. I lined them up for the people I dreamed would one day come to watch my shows. The Parish Theater, I called it, because of those pews.

In 1971, we had our first production, a play called *The Brown Bag Affair.* It was very racy, provocative, a lot of nudity, but the story was powerful, and even though for the first few weeks only a few people showed up to see it, word started to spread. First, we had an audience of ten people, but eventually it grew to twenty, everyone sitting shoulder to shoulder in those long pews. Every few months, we did a new show, and two years after we opened our doors, we were getting regular crowds for every one. The theater wasn't making much money, but we were bringing in enough to keep the plays on. That by itself was some kind of miracle.

Now, twenty years later, I still run the Parish Theater. We do just one production a week. I act in them sometimes, but the real pleasure for me now is giving roles to other actors, watching them perform, especially the young ones. I was like them once. I can relate. And now I think, Okay, *this* is what it is. My life. This country. It took me so long to get started, and I never became a big star, but now I feel proud when I go back to Puerto Rico to visit my old neighborhood in Caguas because in a certain way, I did make it, after all.

A few months ago I met a man who came to the theater. He's younger than me, a gringo, an attorney, so young and handsome. ¡Cielos! We have almost nothing in common, but somehow we're a good fit with each other. He makes me laugh. How can I explain it? He has a spirit. I'm fifty-three years old with wrinkles on my hands. I've never been married in my life, and now this. You never know what life will bring. Dios sabe lo que hace. But that's what makes it so exciting, no? That's what keeps me going. The possibility.

# Alma

One day near the end of January, Maribel and I were sitting at the table, going over her schoolwork, when, three hours before he usually got home, Arturo walked through the front door, slammed it behind him, and marched down the hall.

Maribel looked at me, confused.

"I'll be back," I told her.

I found Arturo in the bathroom, stripping off his clothes, tiny crumbs of mushroom soil raining down to the floor. He turned on the water and, without waiting for it to warm, climbed into the shower, burying his head under the spray.

"Are you okay?" I asked.

He didn't answer.

I rested my hands on the rim of the sink, feeling the cool, smooth porcelain, and stared at myself in the mirror. For a second, fear got the best of me. What was it? Something with the boy?

"Did something happen?" I asked, trying to conceal the anxiety in my voice.

Arturo pulled his head out from under the water, heavy droplets streaming down his face, dripping off the tips of his mustache. "You really want to know?" he said. "I was fired."

"Fired?"

"Yes. Because I changed my shift. The morning when I stayed home for Maribel's first day of school."

"But that was months ago!"

Arturo turned off the water, twisting the handle so hard I thought he would break it. I watched as he picked up his towel from the floor and rubbed himself dry, the hair matted on his barrel chest, his limp penis hanging between his stocky legs.

"I don't understand," I said.

He snapped the towel against the floor. "¡Chingao!"

"It has to be a mistake. They went through all the trouble of getting you a visa. Why would they do that and then turn around and fire you?"

"Because they're cowards."

"What does that mean?"

"The only reason they sponsored our visas was because the government was pressuring them to hire workers with papers. But now everyone's saying it was all talk."

"But why does that mean they have to fire you? What are they going to do? Get rid of everyone they already have and hire people without papers now?"

"Probably. It saves them money that way."

I thought, I could call his boss and explain the situation. Maybe if he knew about Maribel, he would have some sympathy. Maybe if he knew what it meant to us. This wasn't how it was supposed to happen. We had followed the rules. We had said to ourselves, We won't be like everyone else, those people who packed up and went north without waiting first for the proper authorization. We were no less desperate than them. We understood, just as they did, how badly a person could want a thing—money, or peace of mind, or a better education for their injured daughter, or just a chance, a chance! at this thing called life. But we would be different, we said. We would do it the right way. So we had filled out the papers and waited for nearly a year before they let us come. We had waited even though it would have been so much easier not to wait. And for what?

Arturo finished drying himself in silence.

"I worked hard," he said after a long time.

"I know."

"I did what I thought—"

"I know," I said.

We were both quiet for a moment. "Maybe I could look for a job?" I suggested.

"No. Our visas are only for me to work. I have thirty days. If I can find something within thirty days, then we'll stay in status. It can be anything. Just a paycheck and our visas will be good."

I reached toward him, but he stepped back, tense, locked in his thoughts.

"You'll find something," I said.

SO DURING THE DAY, every day, Arturo looked for work. He dressed in his church clothes—black pants and a button-down shirt, a brown belt, his cowboy boots—and walked into store after store, asking for applications. People laughed in his face. They told him, "Haven't you heard that the economy's in the shitter? We can't get *rid* of workers fast enough." They told him, "Crawl back across the river, amigo." And yet, what else could he do but try the next place, and the one after that?

We had to take money from our savings to pay the rent. There was no other choice. Arturo and I tried reasoning with Fito, but Fito was firm. "I feel bad for you," he said. "I do. But I have a mortgage to pay and it depends on collecting the rent." Arturo shook Fito's hand and assured him we would bring him the money soon, even though both Arturo and I feared that might not be true. Two months, we estimated, was as long as we could go without a paycheck coming in.

I made rice and beans and rice and beans and more rice and beans, but since we couldn't afford chiles or ham or anything to spice it up, we soon grew tired of rice and beans. "Oatmeal," I suggested. "We still have oatmeal left." But neither Arturo nor Maribel wanted that either.

We walked around the apartment in the shadows, turning on the lights only after the sun had gone down. We kept the heat off at night. We showered every other day to save on water. I still washed our clothes at the Laundromat, but I carried them home sopping wet and laid them all over the kitchen counters and the floor to let them dry. I would have draped them over the balcony railing except that I was afraid they would freeze stiff. Instead of sitting at the kitchen table at night, drinking tea, now I simply boiled water for Arturo and myself instead, but the water was a poor substitute and trying to pretend otherwise only made me more depressed.

I tried to be at the apartment during the day in case Arturo stopped back at home, either to eat or to drop off applications. I made him food and gave him pep talks, and then he was off again, ready to try somewhere new. I went only as far as the Dollar Tree or the Laundromat, both of which were close enough that I didn't have to be gone for long. The Community House was too out of the way and even though I had gone back to the English class there only a few times, now I stopped going altogether. I still wanted to learn English, though, so I asked Celia if she would come over to teach me a few things. She brought a workbook that she and Rafael had used when they first came to the United States. It had illustrations to show basic vocabulary—words for colors, foods, parts of the body, animals—like a child's book of first words.

"Rafa and I both learned English in school in Panamá," Celia said. "But when we got here, we had to refresh our memory."

We sat at the kitchen table while she said, "Miércoles. Wednesday."

I repeated the words.

"Jueves. Thursday," she said.

I said, "Tursday."

"Not 'Tursday,'" she said. "Thursday. Push your tongue out against the back of your teeth."

"Where is my tongue now?" I asked.

"At the top of your mouth, I think. Push it out."

But I didn't know what she meant and each time I repeated it—"Tursday"—Celia corrected me.

"Thursday."

"Tursday."

"Thursday."

"Tursday."

"No, Thursday. Th th th."

"Thursday," I said.

"You got it!" Celia cheered.

When I didn't have a lesson with Celia, I made it a point to at least sit in front of the television with the dictionary Profesora Shields had given me and look up as many words as I could while they flashed across the closed captioning on the screen.

I learned the phrase "Are you hiring?" and taught Arturo the words. I thought maybe if he approached potential employers in English, he would have a better chance. But after trying it at various places, he said, "I feel silly. I say it and then they answer me in English and there's nowhere to go from there. They look at me like I'm stupid."

"You're not stupid," I told him.

"To them I am," he said.

And yet, despite the stress of the hunt and the anxiety over what it would yield, since that night in the kitchen, I felt closer to Arturo again, if only by inches, and I could tell that he felt closer to me, too. He took my hand sometimes under the blankets while we lay next to each other in bed, and once, while I stood in front of the sink washing the dinner dishes, watching bits of food float in the soapy water, he came up behind me and threaded his arms under mine, cupping my shoulders and resting his chin on the back of my neck, as if he simply wanted to be near me.

Our wedding anniversary was on February 19, and though usually in Pátzcuaro we went out to dinner, we didn't have the money for that here. But Arturo wanted to honor the tradition, so we made a plan to go out for drinks instead. Waters, we decided, since even sodas were beyond our means by then.

We went to the pizza restaurant down the street because Arturo had submitted an application there and I knew he was hoping that if he showed his face again, maybe someone would recognize him and maybe somehow he would walk away with a job. We were down to one week, a mere seven days, before we would lapse out of status.

The restaurant was in the corner of a strip center, a striped vinyl banner above the door heralding its presence and its name. Luigi's. Inside it was filled with square tables and metal-framed chairs, and the aroma in the air was sweet and sharp—tomatoes and cheese.

We had told Maribel on our way there that we were only ordering water.

"Can we order horchata?" she asked as soon as we sat down.

"They don't have horchata here," I said.

"Is this a restaurant?" she asked.

"Yes. But they don't have horchata."

"Do they have pescado blanco?" she asked.

"We're not ordering anything," I said.

"Why not?"

"We're here to celebrate."

"With water," Arturo added.

We ordered three waters without ice and when they came we sat together, sipping out of pebbled red plastic glasses, celebrating in silence, while around us American couples and families ate slices of pizza and drank bottles of beer. I had the feeling that they disapproved of us being there, drinking only water, taking up space. But when I glanced at the people around us, no one was even looking in our direction, and I felt the way I often felt in this country—simultaneously conspicuous and invisible, like an oddity whom everyone noticed but chose to ignore.

And then, the front door opened, and I snapped my head up to see who it was. The boy, I thought. I don't know why. On the walk over, I had been convinced that he was following us, and I had peered over my shoulder, thinking I'd heard the clatter of his skateboard behind us, but all I saw was Arturo giving me a quizzical look. Now though, it was only a young mother who walked in, pushing her child in a stroller. I held the glass to my lips and took a deep breath.

A few minutes later, Arturo broke the silence that had settled over us like fog. "Well," he said. "Nineteen years."

"Nineteen years what?" Maribel asked.

"Nineteen years that your mother and I have been married. She was eighteen when I married her."

"Don't say that," I said. "It makes me feel so old."

"You are old," Maribel said.

Arturo laughed.

"What's funny?" Maribel asked.

"Yes, what's so funny, Arturo?"

"Do you have . . . a joke?" Maribel asked.

"Your father doesn't know any jokes," I said.

"Oh, I know jokes."

"Like what?"

"Here's one I heard on one of the American late-night shows. Why did the bicycle fall down?" He scanned our blank faces, waiting for a response. When he got none, he said, "Because it had two tires."

"That doesn't make sense," I said.

"Well, the audience laughed. Maybe the subtitles were wrong?"

"It was tired?" I said. "That's why it fell down?"

"You think you can do better?" Arturo asked. "Let's see you tell a joke."

"A joke about what?"

"Anything."

"Yes," Maribel said.

I looked around the restaurant for inspiration.

"We're waiting," Arturo said.

"Hold on."

"Maybe you can order one from the menu," Arturo offered. "Waitress, waters for us and one joke for my wife. Skip the straw."

Maribel smiled.

"I'm getting funnier by the minute, Alma. You'd better think of something quick if you want to keep up with me."

I stared at the table and tried to concentrate. Finally, to satisfy them, I told the only joke I knew, one that had made me laugh out loud when I heard it, even though I'd never repeated it myself. I said, "Why didn't Jesus use shampoo?"

"I don't know. Why?" Arturo asked.

"Because of the holes in his hands."

Arturo looked at me in shock. At the sight of his face, I crossed myself. God in heaven, forgive me.

Then Arturo started laughing. Even Maribel, who months earlier never would have been able to process a joke like that, put her hand over her mouth to hold in her laughter.

Arturo raised his glass and toasted. "To the funniest woman I know," he said.

"Thank you," I said.

Arturo frowned. "Nothing about me?"

"Sorry. To the best man I know."

"That's more like it."

"And the best daughter," I added.

"The best!" Arturo said.

I looked at them both—the way Arturo's mustache turned up when he smiled, the way Maribel's face glowed.

"The best," I repeated.

SEVEN MORE DAYS passed. Seven days of knocking on doors and making calls and begging with store owners and anyone who would listen. But at the end of it, Arturo came up empty-handed.

I found him in the morning, the day after the deadline, sitting in the thin blue light, his head bowed, his fingers entwined behind his neck. I went to him and put my hand on his shoulder with all the tenderness I possessed. I wanted to heal him somehow with my touch, to save him from feeling that he had let us down.

He said, "I'm sorry."

"You did everything you could have done," I said.

"If anyone finds out—"

"Who's going to find out?"

"She would have to leave her school, Alma."

"No one's going to find out."

He ruffled his hands up through his hair.

"We haven't done anything wrong, Arturo."

He didn't respond.

"We're not like the rest of them," I went on. "The ones they talk about."

He unclasped his hands and looked at me, his expression sad and weary. "We are now," he said.

AT THE TAIL END of February there was an ice storm. That's what Celia called it. I phoned her not long after it began, when the rapping against our windows got so bad I thought for certain those hundreds of tiny collisions would break the glass. I was home alone—Arturo was still searching for a job, not for our visas now, but because we needed money—and when I heard the light taps followed by great thwacks like horse hooves against the panes, the thought crossed my mind that it was kids in the neighborhood, tossing rocks against the window. But when I looked I saw a glinting silvery spectacle against a white sky. Splinters of rain.

When Celia answered the phone, she said, "It's an ice storm. They'll be sending the children home from school soon, I'm sure. Don't go outside unless you want to fall and break something. The last time this happened, José's walker slipped. He broke his wrist and had to wear a cast for six weeks."

"It's ice?" I asked. "Coming from the sky?"

"I know," Celia said. "Can you imagine?"

"Is it chips of ice?"

"More like spears, I think. Well, that sounds dangerous. More like toothpicks."

"Toothpicks of ice," I repeated.

All winter, we had been anticipating snow—everyone kept saying how strange it was that we hadn't had any yet—but I'd never heard anything about falling ice.

Celia said, "When it's over, it's actually very beautiful. In White Clay Creek Park there's a marsh that freezes, and the children go skating on it. Maybe Maribel would like it. Should we go? It's something to see at least."

"Maribel doesn't know how to skate on ice."

"She doesn't need to. Everyone just slides around in their shoes. Let's go on Sunday, after church. The roads will be clear by then, but the marsh should still be frozen."

"Is it far?"

"A few miles. There used to be a bus, but it doesn't run that route anymore. Maybe we could drive? Oh, it would be fun! You could use a little fun, couldn't you? Rafa hasn't even driven that car since we got it. And then Maribel can say she went ice-skating."

The wonders of this country. In México, men sold ice out of carts they attached to bicycles. Here, it was falling from the sky.

Imagine, I thought, if Lake Pátzcuaro froze all the way through. I wanted to tell my parents that we had walked in our shoes on islands of ice. They wouldn't believe it. They would think we had gone to the moon.

"Yes," I told Celia. "Let's go."

THAT SUNDAY, we all stood in the parking lot, next to Rafael's car, waiting for him to tell us where to sit. He scratched his head and stared at the car.

"You didn't realize this was going to be a problem?" he asked Celia.

"You could have brought it up, too, you know."

"I thought you had a plan," Rafael said.

"I did," Celia said. "That you would drive us. That was my plan."

Rafael said, "Okay, just let me think."

"A once-in-a-lifetime event," Celia said, and Arturo turned to me and chuckled.

Most of the ice on the ground had melted, although the tree branches were still lined with it, bowing under the weight. In the sunlight, telephone wires looked like glass strings high over-head, bushes glistened like cakes made of diamonds, starbursts of frost etched themselves against our windows. At night, the trees clapped together in the wind and made a delicate tinkling sound. We couldn't believe our eyes nor our ears nor the fresh sting in our noses. "What world is this?" I had asked Arturo. And he just shook his head.

Rafael said, "Okay, let's try this." He opened the back door. "Alma, you get in first. Then Celia, you get in next to Alma."

"Who's sitting in the front?" Celia asked.

"I'll sit in the front," Mayor volunteered.

"Arturo can ride in the front with me," Rafael said to Celia. "He's bigger than you."

Celia looked Arturo up and down, then motioned for him to come over to where she was.

"Stand there," she said. She turned so the two of them were back to back. She was a finger width taller than him.

"I think it's you, Arturo," Rafael said.

But Celia wagged her finger. "No. I'm taller than him."

Rafael massaged his temples, as if the whole thing was giving him a headache. "Bueno. You sit in the front. Arturo, please get in next to your wife. Mayor, you go on the other side."

"What about Maribel?" Mayor asked.

"She can sit on her father's lap."

Arturo and I were the only ones in the car so far. "Come here, Mari," Arturo said, patting his thighs. "Let's see if you can fit."

Maribel stuck one of her legs into the car and backed her rear end in through the door, ducking her head to clear the opening. But when she lowered herself onto Arturo's lap, even with one of her legs still outside of the car, she was too high to uncurl her back and neck.

"¡Por favor! She can't sit like that!" Celia said from outside.

"Come back out," Rafael said, extending his hand.

"She can sit on my lap," Mayor offered. "We're both skinny." And when no one said anything, he shrugged and climbed into the car on the other side of me.

Rafael stood, looking at the people and the spaces, as if the whole thing were an elaborate puzzle that he could solve if only he could find the right piece.

"This is ridiculous," Celia finally said. "Maribel, would you mind sitting on Mayor's lap? It's only for a few miles. I'll sit in the front, and Rafa, you drive."

Silently, Maribel walked around the car and climbed in on top of Mayor, the rhinestone butterflies on the back pockets of her jeans resting on his thighs.

Arturo looked at me.

"It's okay," I said, even though I was worried, too, about letting her ride like this. Here the roads seemed clear, but what if farther on they were still icy? I reached over and locked Mayor's door. I clutched Maribel's forearm as if somehow that would protect her in the case of an accident.

Rafael had to rev the engine a few times to get it to start in the cold, and just after it did, someone called from the balcony.

Rafael cranked the window down.

"Is everything all right?" I heard a voice yell. Quisqueya. She said, "I heard some commotion, so I came out to check."

"We're fine," Rafael shouted back.

Quisqueya bent down to peer between the balcony bars. "Who's there?"

"It's the Riveras and us," Rafa called. "We're headed to the park to take the kids skating." I caught a glimpse of her face, which betrayed disappointment mixed with a flash of envy.

Rafael said, "Celia will call you later," and I saw Quisqueya give him a doubtful look as he raised the window.

"I don't need—" she started to say, but the window closed before she finished.

"Why did you tell her I would call her later?" Celia asked.

"Just to get her off our back. What does she care what we're doing?"

"But now I have to call her later!"

Rafael put the car in reverse. "Vidajena, that woman," he said.

"What does that mean?" Mayor asked.

"A nosy person," Rafael said. "Always interfering." He started to pull out. "Okay, enough of this. If we wait much longer, the ice is going to melt. Vámonos."

THERE MUST HAVE BEEN a hundred children at the marsh. As we walked toward the frozen pond, we saw them flailing their arms and squealing as they cast their bodies across the surface, half squatting to steady themselves.

"Will it break?" I asked. "With all those children on top of it?"

"I don't know how it works," Arturo said.

We walked over the brittle grass and when we came to the pond, Maribel crouched down and laid her hand against the surface.

"You can skate on it," Celia said. "See all the kids?"

"Go ahead," Arturo said. "Let's see if you can stand on ice. That's not something any of your friends in Pátzcuaro can say."

We all waited for her to do something, but Maribel simply squatted with her feet rooted to the ground, staring back at us through her sunglasses.

"Come on, Maribel," I said. I meant to sound encouraging, but it came out shrill.

Arturo glared at me, and I looked away from him, embarrassed by my impatience.

"Don't you want to try it?" Mayor asked. He jumped onto the ice and slid with his arms out to the sides. "See? It's fun."

Maribel stood and took a step toward the ice, and Mayor hurried back to help her down. He walked slowly, pulling her along. I held my breath, watching her every step, worried that she might fall. But she was walking on her own before long, one foot carefully in front of the other, and I looked at Arturo and smiled.

"She's doing it," I said.

Rafael and Celia glided out into the middle of the pond together, and cautiously, with his hands in his coat pockets, Arturo stepped onto the ice and twisted his boots in small Z's, staring at his feet.

"How does it feel?" I asked.

"It's like a floor," he said. "Come try it."

Arturo skated backwards on the soles of his boots, looking over his shoulder as he moved to make sure he wasn't about to bump into anyone. I stood on the bank of the marsh and watched him, the way he wobbled and twitched.

And then, out of the corner of my eye, I saw something. I jerked my head around. The boy, I thought. But when I turned, no one was there. Had he been there? I felt sure of it all of a sudden, sure that he was watching us, waiting for his chance. I looked back to where Maribel had been standing with Mayor, but I didn't see her. I didn't see her or Mayor. I scanned the marsh, raking my eyes through all the bodies moving across the ice, the children in their bright coats and wool hats, shrieking and laughing. "Maribel?" I said out loud. "Mari!"

The next thing I knew, Arturo was in front of me again, at the edge of the bank. "What's wrong?" he asked.

"Where did she go?" I said. "Maribel!"

Arturo whipped around. "Mar—" he began to shout. Then he stopped. "She's right there, Alma. She's standing with Mayor."

I tried to focus on where he was pointing. "I don't see her."

"She's right there."

And then: her dark hair, her thin, coltish legs in her slim jeans, her big coat. I blinked and took a long breath, trying to loosen the fist around my heart.

"I didn't see her," I said.

Arturo shook his head. "I don't know what's going on with you."

"I lost track of her."

Arturo stepped off the ice and onto the bank where I was. "No," he said. "It's something else. I don't just mean now."

And for one compact second, for no real reason, I considered telling him about the boy. It was nothing more than a block of words, I thought, that I could hand him, like a gift. But what would he think of me now, knowing that I'd been keeping so much from him for so long? The boy coming to the apartment, me going to Capitol Oaks, finding the boy with Maribel that day. Besides, before we left México I had promised him I would handle everything here. I had promised myself I wouldn't burden him with one more thing. And now here it was: one more thing.

"It's nothing," I said.

"You're lying."

I shook my head, afraid to open my mouth.

"So it's just my imagination, then? Am I going crazy?"

"You're not going crazy."

"So there *is* something?"

"It's just the usual things—you being out of work, and the money. Maybe I'm homesick."

"That's not it," he said.

"I don't know what you want me to say."

"I want you to tell me the truth."

"I am telling you the truth!"

"Come on, Alma! You think I don't know you? You think I

don't breathe you and dream you every single day of my life? You think I haven't been inside you? I know when you're lying to me. There's something else."

And again, for the briefest moment, I thought, How easy it would be. To say, Here. I've been holding on to this all this time, but here, if you want it you can have it. When I look back on it now, I see that I should have done it. In that split second, telling him might have changed our fates.

"There's nothing else," I said.

I gazed out across the pond, to the treeline and the soft wash of sky. I kept my eyes on Maribel, watching her with Mayor, the way she smiled when she was with him, the way he talked to her without judgment or expectation, how at ease she seemed when he was around. I was grateful for those things.

"Look at her," I said.

Arturo turned, and together we watched as Maribel drew out a strand of hair that had blown into her mouth. Mayor said something, and she laughed.

Arturo walked to the edge of the frozen grass and stepped onto the ice again, tapping his boots against its marbled surface. He looked at me with a gentle expression.

"Come on," he said, offering his hand.

I didn't move.

"I'm here," he said. "Whenever you're ready."

I took his hand, feeling his rough, warm skin against mine.

"I'm right here," he said.

I lowered one foot onto the ice. He tugged gently, walking his fingers up to my elbows, easing me down. I picked up my other foot and planted it next to the first as I clung to Arturo's coat sleeves. And then I was standing on the ice, which I was astonished to find felt as firm as the ground, all of me braced in Arturo's arms.

THE SUNDAY AFTER we went skating, Arturo asked to borrow the Toros' radio and we took it home with us after eating lunch at their apartment. Arturo set it on the kitchen table and tuned it to a station playing nothing but the Beatles, which had been his favorite band since he was a boy. He raised the volume and sang along with words he had memorized from a lifetime of listening—"La la la la life goes on!"—smiling wide and clapping. "¡Va!" he shouted sometimes, at me or at Maribel, and he drummed his hands on the table, on the walls, on our rear ends. The Beatles sang in their English accents about the sun coming out after the winter. We sang along, even though we didn't know what some of the words meant. "Little darling . . . It's all right."

And then, in the middle of the revelry, we heard a knock at the door.

"What was that?" Arturo asked.

"What?" I said.

A knock sounded again.

Arturo walked past me to the door and when he returned, he was trailed by Quisqueya.

"Alma," she said, when she saw me. "Buenas."

"Quisqueya says she needs to talk to us," Arturo said.

"Have a seat. Can I get you something? A water?"

"Do you have coffee?"

I started to shake my head—we'd bought neither coffee nor tea in weeks—but then she said, "Oh, don't go to any trouble on my behalf. I mean, if you have some made . . ." She craned her neck to scan the countertop for evidence of a coffeepot while she lowered herself into an empty chair.

"I'll get you water," I said. If it had been anyone else, I would have been embarrassed by not having something more to offer, but there was something strangely pleasurable about having to disappoint someone like Quisqueya.

"Only if it's not too much trouble," Quisqueya said, folding her small hands in her lap.

I took a glass from the cabinet and turned on the tap.

"Maribel, come say hello," Arturo instructed, turning off the music and summoning her from the living room.

Dutifully, Maribel walked over, tucking her hair behind her ears.

"Say hello," Arturo urged.

Maribel stayed quiet.

"It's fine," Quisqueya said. "I understand."

Arturo tightened his jaw. "She's shy," he said.

"Maribel, we need to talk to Quisqueya for a few minutes. Do you want to wait in the bedroom?" I asked.

After she left, Arturo settled himself across from Quisqueya at the kitchen table. I placed the glass of water in front of her. She took a sip and pushed it to the middle of the table. Then she sat, squeezing her fingers in her lap.

Arturo raised his eyebrows at me. I shook my head, as puzzled as him.

"Well," Quisqueya began, "I hate to say anything."

"Is everything all right?" I asked.

"With me? I'm fine. Thank you for asking." She fidgeted while Arturo and I waited.

"Well," she began again, "I was on my way out to the hospital one afternoon. Did you know that I volunteer there? It's nothing, really. I change bedpans and prop up pillows and deliver lunches. Sometimes the patients mistake me for a nurse, but I tell them, please! Nurses do important work. I simply come and do chores. It's nothing. Of course, we are all doing God's work. That's what I think. Even if we contribute in only small ways." She stopped and looked at us.

"What you do is important," I offered, even though I didn't know where this was headed.

"Yes," Quisqueya agreed. She reached for the water glass again, but thought better of it and drew her hand back to her lap.

"I was on my way out a few weeks ago. And you know that the Toros bought a car? I haven't had a chance yet to ride in it myself but . . . oh, of course you know. They took you for a drive, didn't they? Last week? Did you see me? On the balcony? Rafael can be so rude sometimes. And do you know that Celia never called me after that? I hardly see her anymore. It seems she always has plans with other people"—and here, Quisqueya looked pointedly at me—"so there's never really a good time to catch her anymore. It's such a shame. She and I used to be very close."

Arturo looked at me, confused.

"I saw them sitting in the car together," Quisqueya said suddenly.

"Who?" Arturo asked.

"Mayor Toro. And your daughter. They were together in the car."

Quisqueya cast a quick glance down the hallway, then leaned toward us. "They were kissing," she said.

"When?" I asked.

"It was a few weeks ago."

"Kissing?" Arturo said.

"Yes, they were kissing. Mayor Toro and your daughter, Maribel."

"You're sure it was them?" Arturo asked.

"I'm positive. In Rafael's car."

When had they been in Rafael's car? They knew the rule. They had to be here or at the Toros' apartment.

"They spend a lot of time together," Quisqueya said.

"They're friends," Arturo said. I could tell he was upset, but he didn't want to give Quisqueya the satisfaction of knowing it.

"I think they're more than friends."

"Okay," Arturo said. "Is that what you came here to tell us?"

Quisqueya looked momentarily defeated. I could see it in her face. She had been eager to deliver this news. She had been looking forward to see what impact it would make, and now that she saw that it hardly left a dent, she was disappointed.

"No," she said slowly. "There's more."

When she didn't offer anything else, sitting there with her mouth pinched, Arturo said, "And? What is it?"

"It only *started* with a kiss," Quisqueya said. "But then Mayor put his hand on her leg. I could see them through the windshield. They were kissing and then Mayor leaned toward her. And he put his hand on her leg, and . . . it was hard to see everything they were doing, but a few minutes later when Mayor stepped out of the car, his pants were . . . wet."

Arturo pushed himself back from the table and stood.

Quisqueya stopped talking, her eyes wide, her face nearly as red as her hair.

I didn't know what to think. It was too much.

"You're making this up," Arturo said.

"I'm sorry," Quisqueya said, "but I thought you should know. Especially considering . . ."

"Arturo, sit down," I said.

He was pacing in small circles.

"I know how boys can be," Quisqueya said. "Boys Mayor's age—you can't be too careful. Of course Celia always tells me he's so good, but I was over there recently and you should have heard how he talked to me. Very disrespectful. If that's how he treats me, I started to think . . . Well, I was worried about Maribel."

Arturo looked at me as if to ask, Do you believe her?

I don't know, I told him with my eyes. Maybe. I wasn't sure, but I wasn't ready to take any chances, either. If there was even a possibility . . .

"I should go now," Quisqueya said. "Thank you for the water." She waited, as if she expected one of us to escort her to the door. When neither Arturo nor I moved, Quisqueya walked out herself, the click of her shoes echoing down the hall.

# Mayor

Late in February, my dad came home from work one night and said, "It's over."

I was on my way to the kitchen, but I knew enough to tell when I should stay out of his way. A few years ago Enrique and I had devised an alert system where we'd hold up a certain number of fingers to each other to indicate how far up the scale of volatility my dad was. If Enrique had been there that day, I would have rated this a level four, the second-highest possible, which meant "Radioactive. Steer clear." The day he'd grounded me had probably been a level six, off the charts.

From the hallway, I listened as my mom scurried out to meet him. I heard muffled voices. And then, for a long minute, I heard nothing.

"Mayor, come to dinner!" my mom called. She sounded angry.

I walked down the hall slowly, unsure about what to expect, preparing myself to be yelled at again. Maybe I'd messed up something in the car when I snuck in there with Maribel and he'd just now noticed. But my dad had been in the car since then—all of us had gone to White Clay to skate on the marsh the week before—and he hadn't said anything. Or maybe Sra. Rivera finally said something to my mom about how I'd been over there when I wasn't supposed to be. Or maybe anything. You never knew with my dad.

But when I got to the table, he didn't say a word. He was sitting with his arms crossed, still wearing his coat and knit cap, while my mom dumped arroz con guandú onto plates, knocking the side of the spoon against the paila with each motion. I didn't say anything either. I just concentrated on being invisible, lowering myself quietly into a chair, holding my breath.

When she had finished half the food on her plate, my mom looked at my dad and said, "Aren't you going to tell him?"

"Leave it alone, Celia."

"He deserves to know, doesn't he?"

"Know what?" I asked.

"Go to your room," my dad said.

"What did I do?"

"That's how you answer me? When I say go to your room, you go."

"Mayor, stay where you are," my mom said. "He hasn't eaten yet, Rafa. Let him eat."

"Mayor, go to your room," my dad said again.

"Mayor, stay where you are," my mom said.

I waited for my dad to counter, and when he didn't, I hesitantly picked up my fork and poked it into my rice.

I took a few bites while my parents watched me. My mom was curling and uncurling her lips like she wanted to say something. A geyser waiting to spew. After a minute and twenty-two seconds—I watched the time tick by on the clock on the wall—my mom said, "Well, what if you don't find anything?"

"Jesus, Celia!"

"I think it's a legitimate question."

"I've already told you I'll find something."

"But what if it's not for a while?"

"Then it's not for a while."

"Rafa!"

"This woman!" my dad said, looking up at the ceiling and pressing his hands together like he was praying. "Que Dios me ayude."

"Don't say that."

"You don't listen to me."

"You're not telling me anything."

"I'm telling you I'll find something. Do you want me to say it again? I'll find something. I'll find something. Do you hear me?"

After my dad left the table, snatching his pack of cigarettes from on top of the refrigerator and escaping to the balcony, my mom looked at me and said, "Well, I guess you might as well know. It finally happened. Your father lost his job."

THE REST OF the story emerged little by little: The diner was closing. Windows boarded up. Doors locked. Out of business after forty-five years. All that time my dad had spent worrying that he was going to get fired for dropping an omelet or for leaving the freezer door open, and now the reason he'd been axed wasn't even his fault. It was the rotten economy that had landed him in the water and that had capsized the whole ship along with him.

For fifteen years, my dad had been working at that diner. Fifteen years of taking the bus to the same place with leatherette booths and a coffee-stained linoleum counter and wood-paneled walls. He'd started as a busboy, clearing tables and wiping up bits of egg that had been left behind on the tables, and he'd never complained. "I wouldn't have done much better in Panamá," I'd heard him say before. "I didn't have the brains to make much of myself." My dad was smart, though. He'd never gone to college, which gave him the wrong idea about himself, but the only reason he hadn't was because he'd been forced into getting a job after his parents died. He'd waited tables at a roadside restaurant in Panamá, which turned out to be the only experience he needed to find work in the United States.

Eventually my dad worked his way up from busboy to dishwasher to line cook. He flipped thousands of omelets and fried mountains of hash browns. He strained the pulp from the orange juice by hand when they used to do that sort of thing and then dispensed pre-fab OJ from a machine when the management switched to that. He remembered the days when everyone who came in ordered coffee and remembered how the waitresses had complained when everyone started asking for lattes instead. Fifteen years. Six days a week. Early mornings. Up to his elbows in grease. And now it was over. Just like that.

My dad scoured the newspaper every day, searching the classifieds, calling any that sounded promising, and hanging up either in fury or in disappointment. He went all over town, filling out applications to work in the kitchens at the Christiana Hilton, Caffè Gelato, Valle Pizza, Grotto Pizza, Friendly's, Charcoal Pit, Ali Baba, Klondike Kate's, Iron Hill, Home Grown, the Deer Park, and even the restaurant at the Hotel duPont. My mom suggested he go to the Community House to see if someone there could help him, but he hated the idea of it so much, either of my mom interfering or of accepting help from a place that he called "the Handout House," that he shouted at her to keep her big nose out of it, to which my mom said, "Big nose?" to which my dad replied by holding his arm in front of his face to mimic an elephant. My mom didn't even have a big nose, but the two of them were down to cheap shots by then, and my mom ran to the bedroom, where she shut herself away all afternoon. Even when my parents were speaking civilly to one another, they spent the dinner hour complaining about how so far President Obama hadn't done anything and how they saw absolutely zero improvements and about how people were getting desperate and thank God we had the money from Gloria but everyone else was in a tough spot and it had gotten so bad now that people were getting mugged outside of Western Unions for the money they were about to wire to relatives back home. "They're targeting people who look like us," my dad said. "It used to be the Orientals, but the style now is to pick on the Latinos. And the Arabs. At least them I can understand. They did September eleventh. What did we ever do to anyone?"

My dad looked at my mom and me like he honestly expected someone to give him an answer. "'Oriental' is for rugs," I said, repeating something that my social studies teacher, Mr. Perry, had told us once.

"What?"

"You're supposed to say 'Asians,' not 'Orientals.' I don't know if 'Arab' is right, either."

"This is what they teach you at school?" my dad said. "Forget about what to call people. What about the history?"

"They teach us history."

"And has it ever been this bad before in the history of this country?"

"Well, there was the Great Depression."

"I don't know," my dad said. "It seems to me like the world is going to hell."

"Don't say that," my mom said.

"What would you prefer I say?"

"How about something nice for a change?"

"I say nice things."

"When?"

My dad shrugged.

"Exactly," my mom said.

I HADN'T HUNG OUT with William in months, lately because I'd been grounded, but even before that there had been times when he'd invited me to do something—go to Holy Angels to watch the girls in their uniforms or to Bing's to get cinnamon rolls or to a movie at Newark Shopping Center—but I'd shot him down so often that he started snubbing me, acting like he didn't see me when I passed him in the hall at school, walking away if I approached him at his locker, sitting at a table as far from me as he could possibly get in the cafeteria. I figured that with enough time he would get over it, but in the end, I was the one who caved.

"Hey," I said one day in chemistry. We were going through the motions of that day's experiment, sitting side by side while neither of us acknowledged the other's existence. "Is this seriously how it's going to be?"

He pretended like he couldn't hear me.

"Hey," I said louder.

He looked at me.

"You know this is dumb, right?" I said.

"Did you just call me dumb?"

I rolled my eyes. "So you're gonna keep being like this?"

"Like what?"

"Like, not my friend."

"Me? You're the one who keeps dissing."

"I've been grounded."

"So you've said."

"It's true."

"What about before that?"

"I had other plans."

"Yeah. With her."

"I told you that you could come hang out with us if you wanted."

"What do you do with her anyway?"

"What do you mean? We talk."

"She can talk?"

I gave him the finger.

William pulled a beaker out of the clamp and held it up to the light, watching the soft fizz of the chemicals inside.

"What do you want me to say?" I asked.

"Say you're sorry."

"For what?"

He gave me a sideways look. "Seriously, if you don't know, then it's not worth it."

I ran my tongue along my teeth. Fine. If that's what it took. "Sorry," I said.

"Like you mean it."

"You're being a jackass," I said.

William shrugged.

"Sorry," I said again.

He grinned and put the beaker down. "So, amigo, you want to do something after school today?"

"I'm still grounded."

"Fuck that. We just made up! You can't leave me hanging now. We'll go see a movie or something. I'll drive you home after."

I could see how much it meant to him and how crushed he would be if I turned him down. Besides, I'd snuck out that time to see Maribel and had gotten away with it, so maybe I could pull it off again.

"Sure," I told William. "No problem."

THE SECOND I got home that day my mom stood up from the couch and said, "Señora Rivera called me."

That was it. Nothing about where I had been or why I was so late getting home. Nothing about my grounding. I put my backpack on the floor.

My mom frowned. She was twisting a bracelet around her wrist.

"Why?" I asked. Was it Maribel? I wondered all of a sudden. Had something happened to her?

My mom looked like she was about to say something, but then she stopped herself. "We should probably wait for your father."

"But why?"

"We should talk to you together."

Now I was really worried. "Can't you just tell me now? Is something wrong?"

My mom searched my face. Her eyes were heavy and tired and the makeup around them was smudged, like she'd been rubbing at them.

"I don't know," she said.

"Is Maribel okay?"

"Maybe you should go to your room, Mayor."

"Is she okay?"

"Please, Mayor. Don't make me say anything right now. I don't even know what to say. Just wait until your father gets home. He and I need to talk first, and then we'll come find you."

"I'm just asking you if she's okay." That was all I wanted to know. As long as she was okay, I thought, nothing else my mom could say would matter.

"She's fine," my mom said. "Just—" she started, when, behind me, my dad walked in the front door.

He took one look at my mom and said, "What?"

"I need to talk to you," she said.

"What happened?"

"Mayor, go to your room. We'll come see you in a minute."

"Papi's home now. Why can't I just stay here?"

"Mayor, please," my mom said.

My dad cast his gaze at me. "You heard her," he said. "Go."

Angrily, I dragged my backpack across the carpet toward my room.

"Pick it up!" my mom screamed.

Without turning around, I snatched it off the floor and went to my room. I heard my dad say, "Celia, what the hell?" before I shut the door.

I sat on my unmade bed with my elbows on my knees. I got up and kicked my shoes off into the corner. I tried to listen through the door, but I couldn't hear anything. From my pants pocket, my phone vibrated, and when I checked it William had sent me a text. "good movie. Ur mom mad?"

I wrote back: "dont know. sent me 2 my room."

William: "haha. pussy."

Me: "ttyl."

I turned off my phone and threw it on my dresser.

After an eternity, my parents knocked on my door and came in. I could see right away that my mom had been crying. She was clutching a used tissue in one hand, and she stood with her body half hidden behind my dad, who had a dark look in his eyes. I stood in my socks, facing them, waiting for the news, whatever it was.

"We received a call," my dad said, his voice stony.

"I already told him that part," my mom said.

My dad raised his hand to silence her.

"Señora Rivera said that you and Maribel were in my car the other day."

I gulped. "We didn't do anything to it."

"So it's true?"

I nodded.

"Is it my imagination," my dad asked, "or are you still grounded?"

"Yes."

"How did you get the keys?" my mom asked.

"I took them off the windowsill."

My dad looked at me evenly. "Did you kiss Maribel?" he asked.

Flames shot through my cheeks. "What?"

"Did you kiss her in the car?"

"Why?"

"Answer the question, Mayor."

"I don't know. Maybe."

"Maybe yes or maybe no?"

I just stared at them.

"What did you do with her?"

"Nothing."

"Did you kiss her?" my mom asked from behind my dad.

"I mean, yeah, I guess. It wasn't a big deal."

My dad glanced at my mom and for one delirious second I thought I was off the hook, that somehow I'd exonerated myself, and that we could all just go back to business as usual. But then my dad said to me, slowly, gravely, "You are not going to see her anymore."

"What?"

"No more."

"But what does that mean?"

"It means exactly what I said."

I felt a dullness in my chest. "But why?"

"Her parents don't want you to see her," my dad said.

"Because I kissed her?"

"Was there more?"

"I mean, no . . ."

"No?" my mom asked hopefully.

"I swear, there wasn't."

But my dad shook his head. "It doesn't matter. You broke the rules, Mayor. You're only supposed to be with her in one of our apartments, aren't you? I know you might think that's unfair, but that's what the Riveras want for her, so you have to respect it. And on top of that, you're still grounded. Which means you shouldn't have seen her no matter where you were."

"This is because you don't like her," I said.

"No."

"You never liked her!"

"Mayor, calm down," my mom said.

"You don't even know anything about her. I mean, did anyone even ask her what *she* wants?"

My dad shook his head. "You're not going to see her again."

"So that's it?" I said. I felt the whole thing reeling away from me, like a rope slipping through my hands.

"Dios," my mom said. "Qué lío magnífico."

# José Mercado

My wife, Ynez, and I were both brought into the world by way of Puerto Rico, me in 1950, and she five years later. Not long after we were married, I enlisted in the navy. I always wanted to do something heroic. With the navy, I traveled to Vietnam, Grenada, the Persian Gulf, and Bosnia. I was injured in Bosnia, which requires me to use a walker now. But I came home. I came home. And that is all any soldier cares about.

I love the esoteric things in life. My father used to call me an aesthete. He meant it not as a compliment, of course. He was disappointed by my interests and by the fact that they were not the same as his, which were farming and raising livestock. He believed a man should work hard with his hands, that toil and sweat were evidence of a virtuous life. He did not appreciate that I wanted to read books and that I saved money to buy an easel when I turned fifteen and that I would spend the afternoons painting pictures of trees. The only time he was proud of me, in fact, was when I joined the navy. He was an old man by then, nearing death, but I still remember his face when I told him, the way he had smiled with those teeth of his that were brown around the edges, the way the wrinkles rippled up to the surface of his cheeks.

Ynez was not as happy about it. She supported me, but she was worried. We never had children. We knew from the outset and in a terribly selfish way that our interest lay only in each other.

So when she was home during my deployments, she was there alone, and the weight of the solitude depressed her, I think, and gave her wide-open plains upon which her mind would wander, allowing her too much time and space to think about what might be happening to me as well as whether and when I would return.

When I came back from Vietnam, she wept at my feet. I saw clearly the toll it had taken on her. But I wasn't ready to leave the navy. I had witnessed the sort of atrocities during the war that threaten to steal a man's soul. I saw that humans are no better than any animal or brute, and in many cases might be infinitely worse. But often in the span of the same day, I would be restored, too, by the courage of men. And I had come to understand my father's perspective about the gratification of feeling useful, of being in the world under the most demanding circumstances, and learning that I could not only survive but thrive, and that my body, the physical presence of me, could have import.

So eight years later, I left again, but this time while I was away, I wrote Ynez letters. If she heard from me with enough regularity, I thought, it would ease her worry. Over the years, over the subsequent deployments, I sent her hundreds of letters. I wrote two or three a day sometimes. They began as a way to save her, but they saved me also. They helped me to make sense of the things I saw, and from that, I began to make sense of the world and my place within it.

I read a lot of poetry in those days. I took small chapbooks overseas with me, chapbooks bound by staples with covers that were little more than construction paper. I copied the poems down sometimes and included them in my letters. Ynez used to tell me I should write my own poetry, but just because you have the requisite admiration and even ambition to do something doesn't mean you're up to the task of performing it your-self, which was the case for me. I am good at being a reader of poetry, but not at much beyond that.

My eyes have turned against me now, so I am resigned to lis-tening to books on CD. Sometimes Ynez reads poetry aloud to me. I no longer have any of those chapbooks that used to keep me company in so many far-flung places. I usually burned them after I finished them, just to lighten my load. But Ynez borrows books from the library and we sit on the couch and she covers me with an afghan and draws her slender feet up onto the cush-ions and I close my eyes while she reads.

There's an American poet named Marvin Bell who emerged in the late sixties, during the height of the Vietnam War. He has a beautiful poem called "Poem After Carlos Drummond de Andrade," which is a reference to the great Brazilian poet. I love the part that goes:

> And it's life, just life, that makes you breathe deeply, in the air that
> is filled with wood smoke and the dust of the factory, because
> you hurried, and now your lungs heave and fall with the
> nervous excitement of a leaf in spring breezes, though it is
> winter and you are swallowing the dirt of the town.

And then this portion at the end, which means everything to me:

> Life got its tentacles around you, its hooks into your
> heart, and suddenly you come awake as if for the first time,
> and you are standing in a part of the town where the air is
> sweet—your face flushed, your chest thumping, your

stomach a planet, your heart a planet, your every organ a separate planet, all of it of a piece though the pieces turn separately, O silent indications of the inevitable, as among the natural restraints of winter and good sense, life blows you apart in her arms.

# Alma

After we told her that she couldn't see Mayor anymore, Maribel grew moody and sullen. I had witnessed a hint of the same thing ever since Mayor had been grounded, but now it was worse. She hardly spoke. She nodded or shook her head. She held out her hand to indicate that she wanted something. She sat on the ledge at the front window and stared across the parking lot with her chin planted on her knees.

Once, nearly two years ago, Maribel had insisted on painting her fingernails black. She and her friend Abelina hid away in her room and painted each other's nails, and when Maribel came to the dinner table that night, we saw it.

"What did you do to your hands?" Arturo asked.

"I painted my nails," Maribel said, grinning and holding her fingers out like a fan.

"Is it permanent?" Arturo asked.

"It's just nail polish, Papi."

Arturo looked at me as if to ask, Is this something we should be worried about?

I had learned by then that Maribel liked to think of herself as a rebel. And yet she managed only small insurrections. She stayed out too late with her friends. She walked through the middle of the boys' soccer games in the street, impervious to their shouts for her to get out of the way. She painted her fingernails black. And she did it all playfully, good-naturedly, in a way that made it impossible to be angry at her.

At the dinner table, she wiggled her fingers in the air and said, "I think it looks cool."

Arturo glanced at me again. This time, Maribel saw him.

"What?" she said. "It's okay to be different."

"Of course it is," I said.

With a depth of feeling that was lost on her, Arturo said, "We would love you no matter what. Because you're ours."

Maribel tucked a bite of her cuernillo relleno inside her cheek until it bulged. She chewed loudly, smacking her tongue against the roof of her mouth. "Would you love me if I ate like this all the time?" she asked.

I watched Arturo fight a smile. "Yes," he said.

Maribel swallowed and curled her lips back with her fingers. "What if I looked like this?"

Arturo grinned. "Yes."

She tensed the muscles in her neck until every tendon rose to the surface beneath her skin, like strings under a drooping tent. "What if I walked around looking like this all the time?"

"Maribel, stop it," I said.

Arturo looked right at her, struggling to keep a straight face. "No matter what," he said.

It was still the truth, but the way she was acting now had me worried. She had been showing so much improvement—the latest report from the school had said that Maribel could easily answer questions and follow prompts, and that her attention span had increased—and I hoped we hadn't just undermined all of her progress.

"Do you think we did the right thing?" I whispered to Arturo one night when I couldn't sleep. I shoved him awake and said it again.

"What?" he asked.

"About Mayor and Maribel? Do you think we did the right thing?"

"It's the middle of the night, Alma," Arturo said.

I glanced to where Maribel lay, curled up in the sleeping bag, her hair spread like a veil over her face, then I turned back to Arturo. "It seems like it's only made things worse."

Arturo rubbed his eyes. "We've talked about this already. You heard what Quisqueya said."

"We don't even know if she was telling the truth."

"Mayor admitted to his parents that they were in the car together. You're the one who was so upset about that part of it. 'He knows he's not supposed to be outside with her,' you kept saying. As if that was the worst of it. Being outside together?"

"You don't know what it's like out there," I said quietly. "You don't know the sorts of people who are out there."

"What people?"

I looked at his disheveled hair, his heavy eyes fighting the dragging tide of sleep. I said, "Never mind. Let's go back to sleep."

"We did the right thing," Arturo said. "She doesn't know what's best. Especially not now."

"What does that mean?"

"A year ago it would have been different."

"A year ago you would have let her be with Mayor like that?"

"A year ago we weren't here. She wouldn't have known Mayor. But if there had been a Mayor in México, then maybe."

I stared at him, piercing holes through the dark. "Why don't you just say what you mean?" I asked.

He was quiet.

"Say it, Arturo."

"Say what?"

"Say whether you're upset about Mayor and her because she's your daughter or because she's your brain-damaged daughter."

"I never used that word."

"Say it," I insisted.

Arturo propped himself up on his elbow and hissed, "You don't think I have a right to treat her differently now than I would have before the accident? You don't think we have the *responsibility* to do that? She's not the same person, Alma. There's not some piece of her just sitting there, waiting for us to find it again. No matter how much schooling or medical care she gets, we can't just put her back together."

I felt something collapse inside of me. "She's getting better," I said.

Arturo peered past my shoulder at Maribel. "We shouldn't be having this conversation now."

"She was getting better before all of this happened," I said.

"But even if she gets better from now until eternity, she won't be the same person anymore."

"But the doctors said—"

"The doctors said her brain can heal, but they warned us she would never be the same again."

"They didn't say that."

"They did, Alma. You just didn't want to hear that part."

"She's getting better," I said, as if by repeating it enough, I could somehow make it part of the public record, an indisputable fact.

"But don't you understand?" Arturo said. "We don't get her again."

Across the room, Maribel stirred. I smoothed my hand over the rippled sheet, tears burning in my eyes. Arturo had dropped his head back against the mattress, but I could see that his eyes were open and that he was staring at the ceiling. The weight of finality—so heavy that it felt like a physical thing—hung in the air between us. I didn't want to accept that in order to move forward, I had to walk through it. It was so much easier just to believe there was another path that I could take around it and that at the end of that path would be the destination I wanted. It was easier to want to end up at a lie, instead of at the truth, which was just as Arturo said: We wouldn't get her again. Not ever.

# Mayor

In March, my dad landed a job as a newspaper carrier for the
*News Journal*. He'd gone in because he'd heard that they
needed workers on the floor of the press and after burning
through all the restaurants in town, he was getting desperate,
even if it meant applying for jobs he was totally unqualified for.
He got turned down from the floor job pretty quick, apparently.
"They asked me three questions. Then the woman who was
interviewing me started shaking her head, saying, 'No, I'm sorry.
This won't work. We need someone with experience.' Experience!" my dad cried, telling my mom and me the story. "I told
her, 'All I know how to do is make breakfast.'"

My mom frowned. "That's not true. You know how to do other
things." Then she added, "But only a few."

"Well, this lady's eyes lit up. 'Breakfast?' she said. 'Are you a
morning person?' Who can tell me what that phrase means? At
the diner, customers used to come in all the time and say, 'I'm
not a morning person.' Usually right before or right after they
ordered coffee. But what? The world is divided into morning
people and afternoon people and night people?"

"What did you tell her, Rafa?"

"I told the lady, 'Well, I get up in the morning.'"

My mom laughed.

"So the lady asked if I could handle getting up very early.
When I said sure, she asked if I had my own car. 'Brand-new,' I

told her. She asked did I have a license and insurance. When I told her yes, she said, 'Then I have a job for you.'"

My mom beamed. "This is so exciting. You're a newspaper man now."

"It turns out that thing will finally be good for something other than coupons," my dad said.

"Will you deliver *our* newspapers?" my mom asked.

"If you're on my route, yes."

"I want to be on your route," she said, winking at him.

My dad, who looked astonished at first, smiled. He was proud, I think, to know that he'd turned things around, that he'd saved our fortunes, and that he had tugged my mom back over to his side.

The turn of events had put my dad in a good enough mood that he ended my grounding, which would have been great except that I still wasn't allowed to see Maribel, and that was the only thing I really wanted to do. Her parents had started going to a different Mass, so I didn't even see her at church anymore. I missed her. Everything about her. But what could I do?

Then, as I was sitting in social studies one Friday afternoon, it started snowing. I thought I was imagining it at first. All winter long, I'd been waiting for it to snow—not for me, but for Maribel, because I knew she wanted to see it—but now that it was March, I had given up on thinking that it would happen. Through the window, I saw a few flakes, all spread out, drifting down as soft as dust.

I tapped Jaime DeJulio, who sat in front of me. He shrugged me off like a bug had just landed on his shoulder.

"Julio," I whispered.

He turned around. "I told you not to call me that, Minor."

This was his ongoing taunt. Mayor/Minor. Hilarious. It's why I'd started referring to him as Julio, even though I knew it was lame revenge.

I pointed to the window. He looked, but he must not have seen it. "What's your problem?" he asked.

"Snow," I mouthed.

He looked again and grinned. "Hell, yeah."

At the front of the class, Mr. Perry droned on about Amerigo Vespucci and Vasco da Gama and the Great Age of Discovery while I stared out the window. After a while, the snow picked up, falling heavier and steadier.

There were ten minutes left in the period when I raised my hand.

"Mayor?" Mr. Perry called. "Do you have a question?"

"Can I use the bathroom?" I asked.

He shook his head. "You know the policy."

"I can't wait. I *really* need to go."

Mr. Perry frowned. I could see I was getting to him.

"Like, bad," I added.

Annoyed, Mr. Perry pointed to the hall pass propped up in the chalk tray along the blackboard.

I was off before he even had a chance to get back to the lesson.

I FOUND WILLIAM in study hall and convinced him to drive me home.

"I thought we were going to a movie today after school," he said.

"Change of plans," I told him.

I didn't elaborate, and I think the whole way to the apartment William assumed that the two of us were off on some big adventure together, but when we pulled into the parking lot of my building, I told him I needed him to teach me how to drive stick shift. He looked confused.

"I'm taking my dad's car," I said, pointing to where it was parked.

"Why? I can drive us wherever we're going."

"We're not going anywhere," I said.

He stared at me for a second, the dawning of understanding on his face, and then said, "Yeah."

William was awesome, though. After I ran inside and stole the car keys from the windowsill again, the two of us got in my dad's car and took it down to the abandoned auto body shop on the corner, away from where anyone might see us, so that William could give me a crash course in how to drive stick. He walked me through the basics—putting the car in reverse, how to brake, how to shift through the gears—and we drove in circles around the parking lot until finally William said, "I think you're good."

"Really?"

"Good enough, I guess."

"What if I stall?" I asked.

"No problem. Just start the car again and give the finger to any dickheads honking at you from behind."

"So that's it? I'm doing this?"

"That's it, young Jedi. Go forth and prosper."

"You're mixing up your references."

William opened the car door and climbed out. He poked his head back in before he closed it. "This is about her, isn't it?" he asked.

I didn't answer. I didn't want to admit it, and William knew anyway.

"Well," he said, "it was nice having you back for a little while at least."

EVERS WAS OUT near Delaware Park, a line of bare trees at its back, a baseball field off to one side. It was two o'clock, and the snow was falling a little harder by the time I got there. I flipped up the hood of my jacket before I got out of the car. I'd never been to Evers before, but at my school, a security guard roamed the hallways and the grounds all day, so I assumed there would be one here, too, and I was praying to God not to run into him. I cut across the grass to the side of the building. No one else was around. The only sound was the swish of cars whizzing by on the wet street out front.

I crept from one classroom to the next, my adrenaline surging, and peeked through the windows, looking for her. I couldn't believe I was doing this. I'd never skipped out on school before. The snow fell into my eyes, and I kept stopping to blink it away. Classroom after classroom and no sign of her. In the rooms where the kids looked younger, I moved along right away. In rooms where they might have been our age I lingered, even if I didn't see her, just in case she was in the bathroom or something and would appear in the doorway at any minute.

And then, in the eighth or ninth classroom I checked, I saw her. She was sitting in the front row with her chin in her hand. She looked gorgeous, even from that distance, even separated by a pane of glass and a span of air. I curled my fingers over the ledge of bricks jutting out beneath the window, the rough surface burning my fingertips.

As soon as her teacher, who was winding through the row of desks, walked to the corner farthest from me, I tapped the backs of my fingernails against the glass. An aide seated by the chalkboard narrowed her eyes and craned her head toward the windows. I ducked. I stared at my hands against the cold brick and breathed quickly. I tried to flatten myself against the building in case the aide had gotten up and walked toward the noise. It wasn't like I could make myself invisible, though. Should I run? Go back to the car? I didn't know what to do, but in all the time I'd been thinking about it, nothing had happened, either. If the aide had seen me, she'd be shouting out the window by now. I waited another minute before standing again, and this time, when I did, Maribel was staring right at me. Like she was waiting for me. She blinked a few times, as if she couldn't quite believe what she was seeing. I pointed at the sky, at the snow. I pumped my arms overhead in triumph. She smiled and covered her mouth with her hand. She looked to her teacher, pretending for a few seconds that she was paying attention. When she looked at me again, I motioned for her to come outside. She shook her head. I held my hands together as if in prayer. Come on, Maribel, I was thinking. Come on. She blinked fast. Then I saw her get up and say something to the aide, who handed her a small wooden paddle. A hall pass. Yes! I hightailed it back to the parking lot.

I pulled my dad's car up to the entrance. I didn't want to turn it off because I'd only have to go through the process of starting it up again, and I didn't know how to idle it without stalling, so I decided to drive in circles around the bus lane and back up to the entrance until Maribel came out. I didn't see her at first, but then she walked out from around the side of the building—maybe she'd had to use that door so no one would notice her—smiling like I had never seen her smile before, holding her hands up to feel the flakes land on her palms. I slowed down as much as I could and leaned over to roll down the passenger window. I had this idea that if I went slow enough, she would jump in and I wouldn't have to stop. Like we were in some kind of slow-motion action movie. I was going to yell out and explain it all to her, but while I was coordinating the pedals and the steering and my tilting body at the same time, I stalled the car. Maribel acted like she didn't even notice. She just walked over and climbed in.

"It's snowing," I said, like it wasn't obvious.

"It's snowing," Maribel repeated in wonder. She wiped her hands on her pants.

This was the thing about Maribel: No matter how many times I proved it, she didn't think I was an idiot. She just took me. She took me in. Such a simple fucking thing.

"Where's your coat?" I asked. "And your sunglasses?"

She pointed toward the school.

"Well, are you cold?"

"No," she said. Then she leaned forward and looked out the windshield, twisting her neck to gaze up at the sky.

"I thought we could go somewhere," I said.

"Where?"

"Just a place I know. It's really cool. Especially in the snow."

"Is it okay?" she asked.

I didn't know what she was talking about. Was she asking if it was okay for her to leave school? Probably not. It wasn't really okay for me, either, but I didn't want to think about it.

"Everything's okay," I said.

We drove for at least a mile without speaking. Which was fine with me. I felt electric just at seeing her again, at sharing the air with her, at anything and everything.

On the way out of the school parking lot, the car had lurched and sputtered as I got it up to speed, but once we were in fourth gear, I just squeezed my hands around the steering wheel and stayed in the same lane, cruising along down Route 7, toward Route 1. The snow was still falling, dissolving against the windshield, leaving wet asterisks on the glass. The sky was as pale as salt. Maribel kept her face against the window, rapt and in awe. I glanced at her a few times, but mostly I fixed my eyes on the road. We sped by Chili's and Borders and Christiana Mall, and eventually, the snow started falling harder, white dashes shooting at the car and past the windows like light trailing from a thousand stars. A few miles later, I got confident enough that I turned on the radio, but after bouncing around through about twenty different stations, I clicked it back off again.

"I think I should start a radio station," Maribel said suddenly.

"What kind of radio station?"

"I like music."

"Are you talking about a radio station at your school? Do they have that?"

"I could do it."

"Sure, why not?"

"I could."

"I believe you."

I felt her staring at me.

"What?" I asked.

"You're the only one who thinks I can do anything," she said.

We drove for the next hour and a half and the snow kept falling, even though it wasn't sticking to the pavement, only the grass. I stayed in the right lane, letting people pass me, and focused on keeping the car steady even though I was practically shaking with the thrill of being out on the road like we were.

My cell phone rang at one point, not long after I should've been home from school. I fished it out of my pocket and looked at the screen: home. I turned it off. I knew I was in for a mountain of shit when I got home—for seeing Maribel, for taking my dad's car, for driving with nothing but my permit folded up in my wallet—but I didn't care. Maribel and I deserved to be together and she deserved to see the snow if she wanted to and nobody was going to hold us back. I was her one chance. I wanted to give her the thing that it seemed like everyone else wanted to keep from her: freedom. Besides, by now the damage was done. If I'd turned around that very second and taken her home and parked my dad's car in the lot and walked back into the apartment, the mountain of shit wouldn't have been any smaller.

"I'm hungry," Maribel said after a while.

"I have some Starbursts in my backpack," I said. "You can have them."

"What are they?"

"You've never had Starbursts? They're fruity. Like candy. But chewy."

She didn't say anything.

"You don't want them?"

"Do you have French fries?"

I laughed. "I didn't even know you liked French fries."

"I have them at school sometimes."

"Cafeteria fries? Are you kidding me? That's like eating earwax or something. Listen, I'm going to do you a favor and introduce you to real fries. You won't know what hit you."

I pulled off at the next exit. Straight ahead, the golden arches hovered high above a McDonald's, its roof covered with splotches of snow. The car skidded as I turned and the rosary my mom had hung on the rearview mirror knocked against the glass. I tried to downshift, and the car made this horrible grinding sound, but somehow I recovered and before long we were coasting into the drive-thru lane. I pulled up to the speaker box, thinking I could just shout my order and circle around without stopping the car, but of course it didn't work out that way. The car clunked and stalled, and Maribel and I were just sitting there, waiting for a voice to come through the speaker. When it did, I yelled out that we needed an order of large fries, and then I depressed the clutch and turned the car on again. We drove around to the first window slowly—I was concentrating on staying in the drive-thru lane without bumping up onto the curb—and I handed over a five-dollar bill, all the money I had with me. This time I just kept the clutch down until I got my change, then let it go again and rolled up to the second window, where I grabbed the bag of fries from a guy who was standing there dangling them out the window.

By the time we left, I was feeling pretty good. If I didn't say so myself, I was getting the hang of driving stick.

Maribel held the warm paper bag on her lap until we got back on the highway. Then she said, "Can I have one now?"

"Sure," I said. "They're probably still really hot, so be careful."

Maribel pulled out a fry and bit into it.

"So?" I asked, when she didn't say anything.

"Cafeteria fries suck," she said, and I busted out laughing while she finished that one and reached for another. Then another. Then another. She was going through them so fast I had to tell her to save some for me.

It was close to five o'clock by the time we got to Cape Henlopen. I parked on the street, near the outdoor showers where people washed the sand off their feet before walking to their cars during the summer.

"You ready to get out?" I asked her.

"Where are we?"

"You'll see. Come on."

I wriggled out of my coat and handed it to her even though it was about three sizes too big for her. The sleeves covered her hands and the body of it reached almost to her knees. It reminded me of that day I first met her in the Dollar Tree. She'd been wearing that yellow sweater. She'd been swimming in it. Lost in it. Now she was lost in me. I shook my head and smiled. She made me think the craziest stuff, but I didn't even care.

Maribel and I ducked under the lowered parking gates and walked across the empty lot, our sneakers making prints in the snow, our breath heavy in the air.

The sand, when we came to it, was covered by a dusting of snow. The barreling ocean waves were a silvery blue. We stood side by side and looked out at the vastness, the possibility of everything out there. Within the universe, I felt like a speck, but within myself I felt gigantic, the salt air filling my lungs, the roaring of the waves rushing in my ears.

"It's so beautiful," Maribel murmured.

I kept my hands balled in the pockets of my jeans while the cold air knifed at my lungs.

"Thank you," she said.

"For what?"

"This." She held her arm up, the end of the coat sleeve flopping.

"Yeah," I said, like it was no problem, which in a way it wasn't. Forget about the trouble we were in, or who might be looking for us, or how, after this, it would probably be even harder to see her again. Forget all of that. I would have done anything for her.

I shifted my weight from side to side and clapped the edges of my sneakers together, knocking the wet sand off. I was freezing without my coat, but there was no way I was going to admit it. Goose bumps pricked up on my skin under my shirt, and a shiver spread across my back.

Maribel crouched down and ran her hand along the sand, barely skimming the surface. "So beautiful," she said again.

I put my hand on her head, on her damp hair, and when I squatted beside her, she looked at me with her golden brown eyes and her long black eyelashes. I reached under her hair and put my hands behind her neck and kissed her. Her face was moist from the falling snow. Maybe I should have stopped, I don't know. I should've given her a chance to come up for air or to protest or whatever. But when she put her hands on my shoulders, pressing her mouth to mine, I knew she wanted to be there as much as I did. I kissed her again and again and again, greedily, like I was making up for the time I'd lost, like I was making up for all the times I might not get to kiss her again once our parents found out what we'd done, like I was making up for my whole life when I hadn't known her, which seemed unbeliev-able and like a crime. And by the time I finally pulled away, I wanted to devour her. I wanted to tackle her to the ground. I wanted to put my hands along every inch of her. I felt crazy—spinning lights, blurry vision, pounding ears—with want. Her face was flushed, and I was breathing fast. We were kneeling in front of each other. I slid my arms up under her shirt and felt her ribs and her hot skin under my hands. My fingertips brushed along her bra and I reached around to fumble with the hook until I gave up and lifted the whole band up over her breasts. I laid my hands on them, the softest things I'd ever felt, and she took a sharp breath. "Are you okay?" I asked, and she nodded. Under my pants, I could feel myself getting hard. I didn't want it to happen again, though, the way it had that day in the car. I didn't want Maribel to think I had a problem or something. So I dropped my hands to her waist and tried to take a breath, to calm down and just look at her. Maribel blinked. "You have snow in your hair," she said. I smiled. "So do you." I reached out and lifted a few strands of her hair, drawing them across my tongue, through my teeth, tasting her shampoo and the icy flavor of snow. I was shaking and my skin tingled. Maribel unzipped my coat and spread it open like wings, folding it around me as far as it would reach. I inched closer to her on my knees through the sand, and the two of us crouched together, huddled in my coat, listening to the crashing waves, our breath pulsing into the salty air, watching as the snow landed on the water and melted away. And then Maribel fell backwards, right onto her ass. She started laughing. "I knew it wouldn't last," she said. I knew it, too. But I wished like hell it would.

# Micho Alvarez

I came from México, but there's a lot of people here who, when they hear that, they think I crawled out of hell. They hear "México," and they think: bad, devil, I don't know. They got some crazy ideas. Any of them ever been to México? And if they say, yeah, I went to Acapulco back in the day or I been to Cancún, papi, then that shit don't count. You went to a resort? Congratulations. But you didn't go to México. And that's the problem, you know? These people are listening to the media, and the media, let me tell you, has some fucked-up ideas about us. About all the brown-skinned people, but especially about the Mexicans. You listen to the media, you'll learn that we're all gangbangers, we're all drug dealers, we're tossing bodies in vats of acid, we want to destroy America, we still think Texas belongs to us, we all have swine flu, we carry machine guns under our coats, we don't pay any taxes, we're lazy, we're stupid, we're all wetbacks who crossed the border illegally. I swear to God, I'm so tired of being called a spic, a nethead, a cholo, all this stuff. Happens to me all the time. I walk into a store and the employees either ignore me or they're hovering over every move I make because they think I'm going to steal something. I understand I might not look like much. I work as a photographer, so I'm not in a business suit or nothing, but I have enough money to be in any store and even if I didn't, I have the right to be in any store. I feel like telling them sometimes, You don't know me, man. I'm a citizen here!

But I shouldn't have to tell anyone that. I want to be given the benefit of the doubt. When I walk down the street, I don't want people to look at me and see a criminal or someone that they can spit on or beat up. I want them to see a guy who has just as much right to be here as they do, or a guy who works hard, or a guy who loves his family, or a guy who's just trying to do the right things. I wish just one of those people, just one, would actually talk to me, talk to my friends, man. And yes, you can talk to us in English. I know English better than you, I bet. But none of them even want to try. We're the unknown Americans, the ones no one even wants to know, because they've been told they're supposed to be scared of us and because maybe if they did take the time to get to know us, they might realize that we're not that bad, maybe even that we're a lot like them. And who would they hate then?

It's fucked up. The whole thing is very, very complicated. I mean, does anyone ever talk about *why* people are crossing? I can promise you it's not with some grand ambition to come here and ruin everything for the gringo chingaos. People are desperate, man. We're talking about people who can't even get a toilet that works, and the government is so corrupt that when they have money, instead of sharing it, instead of using it in ways that would help their own citizens, they hold on to it and encourage people to go north instead. What choice do people have in the face of that? Like they really want to be tied to the underside of a car or stuffed into a trunk like a rug or walking in nothing but some sorry-ass sandals through the burning sand for days, a bottle of hot water in their hands? Half of them ending up dead, or burned up so bad that when someone finds them, their skin is black and their lips are cracked open? Another half of them drowning in rivers. And half after that picked up by la migra and sent back to where they came from, or beaten, or arrested. The women raped in the ass. And for what? To come here and make beds in a hotel along the highway? To be separated from their families?

And then there are a lot of people who come here because they actually want to try to do something good in this country. In my case, I was working at a newspaper in Sinaloa for years, trying to report on the drug war, trying to make people there aware of what was happening in their own backyard, but my bosses only had an appetite for the macabre. They kept sending me out to take photos of crime scenes that they'd plaster on the front pages. I did it at first because I thought, you know, that's what people needed to see. Maybe people would be shocked into action. But after a while I realized that it was all just spectacle. Photos of decapitated bodies weren't helping anyone. So I wanted to come to the other side, across the border. No one here wants to admit it, but the United States is part of México's problem. The United States is feeding the beast, man. I thought maybe if I came here, I could make a difference.

Now I work with a group in Wilmington that's advocating for legislation reform for immigrants. I do all the photographs for their newsletter and their website. Pictures of people's living conditions or of some bodily harm that they suffered because they got jumped just for being brown in this country. I don't know. We don't make much progress most of the time. But what else am I gonna do? I gotta fight for what I believe in.

# Alma

That Friday I waited by the front window for Maribel's bus to bring her home from school. Tiny flowers of frost were etched across the windowpane, and I puffed my breath against the glass, watching it fog up and dragging my finger through the condensation.

I checked the clock on the oven. It was an old oven, scabbed with rust, and I remembered my dismay at seeing it when we first arrived. Nothing at all like the tile and clay oven I had in Pátzcuaro with its wide wood mantel. I watched the hands on the clock tick around calmly. It's still early, I told myself. I bit my thumbnail and waited. And yet, after ten more minutes, there was no sign of her.

I put on my coat and boots and walked downstairs, standing under the balcony overhang, looking around. The grass was ragged and soggy along the edge of the asphalt. Food wrappers littered the ground. I took a deep breath to calm myself and walked to the road, craning my neck to look for her bus.

When I didn't see it, I cut back through the parking lot and headed toward the Toros' apartment.

Celia looked surprised to see me when she answered the door. I hadn't talked to her since I'd called her to tell her that we didn't want Maribel spending time with Mayor anymore. She had defended Mayor at first, reminding me that Quisqueya was a gossip and assuring me that Mayor never caused any trouble.

But later Rafael had called back and told us that Mayor admitted he'd been in the car with Maribel. Rafael apologized on behalf of himself and Celia and said that they had made sure Mayor understood he had to stay away from Maribel.

Now, though, the friction was unmistakable.

"I was on my way out," Celia said.

She was wearing gold earrings and a butterscotch-colored sweater. Her hair was hair-sprayed stiff.

"Have you seen Maribel?" I asked.

"Maribel? No."

"She's not here?"

"No."

My stomach turned. "Her bus didn't come today," I said.

Celia's face betrayed a flash of concern. "When was it supposed to come?"

"Fifteen minutes ago. Maybe twenty by now."

"Did she have something after school? A meeting or a club?"

"No."

"I don't know, Alma."

"Is Mayor here?" I asked.

Celia tensed. She pulled back her shoulders. "No," she said. "But he's not with her. He knows the rule."

"Maybe he's heard something."

"Well, he was going to a movie with his friend William after school today. I can ask him when he gets home." Celia leaned forward and stuck her head out past the door frame. "Is that snow?" she asked.

"What?"

"It's snowing. When did that start?"

I turned and saw brief glints of something, like dust lit by sunlight. I was so distracted that I hadn't registered them.

"Dios, qué vaina," Celia said. "All winter long, nothing. And now this! At the end of March!"

I was quiet, catching sight of the flakes and then losing them again, feeling myself burrow further into fear. Where was she? I didn't want to think what I was thinking. Had that boy come for her again? Had he taken her somewhere? And what was he doing to her if he had? I felt it, then, the full weight of my terror. I felt it low and round in my belly, thin and quivering through my chest. An anguished sound escaped my lips.

"Alma!" Celia said, startled.

"I'm sorry."

"You have to relax. I'm sure she's fine. Maybe the bus is stuck in traffic."

I nodded, unconvinced.

And then the two of us just stood there until finally Celia dropped her shoulders and looked at me with sympathy. "Come inside," she said.

"I thought you were on your way out."

"Come inside," she said again, "I'll make coffee. We'll wait for her together."

Once we were in the apartment, Celia tried to call Mayor, but she only got his voice mail. "He must have turned his phone off in the movie," she said. "He'll check it when he comes out."

I sat on the couch and stared through the window at the white sky, the empty parking lot, the faded asphalt, while Celia brewed a pot of coffee. I forced myself to imagine scenarios in which Maribel was fine: She was sitting on the bus, twisting her hair between her fingers, staring out the window at the traffic on the street; she was asleep in the bus seat, oblivious to the delay; she was only a block from our apartment, pulling her backpack onto her shoulders, preparing to get off. I said to myself: You didn't have a bad feeling before the accident, and then she wasn't fine. Maybe because you have a bad feeling now, it means she *is* fine. I didn't care that it made no sense.

"I need to call Arturo," I said suddenly, reaching for the phone in my coat pocket. But when I looked at it, the screen was black, out of minutes. How long had it been like that? I dropped the phone back in my pocket and asked Celia if I could use her house line instead.

"Of course," she said, handing me the receiver.

"Bueno," Arturo said when he answered. He was out, as he had been for forever it seemed, still looking for a job.

"It's me, Arturo. You need to come home," I said.

"Why? What happened?"

"It's Maribel."

"What happened?" he said again.

"She didn't come home from school."

"What do you mean? Did you call the school?"

I was embarrassed to realize that I hadn't, and I didn't want to admit it to him now.

"Come home, Arturo. Please."

"I'll be right there," he said.

I did call the school as soon as we hung up, but no one answered, and when I passed the phone to Celia so that she could listen to the recording that started playing, she reported that it simply gave the school hours and said that there were no after-school programs that day. I thought of calling Phyllis, too, but her number was in my dead cell phone.

By the time Arturo arrived, not more than ten minutes later, I was pacing outside, knotted with worry, every knot pulled so tight that it had begun to fray. The snow fell lightly, like weightless kisses, although I barely noticed it. I ran to him as soon as I saw him. His face clouded and he put his hands on my shoulders.

"Her bus didn't come," I said. My lips felt numb, but not because of the cold.

"Was there an accident?"

"I don't know."

"Did you call the police?"

"The police?"

"She was supposed to be home half an hour ago! Who knows what could have happened?"

"I didn't know if I was allowed—"

"To call the police? Why?"

I stared at him. I didn't want to say.

"Alma! Use your head! Let them deport us if they want."

He stormed past me, toward our apartment.

"Arturo!" I yelled after him.

He stopped and turned.

"I need to tell you something." Tears were forming in my eyes, but I had to say it. I had no choice now. What did it matter, my instinct to protect him, my misguided idea that somehow by keeping all of this from him, I could prove that I was capable, I could prove that I could take care of our daughter even though I had failed her so terribly before? If she was missing, what did any of it matter?

"There's a boy . . ."

Arturo looked like he was annoyed that I was changing the subject. "What are you talking about?"

"He lives in Capitol Oaks."

"Who?"

"You saw him. A long time ago when we went to the gas station. He was there."

"Who was there?"

"I don't know his name. But he came here one day."

Arturo shook his head as if he were giving up on trying to understand me.

"I found him with her," I said, and pointed to the side of the building. "Over there. I think he'd been after her since the beginning. He had her against the wall."

A darkness settled over Arturo's face. "What do you mean? What was he doing?"

"He had her shirt up."

"When?"

I didn't answer.

"When, Alma? When did this happen?"

"I told him to stay away from her."

"When?"

"A few months ago."

"And you're just telling me now?"

"I thought I could handle it."

"Handle it? Alma!"

"I went over to his house. I told him to leave her alone."

Arturo stared at me with such incredulity it was almost horror. As if I were someone he didn't recognize. "Did he hurt her?" he asked.

"No. I don't think so."

"But you said—"

"I got here in time."

"But where were you? Why weren't you with her?"

There was nothing I could say to that. I had no defense.

"You lied to me," Arturo said.

"I was trying not to worry you."

He sputtered, a sound that verged on laughter, and tipped his head back, gazing at the faded gray sky. The snow was falling steadily now and flakes the size of postage stamps landed on his face, on his hair.

"I wanted to make it up to you," I said.

I waited, but he just kept his eyes trained on the faraway sky.

"I was the one holding the ladder."

Arturo lowered his head and looked at me. "What?"

"That day. I was the one who let her go up there. One second she was on the ladder and she was our perfect daughter, and the next second—"

"She wasn't perfect," Arturo said.

"But I knew you didn't want her up there—you told her not to go up there—and I let her go anyway."

"So?"

"So she fell, Arturo! And it was my fault."

"That's what you think?"

"That's what you told me! In the hospital. Afterwards."

Arturo looked confused.

"You said I was supposed to be holding the ladder. You accused me of letting it go."

"You think I blame you for what happened?"

"We both know it was because of me."

"Well, I'm the one who told you both to come with me that day."

"You didn't know what would happen."

"Neither did you. That's what I'm saying!"

"But it's different."

"No, it's not different. You say you let her go up there, but how could you have known she would fall?"

"But I was the one holding the ladder."

"Did you take your hands off it? Did you move it on purpose?"

I shook my head.

"It wasn't your fault, Alma."

"Everything changed because of me," I said.

He looked at me with sadness, maybe even mercy. "It wasn't your fault," he said again. "You have to let it go."

"But—"

"Whatever I said back then . . . I was upset, Alma. I wasn't thinking straight."

I bit my lip.

"Listen to me," Arturo said. "It's you. It's you who needs to forgive yourself."

I couldn't speak. Tears from a wellspring deep and dark streamed down my face.

"Do you hear me?" Arturo asked. "Forgive yourself."

I nodded and felt a distant sort of release, as if something inside of me was draining away.

"Now," Arturo said, "we're going to find her."

INSIDE THE APARTMENT, Arturo called the police. They said that the school had already notified them and that they had a patrol car out looking. They seemed surprised that no one from the school had been in touch with us. They told him, "Kids this age. You'll see. She'll probably walk through your front door before we even get a chance to track her down."

But she didn't, and Arturo wasn't going to wait. He collected change for the bus, put on his cowboy hat, and started toward the front door.

"Where are you going?" I asked.

"I'm going to find that boy."

"And then what?"

"And then I'm going to make him tell me where the hell our daughter is."

"It's snowing outside," I said stupidly, as if that made a difference.

Arturo zipped his coat. "You stay here," he said. "In case she comes home." He opened the door. "I'll be back soon."

# Mayor

Daylight had started to fade by the time Maribel and I got back in the car. We'd driven a few miles, headed toward home, when the snow picked up for real. It started swirling around in gusts and falling so heavily that I had to turn the windshield wipers to the highest setting, and even then I had trouble seeing the road. I couldn't make out any of the shops and restaurants along the side of it, either. Whole clumps of snow were blowing off the trees and off roofs. Streetlights looked like giant cotton balls.

Before we even made it to the highway, the car was skidding all over the place, the tires spinning like they weren't touching the ground. We passed two cars that had pulled off onto the shoulder to wait it out, which seemed like a pretty good idea, so I did it, too.

Maribel didn't ask any questions, and I realized, after I stopped the car and actually took a second to look at her, that it was because she'd fallen asleep. Without much of anything else to do, I rested my own head against the steering wheel and watched her for a while. She was still wearing my coat and her hair was wavy from the snow. Her hands were resting palm up on her lap.

Outside, the wind howled, and every few minutes a car crept by with its high beams on. The snow will let up soon, I told myself. At least, I hoped so. I mean, I really hoped this wasn't the start of some blizzard that was going to bury us alive on the side of the road. I got a little freaked out at the thought of it and started wondering whether there was a flashlight in the glove compartment and how long two people could survive on a handful of Starbursts. But then I told myself to relax. We were, like, a few hundred feet from the nearest house. It wasn't exactly the tundra.

The heaviest part of the storm passed eventually, but I have no idea when. I fell asleep, too, waking myself up when my head rolled onto the horn, which let out a long honk that cut through the night air. At the sound of it, Maribel startled.

"Where are we?" she asked.

"We're in the car," I said. My breath tasted sour, and I turned my head so she wouldn't catch a whiff of it.

"But where are we?"

"We were on our way home, but the snow was crazy, so I pulled over. And then I guess I fell asleep."

"It's not snowing now," she said.

I looked out the window. It was completely dark and everything outside was calm, like the snow had formed a cocoon over the world. Maribel pulled her hair off her face, and I saw an indentation along her cheek where she'd been resting it against the seat belt.

I put the key in the ignition. The car grumbled but didn't start. I tried again. Nothing. I felt myself start to panic a little, but on the third try, the car came to life. I turned the heat on and held my hand in front of the vent until, after a minute, warm air pulsed through.

"Are you cold?" I asked.

"No," Maribel said.

The clock on the dashboard said 1:14 a.m. Shit. We were in for it. Really, really in for it.

I was about to put the car in gear so we could nose back onto the road when Maribel said, "He pushed me against the wall."

"What?"

"He told me he had something to show me."

I didn't know what she was talking about.

"He took my coat off and pushed me against the wall."

And then somehow I got it. A prickle shot up the back of my neck. She was talking about Garrett Miller. "What did he do to you?" I asked.

"He started taking my shirt off."

"What did he do?" I asked again, even though I wasn't sure I wanted to hear the answer.

She turned and gazed out the passenger side window, her arms clutched around her.

"Maribel?"

"My mom came," she said.

"Did he hurt you?"

"My mom came," she said again.

And then we just sat there. I didn't know why she was telling me now, after all this time. When she turned back to me, she picked up my hand and ran her thumb against my open palm. I closed my fingers and squeezed, pretending like somehow if I squeezed hard enough, I could hold on to her forever.

MY DAD WAS OUTSIDE smoking a cigarette when Maribel and I pulled into the parking lot of the building. It was the dead of night, and the headlights lit him up in the dark. I got so nervous when I saw him that I stalled a few feet before the space. My dad threw his cigarette into the snow and strode over, yanking open the driver's-side door.

"Get out," he said.

I did. Maribel had fallen asleep again on the drive home and she was curled into the passenger's-side seat.

"Give me the keys," my dad said.

I handed them over. I couldn't bring myself to look him in the eye.

"Now get in the backseat," he ordered.

I didn't have the guts to ask why, but I thought I should probably just do whatever he asked, so I climbed in the back while my dad got into the driver's seat and tore out of the lot.

It was a quiet drive. Not a single other car was on the road. My dad was flying—long grooves of slush that ribbed the pavement sprayed up onto the car—and the whole time I was shaking in the backseat like there was an earthquake under my skin. I had no idea where he was taking us, not to mention what might be open in the middle of the night, so I figured maybe he just wanted to drive around for a while until he collected himself. Maybe there was a lecture coming, and he was composing it in his head. Maybe he wanted to get Maribel and me away from the apartment so that none of our neighbors would hear what he was about to unleash on us. Maybe Maribel's parents and my parents had decided between them that my father would be the one who would reprimand us when we finally came home. But after ten minutes in the car, when we pulled up to Christiana Hospital, I had a sinking feeling that I'd gotten it all wrong.

"Wake her up," my dad said after he parked. "We're going inside."

I tapped Maribel on the shoulder. "We need to get out of the car," I said.

"What?"

"You fell asleep again. We're back in Newark. My dad drove us to the hospital and now he wants us to get out of the car."

"Hospital?"

"Yeah. I have no idea what's going on. But he wants us to go inside with him."

I thought, Maybe he's going to take us to see patients who were barely hanging on after car accidents as a way to teach Maribel and me a lesson about what could have happened to us.

My dad lit another cigarette as he cut across the dark, snowy parking lot to the entrance at the emergency room. Maribel and I followed. The doors slid open when we reached them, and my dad stubbed out his cigarette in a standing ashtray before we walked inside.

The second I saw my mom sitting in the waiting room, I knew it was bad. My dad walked straight over and put his hand on her shoulder. She jerked her head up, frightened. "Nothing yet," she said.

My dad nodded toward Maribel and me. "They just got back."

"One good thing," my mom said.

But she didn't get up like I thought she would.

"They're okay," my dad said.

It was only then that my mom looked at me. She curled her lips in between her teeth and blinked fast. Her nostrils flared, and I thought she was going to cry, but she just nodded and turned away again.

My dad sat down next to her and balanced his elbows on his knees, tenting his fingers and staring through them to the white floor, to the radiators along the baseboards, to what? I had no idea.

A fat woman with a Phillies baseball cap and a plastic bag on her lap sat in a chair against the wall. A tattooed man in jeans and a jean jacket—his legs outstretched, his ankles crossed—was sleeping a few seats down.

"What's going on?" Maribel asked me.

"I don't know," I said.

"What's going on?" Maribel asked, louder now.

I saw my mom form her hands into fists and then let them go again. She looked at my dad in agony, which was the same way he was looking back at her. They seemed to be questioning each other, and from the expression on both of their faces I doubted either had the answers the other was searching for.

Finally my mom locked her gaze on Maribel. She reached her hand out, but Maribel didn't take it. "It's your father," my mom said. "We don't know the details yet, but they brought him here. He had surgery and now we're just waiting. Your mother is with him."

"My father?" Maribel repeated.

"What happened to him?" I asked

"We tried to call you," my mom said, "but your phone was off. We called you a hundred times."

"I didn't know . . ."

"We called the police, too."

"The police—why?"

"Why?" my dad said. "Because when I came home, the car—my car—was missing. I thought someone had stolen it."

"I'm surprised they didn't find you," my mom said.

"What happened?" I asked.

Again, the agony on her face. Her mouth tightened into a lock. "We don't know anything yet," my dad said. "Just sit down."

"Ven, hija," my mom said, reaching her arm out to draw Maribel in. Maribel took a step away and lowered herself into a chair. When I didn't move, my mom said, "Please, Mayor. Just sit down. There's nothing you can do. There's nothing else to know yet."

WE STAYED IN those seats for hours. A nurse took Maribel back to the surgical waiting area, where Sra. Rivera was, while my mom and dad and I stayed put, waiting for word.

A television mounted in the corner was playing ESPN, and I stared at it until I couldn't anymore. I kept pulling out my phone, checking the time. My dad walked out through the automatic doors at the entrance to smoke, and each time he did, I looked out at the sky, which lightened little by little with the coming dawn. My mom kept filling paper cups with coffee from the vending machine and then she'd sit down and drink it, staring at the floor, and stand up and get another.

Finally, by the time my dad was down to his last cigarette and my mom was out of money for more coffee and my ass was numb from sitting in one spot for so long, a doctor—a tubby, middle-aged guy in green scrubs and a pair of glasses hanging by a strap around his neck—came out and told us that Sr. Rivera was in recovery but that he hadn't woken up yet.

"What happens now?" my mom asked.

"We wait," the doctor said.

"Is he going to be okay?"

"We've done everything we can."

We headed home after that, trudging through the parking lot in the white early-morning sunlight, the air as thin as paper, while my mom said, "Shouldn't he be able to tell us more?

'Everything we can.' What does that mean?" But my dad didn't have an answer, and neither did I.

I still didn't know what had happened—every time I asked, my dad cut me off with some variation on "Let's just wait. There's no use worrying before we know anything"—except that I knew it was bad enough to land Sr. Rivera in surgery and bad enough that my parents didn't want to talk about it. I didn't need to know much more than that to feel sick to my stomach. Whatever was happening was all my fault. I knew it. I'd taken Maribel away because why? Because I'd wanted to see her? Because I was trying to be romantic? Because I was trying to free her from the confines of her life? Because I'd wanted to show her the snow on the ocean, the thing that had made my mom fall in love with this country, and I had wanted to make Maribel fall in love, too? With me?

My parents wouldn't tell me anything, so all Saturday morning I waited for news. My mom wanted me to try to sleep, so I went to my room for a while, but all I managed to do was sit up in bed—awake and fully dressed—waiting for the phone to ring so that maybe my mom would answer it and I could overhear what was going on. As soon as my dad came home from his newspaper shift, he asked if my mom had heard anything, but she told him no. By then my mom was sitting at the kitchen table with the telephone next to her elbow. Her eyes were red. Her hair was flattened at the back.

"Can't you just tell me?" I said.

My mom started crying.

"What? Did something go wrong?" I asked.

"Everything went wrong," she said.

"Did he have a heart attack or something? Or did he fall on the ice and crack his head? Just tell me. Please, Mami."

She cried for a while longer, then wiped her cheeks with the heel of her hand. "He was trying to find Maribel," she said. She looked at me, her eyes wet, her cheeks broken out the way they always got when she cried. "They shot him."

"What?"

"They shot him."

"Who shot him?"

"I don't know, Mayor. I wasn't there."

"Like with a gun?"

"Oh my God," she said, and threw her hand over her mouth, like hearing me actually say it out loud was too much for her. She pushed away from the table and ran to the bathroom where, even after she closed the door behind her, I heard her heaving and coughing. I stood there like an idiot, blinking. I felt—what? Nothing. The blankness of incomprehension. They shot him, I kept repeating to myself. They shot him.

THE PHONE STAYED QUIET most of the day, even though the doorbell kept ringing. Quisqueya and Nelia came over to see if my mom knew anything, and when she told them she didn't, the two of them chattered on about what they'd heard. Micho stopped by and told us a story about a buddy of his who got shot in Afghanistan and survived. "Lucky bastard," he said. "God gives out a few free passes like that every year. Saves them for the best people. But listen, Arturo will be fine. He's one of the best people." Sr. Mercado dropped in, and then Benny, and I hung around enough that little by little the story emerged: Sr. Rivera had gone to Capitol Oaks. There had been a confrontation, and at some point a man walked out with a shotgun in his hand. He fired, and that was that.

I couldn't stop myself from imagining it, like some sort of television show. I saw Sr. Rivera in his jeans and cowboy boots, his hair wet from the snow, combed to the side like he always wore it, wandering down Kirkwood Highway, peeking behind the Steak 'n Shake and the bowling alley and the Panera Bread, looking for Maribel. I felt his breath in the air as he walked. I heard the hard soles of his boots on the pavement. I saw him approach Capitol Oaks and walk past the entrance, shouting Maribel's name into the cold. I saw people in their houses, pulling back their blinds, peeking out their windows at the noise. And I saw someone come outside—Garrett Miller, I thought, because I had the feeling that somehow all of this had to do with him. In my mind, I heard Sr. Rivera ask him about Maribel, and I saw Garrett screw up his face because he didn't understand what Sr. Rivera was saying. But Benny had said it was a man—a man—who came out with a shotgun. So what had happened then? Maybe Garrett's dad saw Sr. Rivera on his front lawn. Maybe he was drunk or high or maybe he was just pissed off. He came outside, carrying the gun, pointing it toward Sr. Rivera.

Sr. Rivera stepped back, raising his hands in the air to show he meant no harm. "I'm looking for my daughter," he said in Spanish.

Garrett's dad didn't understand. "We speak English here," he said. He came closer, holding the barrel of the gun in line with the tip of Sr. Rivera's nose.

"Where is she?" Sr. Rivera managed to say.

What could Garrett's dad have said in return? "Get off my property." "Shut up." "You fuckhead." "This is what you get." What could he have been thinking?

"Please," Sr. Rivera said, in English this time, one of the few words he knew.

And then Garrett's dad pulled the trigger.

THE HOURS WERE like mountains we had to climb, enormous and exhausting. One after the other, and still no word from the hospital.

My mom foraged through her closet for clothes she could give the Riveras when they got home, even though my dad looked at her like she was crazy and asked, "What do they need with clothes?" My mom said, "I don't know. I just want to do something!"

She devoted herself to the kitchen after that, preparing meals that she spooned into plastic containers and the tins usually reserved for Christmas cookies. She taped notes to the top that detailed what was inside and how to reheat it, and saved it all in our freezer to be delivered when the Riveras returned home.

My dad paced around the house with a drink permanently in his hand and a cigarette permanently in his mouth. He didn't even bother to smoke outside, and my mom didn't bother to make him. He would wander to the couch, sit for a while, stand up, then check the phone again to make sure it still had a dial tone. When he heard it, he would put the receiver back down and stare at it, like he was trying to exert some kind of mind control over it to make it ring.

And me? I was mired in a feeling that was heavy and sick. Once, I walked out onto the balcony and looked up at the Riveras' door, where bouquets of flowers wrapped in cellophane were piled at the threshold. I ran over and started kicking the shit out of those flowers until my dad came out and asked me what I was doing.

I didn't have an answer, at least not one that I could articulate.

My dad said, "He's going to be fine."

I tried to slow my breathing.

"He has to be," he said.

BUT HE WASN'T. Close to eight o'clock that night, the phone finally rang and when my dad, who answered it at my mom's terrified urging, hung up, he shook his head.

"No!" my mom wailed. "Rafa, no!"

"He died," my dad said.

"Who was on the phone?" my mom managed to ask.

"A nurse."

My head was pounding.

"He died," my dad repeated in disbelief.

"No," my mom said again. "No, no, no, no, no!" She dropped her head into her hands.

I couldn't swallow. It had to be wrong. We had to be able to rewind. It couldn't be real. It felt so weightless. It felt like an idea, a particle of dust floating around in the air that hadn't landed yet. There was still time to catch it. There was still time to stop it, right? It had to be a mistake. I tried to swallow again, but my throat was huge.

IT WAS MY DAD who drove Maribel and Sra. Rivera from the hospital back to the apartment.

When he returned, my mom asked, "Where are they?"

"What do you mean? I drove them back."

"But I thought you would bring them here."

"They're going to bed."

"They can't stay in that apartment tonight. They can't be alone at a time like this."

"They're tired, Celia. You should have seen them. They need to sleep."

"But in that apartment?"

"They have each other."

"That's not good enough."

"You're right. It's not. But what can we do? Listen to me. They were calm in the car on the way home. Neither of them said anything except to thank me for coming to get them. You can go over there first thing in the morning. Just let them get some sleep."

"They're our friends!"

"Alma is a strong woman. They're going to be okay."

My mom let out a shaky sigh.

"Tomorrow. You can go see them tomorrow."

AS SOON AS the sun came up, my mom and I went over. Sra. Rivera answered the door and my mom fell onto her in a crushing hug. "¡Qué horror!" my mom cried into Sra. Rivera's neck. I crept past the two of them to the bedroom where, through the open doorway, I saw Maribel sitting on the floor, her legs extended in a narrow V. I hesitated for a second, waiting to see if she would look up. I thought I might be able to tell from her expression whether it was okay for me to go in. But she was just moving her feet from side to side, staring absently at her toes. I went and sat down next to her, straightening my legs in the same way, and tapped the side of my sneaker against her foot. I didn't say anything because there wasn't anything to say. I just sat, listening to the muffled sounds of our moms from the other room—low voices and sniffling and even, once or twice, what I could have sworn was laughter.

After a long time, Maribel said, "Do you think it was my fault?"

"What happened to your dad?"

She nodded.

I looked at her face. I could see that she was going to live with that question for a long time. I'd been living with it for less than a day myself and it was tearing me up. But I said the only thing I could. "No. It was just what happened. That's all."

"But we left México because—"

"No, Maribel. It was just what happened. It had nothing to do with you."

"Then was it our fault?"

I shook my head.

"But the only reason—"

"Listen to me. You can't do that. You can't think like that."

I was trying to comfort her, but both of us were trying to make sense of it. And sitting there, I started thinking, Who can say whose fault it is? Who can say who set this whole thing in motion? Maybe it *was* Maribel. Maybe it was me. Maybe if I hadn't left school that day, or if I had answered my stupid phone when it rang, or if I hadn't fallen asleep in the car on the way home, none of this would have happened. But maybe if our parents hadn't forbidden us from seeing each other, I wouldn't have needed to steal her away like I did in the first place. Maybe if my dad had never bought that car, I wouldn't have had a way to get to the beach. Maybe it was my tía Gloria's fault for giving my dad the money that allowed him to buy it. Maybe it was my tío Esteban's fault for being a jerk who she would need to divorce to get that money. You could trace it back infinitely. All these different veins, but who knew which one led to the heart? And then again, maybe it had nothing to do with any of us. Maybe God had a plan and He knew from the second the Riveras set foot here that He was putting them on a path toward this. Or maybe it really was completely random, just something that happened.

I DIDN'T KNOW IT THEN, how close to the end I was with her. I mean, I should've been able to figure out that they'd go back to México. I just didn't know how soon. I didn't know that the last time I'd see Maribel would be just a week later, when I'd find her sitting on the curb outside our building next to a full-size mattress.

I went outside and sat next to her, the cement cold through my pants, the ground mostly clear by then except for a few patches of dirty snow.

"What are you doing out here?" I asked.

"Nothing."

"I thought you weren't allowed outside by yourself."

"My mom is sleeping."

I peeked at the mattress. "On the floor?"

"She doesn't want to sleep in the bed anymore."

"Oh."

"We're leaving tomorrow," Maribel said.

"Tomorrow?" I said, looking at her.

"My mom wants to go back."

"So that's it?"

"She says we have to."

The melting snow trickled into the street grate next to us. I didn't know how to comprehend it, really, the fact that she was leaving. I mean, all my life people had been coming and going—neighbors came and left, kids at school showed up and were gone again the next year, but the difference was that none of them had been her.

The green notebook I had gotten so used to seeing her carry around was on top of the mattress. Maribel picked it up and thrust it toward me. "Here," she said.

"What? Did you write me a letter or something?" I asked. I was only half joking, hoping that maybe she had.

But when I took the notebook and flipped through it, there was nothing but the lists she kept and her notes to herself. I closed the cover and fingered one of the rounded corners, feathered and frayed from overuse. I tried to hand it back to her, but she shook her head.

"You don't want it?" I asked.

"Not anymore," she said.

It seemed like a measure of something, evidence of how far she'd come. She hadn't even talked that first time I'd seen her in the Dollar Tree, hadn't even made eye contact.

"You could come back one day," I said. "Or I could come there."

"Maybe."

"I could find you."

Maribel shook her head. "Finding is for things that are lost. You don't need to find me, Mayor."

She had her hands on her knees and I touched my fingers to her knuckles, tracing the peaks and valleys, staring at her skin. The only girl who had ever liked me. It wasn't fair, I kept thinking, even though I had no right to complain. There were worse things, way worse, that happened in the world. If I hadn't known that before, I knew it now.

They were gone by the time I got up the next morning. I didn't want to wake up early just to see them leave. I thought it would come pretty close to wrecking me to stand at the front window and watch them—two of them this time—walk out with their things in their arms. Besides, I could imagine it well enough. Maribel and her mom climbing into a truck similar to the one they had climbed out of seven months earlier. Maribel with sleepy eyes and uncombed hair, sitting cross-legged on the seat, turning around and looking back for me. But it would be okay, I told myself, that she wouldn't find me. It was like she had said—finding is for things that are lost. We would be thousands of miles apart from now on and we would go on with our lives and get older and change and grow, but we would never have to look for each other. Inside each of us, I was pretty sure, was a place for the other. Nothing that had happened and nothing that would ever happen would make that less true.

# Alma

I detached from myself. I saw my life as a spectator would, from outside, from a distance so remote that I couldn't feel any of it. "Señora Rivera," they said, "we're sorry. The surgery was more complicated than we anticipated. There was nothing we could do." The translator at the hospital, a woman about my age with a wide, round face, cried as she delivered the news. I stared at her hands trembling against her chest as she spoke. "Mi más sentido pésame," she added, on behalf of herself. I reached out and gave her a hug. I saw myself doing this, but I didn't feel her shaking in my arms. I went to Maribel. I saw myself walking, but I didn't feel my feet upon the thin carpet. "It's time to go," I told her. I saw myself talking, but I didn't feel the words crawling up through my throat.

"Is the surgery over?" Maribel asked.

"Yes," I said. "Get your things."

"Are we going to see him?"

She looked so hopeful, so nervous. She stared, waiting for me to say more. Are we going to see him? Are we going to see him? Had she really asked that? Are we going to see him? My God! I blinked and came back to myself. Are we going to see him? What a simple question to break my heart.

"No," I said, the word as fragile as an egg.

"Why not?"

My breath rose up through my lungs and emptied out again. Blood swept through my veins. My lips were dry.

"Is he . . . resting?" she asked.

He was, in a manner of speaking. So I said, "Yes." Then, "No. No. Maribel, come here." I pulled her to my hip, feeling her wiry, warm body against mine. "The surgery didn't go well," I said.

"Why?"

"He . . ." I took another breath. "He didn't make it."

Maribel closed her eyes, and I tightened my hold on her. "What does that mean?" she asked.

"He—" I started. But I couldn't go on. There weren't enough words in Spanish, not enough words in English no matter how many classes I might have gone to, not enough words in any language on earth, not the right words, nothing to match the depths of what I felt. My tongue fumbled against the back of my teeth, trying to give shape and sound to what had happened, struggling to explain, when Maribel opened her eyes and said, "He died?"

When I nodded, she let out a sound like a baby seal. I felt tears gathering at the edges of my eyes. And then, as quickly as a gasp, the world shrank, and I felt the ground open up beneath me.

IF I SLEPT AT ALL, I slept on the floor. Of course, that first night home I didn't sleep. I lay on the floor next to the mattress and shivered under a blanket. I stood up in the middle of the night and looked at the bed to see if it had all been a dream. Maribel was tucked into her sleeping bag against the wall, but Arturo wasn't where he was supposed to be. He wasn't breathing long, rhythmic breaths, lying on his back. He wasn't in his undershirt and briefs, the comforter pulled to his chin. He wasn't there.

I wrapped the blanket around me and stood at the window, my hair loose over my shoulders. If I turned my head enough, I could see the street and the traffic lights and an occasional semi-truck driving through town. I stood at the window for hours that first night. There was no comfort in it. Cold air slipped through the window sash and cut across my skin like razor blades. The caulk Arturo had tried to apply lay splintered in the seams. I stood there and thought about what must have happened, about what it must have been like, although I tried very hard not to imagine what he must have felt. At the hospital, Officer Mora, the same officer I had spoken with at the station months earlier, tried to console me. He had knocked on our apartment door only minutes after Arturo had left. He had told me he was there about Maribel. He had asked, "Do you think it had something to do with that boy, the one you told me about?" I explained that Arturo had gone to find him. "He lives in Capitol Oaks," I said, and Officer Mora pulled the radio off the belt of his pants. He spoke into it in English, then clipped it back on and said, "I'll head over there now." Which is what he and another officer did. Only by the time they arrived, it was too late. They found Arturo on the ground. They called for an ambulance. They found the boy and his father standing outside, a gun still in the father's hands. All of this Officer Mora told me later, at the hospital. He said that the boy's father—his name was Leon Miller— was in custody and would be charged. The boy—his name was Garrett—had witnessed the whole thing.

"What happens now?" I asked.

"Mr. Miller will probably be locked up for a long time. We're trying to determine if the kid was involved, but so far it doesn't seem like it. We haven't been able to track down his mother yet, either." Officer Mora looked me in the eye. "I'm sorry about before," he said, "when you came to the station." His face was grave. "We're going to get justice for you now, though, I'll make sure of it."

But it was only a word—justice. It was only a concept, and it wasn't enough.

As I stood at the window, I thought, If I saw the boy or his father now, I would take a gun and kill them myself. But of course I didn't have a gun. I would throw my heavy winter boots at them. I would tear at their flesh with my teeth if I knew it would make a difference. But of course, it wouldn't make a difference.

I leaned against the glass until daybreak, until the sky began to lighten over the earth. When it did, I thought, Maybe it's over now. I turned back toward the bed to see if maybe, just maybe, he was stirring, stretching his arms overhead and rubbing his eyes. To see if he would swing his legs over the side of the mattress and stand up and wander to the bathroom and shave his face, the smell of soap wafting out to the hallway. But when I turned, there was only the sheet thrown back, the mattress still depressed from where he had last lain.

CELIA CAME OVER the morning after—everything to me now was either before or after, the way that previously my life had been divided by the accident—and sobbed into my shoulder. She apologized over and over, and though at first I mistook her apologies for condolences, I realized soon enough that she believed she had a role in what had happened—or maybe that Mayor did—and I had to tell her, "No. Stop. Please." Because while it was true that Mayor had taken Maribel away, he hadn't done this.

Still, Celia kept coming every day, sometimes twice a day. She stayed for hours at a time. She brought empanadas and sugared breads wrapped in tinfoil, arroz con pollo and chicken soup packaged in plastic containers. She brought brown paper bags filled with clothes we didn't need and could barely use. She brought the prayer notes from Mass where Arturo had been listed that first Sunday in the bulletin.

"Father Finnegan did a beautiful service," Celia reported. "He asked if there was anything he could do. He wanted me to remind you that his door is open. If you want to talk."

"I know."

Celia put her hand on mine and left the prayer notes on the counter.

On Monday, a woman from the hospital called to ask what I wanted to do with the body. The question was so absurd it made me laugh.

"What do I want to do with it?" I said. "I want to bring it back to life."

When I told this to Celia, she laughed, too. "Of course! What else would you want to do with it?"

"Exactly!"

"What did she say then?"

"She said she was sorry and that what she meant was whether I knew where I would like to bury him. So I said, 'I would not like to bury him!'"

"Oh, Alma."

"What questions!" I said, shaking my head.

Celia twisted the coffee mug in her hands. "But you'll have to make a decision, won't you?"

"I want him buried in México," I said. I didn't tell her that I wanted him in the Panteón Municipal, where we could celebrate him on el Día de Muertos. I wanted to bake pan de muerto and prepare calabaza en tacha for him. I wanted to make an ofrenda with the cempasúchil flowers that grew in our yard. I wanted to put candles on his tomb. I wanted to honor him. I wanted him near me.

Celia said, "Of course he should be buried in México."

"But the woman from the hospital said it would cost five thousand dollars to send his body there."

"Five thousand dollars! Qué escándalo. What are they going to do? Build a house around him?"

"I told the woman, 'Thank you, but I'll carry him to México myself if I have to.'"

Celia nodded.

"He has to go back with me. I need him—" The inside of my nose, the whole inside of my face, burned. I clenched my teeth until I could go on. "I need him with me."

Celia looked at me sadly. "So you're going back?"

"I don't know what else to do. We're not even in status. The police know that now. They're going to send us back anyway if we don't leave ourselves."

"Where will you go?"

"We still have our house. My parents have been checking on it since we left. They're waiting for us."

"And then?"

"I don't know. I can barely even believe that the days will go on. It seems like it should all stop somehow."

"But it doesn't," Celia said.

"No," I said. "For us it doesn't."

· · ·

I WELCOMED VISITORS. They made the passage of time tolerable. Gustavo Milhojas came over with a bouquet of flowers in his arms.

"They're marigolds," he said, handing them to me. "The girl at the flower shop said they were the right kind."

I raised them to my face, inhaling their grassy scent.

"Come in," I said.

Nelia Zafón stopped by with a greeting card that had an illustration of seagulls flying over a crucifix.

"I saw this in Walmart yesterday and thought of you," she said. "They have a good selection of cards in Spanish."

I opened it and read: "Con el pésame más profundo y las bendiciones de Dios por la pérdida de alguien tan querido para ti."

"Come in," I said.

Micho Alvarez knocked on our door, balancing a photograph on his open palm.

"I meant to give this to you sooner," he said. "I had it developed a while ago. It's from Christmas." He handed me a photograph of Maribel, Arturo, and me, smiling in our winter coats in front of the Toros' door. Looking at it, the most exquisite pain seared across my chest.

"Come in," I said.

Fito arrived and stood in the doorway, stricken, the skin on his face sagging. I waited for him to speak and when he didn't, I said, "It's okay."

Quisqueya never stopped by, but I saw her on the balcony one morning and raised a hand in greeting. She waved back, but hurried into her apartment. I understood. For her and any others who didn't come over, I understood. They simply didn't know what to say.

José Mercado and his wife, Ynez, came over without anything but condolences, and after I invited them in, they talked for an hour about what a good man Arturo was and how much they had liked him and how he had helped José carry paper bags of groceries into their apartment on more than one occasion. I hadn't known anything about the groceries, but I wasn't surprised, either. It sounded just like Arturo.

"Not that he was a saint," I told them. "He never cleaned his mustache clippings out of the sink."

"That sounds familiar," Ynez said, poking her husband in the side. She had long gray hair that she wore in a low bun. Her face was gentle and kind, pleated with wrinkles.

"Arturo was stubborn, too," I said. "He threw his back out once trying to raise cinder blocks over his head in a contest with his friends. This was in Pátzcuaro. I kept telling him he was lifting too many at once. 'It's too heavy,' I said. But he wouldn't listen to me. He just wanted to prove he could do it."

"Men," Ynez said, nodding in amusement.

"You're more stubborn than me!" José said.

Ynez looked at me. "You see? Stubborn even in his belief that he's not stubborn."

I smiled.

And in this way, the days passed.

But when no one was there, no one but Maribel and me, the days vibrated with sadness. I had called Phyllis, the school district translator, and told her that I was keeping Maribel home with me. "I don't want her out of my sight," I said.

"Is she ever coming back to the school?" Phyllis asked.

"No."

"Her teacher will be sorry to hear that."

"I'll find something for her in México," I said. "I know it won't be the same. But I'm not giving up on her."

And because through the phone I could feel Phyllis's sympathy, I added, "I promise."

"She did well here," Phyllis said. "Maribel's a different girl now than when you arrived."

"We're both different now," I said.

When no one came over, Maribel and I watched television, hours and hours of it, finding small comfort in its ability to numb, to keep us from losing our minds. And yet, sometimes out of nowhere, Maribel asked where he was, or when he was getting home from work, and I had to remind her, "No, hija. No." I would hold her hands in mine and explain everything again. I hugged her and let her cry as often as she wanted. Once, because repeating it was too much to bear, I let impatience get the best of me. I snapped, "Stop asking me that!" She looked at me so woefully that I collapsed in shame and said "I'm sorry" again and again, repeating it until I hoped maybe she believed me.

When I wasn't watching television or receiving guests, I spent time packing, preparing for the journey back to Pátzcuaro. I stood in our bedroom and looked at Arturo's clothes folded in neat towers on the floor. I took his shirts and his underwear, his socks and undershirts, and stuffed them all into plastic trash bags. I held up the one extra pair of jeans he had besides the ones he had been wearing that night. These were Wrangler, and he rarely wore them because the others were Levi's, which he claimed were better, but he'd kept the Wranglers for years anyway. They were stiff and smelled of detergent. I shoved them in the bag. I took his razor from the shower floor, bits of his black hair still caked between the blades. I took his toothbrush from the sink counter and sucked on the bristles, trying to find the taste of him, but there was only the flavor of watery mint toothpaste. From behind the faucet, I took the scissors he used to trim his mustache and slipped them into the bag, too. I pulled the sheets off the bed with the idea that I could gather up the imprint of him and save it. I thought, I can unfurl the sheets on our old bed at home. I can lie in the creases formed by his body. I can sleep with him again. I plucked his used toothpicks out of the trash and clutched them in my hand before dropping them all into a bag. I watched them scatter and sink into the crevices of the things I had already packed. And then I came across his hat, the cowboy hat that he'd worn for almost as long as I'd known him. At the hospital, they had given it to me when we left. I remembered when he had bought it, how proud he had been because it was a good hat, finely woven and crisp. Now it was soft, and dirt had settled into the notches where the pale straw fibers crossed each other, especially in the crown. Parts of the brim were frayed. I put it over my face like a mask, feeling the sweatband, soft as felt, against my cheeks. I took a deep breath. And there he was. The smell of him. I closed my eyes and felt myself sway. There he was. ¡Dios! I put the hat on my head.

I learned something about grief. I had heard people say that when someone dies, it leaves a hole in the world. But it doesn't, I realized. Arturo was still everywhere. Something would happen and I would think, Wait until I tell Arturo. I kept turning around, expecting to see him. If he had disappeared completely, I thought, it might be easier. If I had no knowledge that he had ever existed, no evidence that he was ever a part of our lives, it might have been bearable. And how wrong that sounded: part of our lives. As if he was something with boundaries, something that hadn't permeated us, flowed through us and in us and all around us. I learned something about grief. When someone dies, it doesn't leave a hole, and that's the agony.

Two days before the scheduled burial, I started packing everything in the kitchen. I had spoken to someone at a funeral home that partnered with the hospital and confirmed yes, we would lay Arturo to rest there. For a week, his body had been in the morgue, waiting to be taken *someplace*. The burial felt wrong, but what could I do? I didn't have the money to fly him back. I had no way of getting it. I called my parents, who cried and cursed the heavens when they heard the news, but they had nothing either. I was told I couldn't drive him because it was against the law and the authorities would take him at the border rather than let his body cross. I didn't know any other way to get him from here to there. It would have to be this. Arturo would be buried on Thursday morning at the All Saints Cemetery. He would be lowered into the ground in a casket I could barely afford, even though I had instructed the funeral home to use the most inexpensive one they could. "There's no shame in a pine box," I told them. In fact, I thought Arturo, who had been so humble, would have appreciated it.

I put most of the silverware, loose and clattering, in bags. I packed the comal, the escobeta brush, the plastic baggies filled with spices we had brought, the molcajete and pestel. Except for the coffee mugs, which I thought we would use until the very end, I packed every cup. And then I started with the dishes.

I pulled the top plate from the stack. It was solid green and glazed with a clear lacquer. I held it in my hands and remembered when we had come, how carefully I had set the plates in the cabinet once they were unpacked. How carefully I had set up our lives here. How naïve I had been to think I could control any of it.

And then I let the plate drop on the floor. It plummeted straight down from my open hands and landed with a crash, shards of ceramic bursting apart and skittering across the floor.

"What was that?" Maribel asked from the other room.

I didn't answer. I took another plate from the cabinet and dropped it, too, watching it bloom at my feet. Then another. Then another. I thought suddenly, What is the meaning of all these *things*? All these bags and bags I've been packing? We could take everything we have with us. We could take every single thing that every single person in the world has ever had. But none of it would mean anything to me. Because no matter how much I took and no matter how much I had for the rest of my life, I didn't have *him* anymore. I could have piled everything from here straight to heaven. None of it was him.

Calmly, I pulled the rest of the plates out one by one. I dropped them all and watched the shards spin across the floor. I did this not in anger, but in the spirit of release. Vaguely, I noticed Maribel standing at the edge of the show. I heard her asking questions. I kept going.

After I dropped the last of them—six in all—I looked up.

"Why did you do that?" Maribel asked.

"It made me feel better."

"It was so loud."

"It's done now," I said.

I swept the pieces into the trash can. I took most of the garbage bags that I had piled in the hallway out to the Dumpster in the alley. Maribel helped me carry the mattress down to the parking lot, where we left it. Somebody else could have all of it if they wanted. I didn't need it anymore.

CELIA CAME OVER early the next morning, dressed in her bathrobe and slippers. Her hair was in rollers. There was a chill in the air and she shivered when I opened the door.

"You look awful," she said when she saw me.

"I haven't been sleeping."

"You should take medicine. Like a Tylenol PM. I use it sometimes when I'm anxious."

"It works?"

"De maravilla."

"Come in," I told her. "Maribel's still sleeping."

"No. I need to go home and get dressed. We're going to eight o'clock Mass. Actually, you know what? You should come. We could go together."

"No, thank you."

"It might make you feel better to get out."

"Are you sure you don't want to come in?"

"I just came to give you something," Celia said. She pulled a plain white envelope from her bathrobe pocket and handed it to me.

"What is it?"

"Look inside."

I lifted the flap and saw the edges of bills—there must have been a hundred of them—open like a fan.

"We took up a collection," she said. "Everyone chipped in. The teachers at Maribel's school, the receptionist in the school district office. Oh, and the translator there, too. Arturo's coworkers at the mushroom farm, the manager at Gigante, a teacher from the Community House, the translator and some of the nurses from the hospital. The church made a nice donation, and Father Finnegan added more on top of that. Plus, everyone in the building."

I stared at the money, overcome.

"Mostly it's just a little bit from each person," Celia went on. "Twenty dollars here, ten dollars there."

I couldn't speak.

"But Rafa and I talked it over. You know we got some money recently? From my sister? Of course there was hardly any discussion. The bigger bills are from us, so you can afford to fly Arturo back to México. I hope it's not too late."

The envelope felt weightless in my hand.

"It's five thousand one hundred thirty-two dollars," she said.

"You did this?"

"We all did. I just mentioned the idea to a few people in the building first. But word spread. And before I knew it people were contacting me to find out how they could contribute. People I didn't even know you knew."

I stared at the envelope.

"Everyone loved him, Alma."

Until that moment, tears had welled in my eyes, but I had beaten them back with furious blinking or distraction. Somehow I had managed not to cry. But right then I broke down. I fell on Celia and cried with more gratitude and happiness than I knew I was capable of feeling anymore.

WE LEFT TWO DAYS LATER in a black pickup truck, driven by a man Rafael had found who took people to and from the border. Apparently he had family in Texas, so he didn't mind the trip.

"How much does he charge?" I asked Rafael.

"Nothing," Rafael said. "He's doing it as a favor to me. I used to give him free breakfast when he stopped at the diner on his way up 95. Don't worry about it."

I knew he was lying. It had to have cost something. But I let it go.

Maribel and I sat in the back with a blanket draped over our laps. I had Arturo's hat on my head, my purse at my feet. Everything else—what little we were taking with us—was once again in plastic trash bags in the bed of the truck.

The man was quiet. He looked like a gringo, but what did I know? He didn't introduce himself nor turn on the radio nor talk on his phone. He just chewed sunflower seeds that he kept in a plastic cup between his legs and flicked the shells out through the window, which he left rolled down. I was grateful for his indifference to us. To him we could have been anyone. We weren't people who were grieving, or who needed to be taken care of, or who were to be pitied. We were simply people who needed to get from one place to another. In a way, it was a relief to have the privacy of our mourning.

It was early when we pulled out of the parking lot. The air was hazy. Feeble sunlight pressed through the filter of clouds. We drove past the pancake restaurant and the Red Lobster, the Dunkin' Donuts and the Rita's Italian Ice, the bowling alley and the Sears, the David's Bridal with its white gowns in the windows and the Walmart next to the highway. Within minutes we were on I-95, heading south.

All morning, I stared out the window as the world rushed by. We drove over the Susquehanna River, where the water was a ribbon, wide and flat. We passed red barns and stone mills, small white houses with black shutters and houses with wooden fences around their sprawling land, everything silent and still. We passed roadside restaurants advertising breakfast specials and movie theaters with the show times listed on towering signs near the edge of the highway. We drove through the Baltimore Harbor Tunnel and then along the outskirts of Washington, D.C., where we passed a temple with gold spires striking up into the air.

I tried not to think, but of course that was impossible. Why hadn't I simply told Arturo about the boy in the beginning? Would it have made a difference? There was no way to know the answer, and yet I remembered what Arturo had said, one of the last things he had told me, as if somehow he had known to offer me absolution in advance: Forgive yourself. Was that possible? Was it possible now, in this, too?

By noon, the sun was high in the blue sky. It shone like honey. It lay upon slender blades of grass, and draped over the hood of the truck. I leaned my head against the warm window and looked at the road stretched out before us and at the land rolling away endlessly on either side. I looked at the billboards and at the trees between them, remembering how when we had come, seven months ago, the trees had been full of green leaves and small berries, their branches so delicate and thin, bobbing in the breeze like something joyful. I stared at them now, leafless at the end of winter, and saw the same thing. To my surprise. I saw trees that looked happy, trees that looked hopeful, their naked branches suspended in reach toward the sky. Spring would come soon, I thought, and fill them up again.

We were six hours into a nearly fifty-hour trip. At the end of it we would be home, and Arturo would be there to meet us. I had canceled the arrangements with the funeral parlor and told them instead to prepare the casket for transport. I had called the consulate, filled out the papers, gotten them notarized and translated into Spanish. I had paid everyone their money. I had done it all urgently, as if my life depended on it. Which, in a way, it did. But it was worth it. Arturo was going with us to the wide, silent lake and the butterfly fishermen who glided over its surface. To the red tile roofs and the rough adobe walls of both his childhood and mine. To the cobblestone streets and the brilliant sunshine and the arched doorways and the flowers spilling over people's roofs. To the market in La Boca and the bench in Plaza Grande where the two of us ate ice cream on our first date while the late-day sun quavered above us, sliding down slowly against the curve of the sky. To the basilica and the cathedral and the painted store names in red and black. To the dirt and the wandering dogs. To our friends and generations of our families. To that stupid glass bowl that he missed so much. To home. Our home.

Somewhere in the mountains of Virginia, where the road grew narrower and hillier, Maribel complained that her stomach hurt. Without a word, the man pulled the truck over.

"Come on out, hija," I told her, opening the back door.

She threw up in the pebbles and the dirt along the shoulder while I held her hair and rubbed slow circles on her back.

"A napkin," the man said in Spanish, holding a crumpled tissue across the seat to me.

I wiped Maribel's mouth. "Are you okay?" I asked.

"Do I have any in my hair?"

I opened my palm and looked at the strands, long and dark and tangled. "No," I said.

"I want to get it cut when we get home."

"Your hair?"

"It looks bad."

I cupped my hand against the back of her head. "You look beautiful."

"And I want to dye it purple."

Suddenly, out of nowhere, there she was. My Maribel. The one who once upon a time had painted her nails black and now wanted to dye her hair purple. The one determined to assert her independence and throw her arms around life. There she was again. The person Arturo and I had been waiting for, the reason for all of this.

And as I looked at her I saw that maybe she had been here all along. Not exactly the girl she used to be before the accident, which was the girl I thought I had been searching for, but my Maribel, brave and impetuous and kind. All this time I had been buried too far under my guilt to see her. I had been preoccupied with getting us to the United States because I wanted it to make her whole again. I believed that I had lost my daughter and that if I did the right things and brought us to the right place, I could recover the girl she used to be. What I didn't understand—what I suddenly realized now—was that if I stopped moving backwards, trying to recapture the past, there might be a future waiting for me, waiting for us, a future that would reveal itself if only I turned around and looked, and that once I did, I could start to move toward it.

"We can call Angelina when we get back," I said. "You remember Angelina?"

"From the salon?" Maribel said.

And I nodded, marveling that she knew. Only a few months earlier, that might not have been the case.

I said, "It feels like a long time, doesn't it, that we've been gone?"

"Yes," Maribel said.

"It will be good to see it all again."

The sky was dark by the time we got to Tennessee. I stared at the tall overhead highway lights as we drove beneath them. Loud semi-trucks passed us in the right lane, and each time I looked at the driver perched up high, wondering where he was going. After we'd eaten some of the crackers and drunk the bottled water that Celia had thrust into my arms when she and Rafael had said good-bye, Maribel fell asleep again, lulled by the sound of the road, and I closed my eyes, too.

When I woke in the morning, we were in Arkansas. I asked the man and that's what he told me. I thought we would have been farther by then, but perhaps the driver had pulled over the truck for a time to sleep himself. The land in Arkansas was lime green and lush, flat and boundless. Tiny buds stood on the heads of blades of grass all over the fields. They swayed whenever there was a breeze or a gust of wind. I remembered that I had said to Arturo many months ago, as we came through in the opposite direction, that it was all so beautiful.

"Every place is beautiful," he had said, "if you give it a chance."

"You sound like a priest," I told him.

"I could be a priest," he said.

"And then what would happen to me?" I had teased him. We had been happy at certain moments during the drive, buoyed with optimism. "A priest can't be married, you know."

Arturo looked very solemn. He put his hand on my knee. He said, "Then I could not be a priest."

I remember I had laughed.

After Arkansas, I knew, we would drive down through Texas, past the hundreds of strip malls and armadillos baking on the side of the road. We would cross the border into México and take a series of buses back to Pátzcuaro. Out of one world and into the next. Just like that. Like Arturo. Our journey would continue, and Arturo's would, too, even though for now he was headed to one destination and Maribel and I to another. Later, much later, I would find my way to him. We would be in the same place again. That much I knew was true.

I looked at Maribel next to me, staring absently out the window, the blanket balled on the seat between us.

"How's your stomach?" I asked.

She turned and gave me a small smile. "I'm fine," she said.

It was what I had been waiting to hear the whole time.

# Arturo Rivera

Iwas born in Pátzcuaro, Michoacán, México. I lived there all my life until I came here. Other people from our town had gone north. Most of them left because they wanted a better life. That's what they said. A better life. But it wasn't like that for us. We had a good life, a beautiful life. We lived in a house that I built. We married in the town square when Alma and I were young, when people told us we didn't know anything yet about the world. But we knew. Because the world to us was each other. And then we had Maribel. And our world grew larger.

We came here for her.

I think about God sometimes, whether He's watching us. Was this what He wanted? Was it all for some greater reason that I don't understand? Were we supposed to come here, to the United States? Is there something better waiting for us here that God in His infinite vision can see? Is there something ahead of us that will help all of this make sense finally? I don't know. I don't know the answers.

I don't want to sound ungrateful. We are happy here in many ways. We've met good people. We haven't been here long, but the people in the building where we live have become like a family to us. The teachers at Maribel's school have helped her tremendously. She's getting better, they say. And Alma and I can tell. Maribel has a light in her eyes now. We see that, and nothing—not a single thing—brings us more joy.

Maybe it's the instinct of every immigrant, born of necessity or of longing: Someplace else will be better than here. And the condition: if only I can get to that place.

It took us a long time to be able to come. We applied and waited to be approved. We traveled for days. We left a lot of things behind—not only physical objects, but our friends and of course our families, pieces of ourselves—all for the chance to see that light in Maribel's eyes. It's been difficult, yes, but I would do it all again. People do what they have to in this life. We try to get from one end of it to the other with dignity and with honor. We do the best we can.

I'm overcome when I think about this place and about what it's given us. Maribel is getting stronger. I can see it. Every day a little bit more. A safe area to live. Such good friends. It's incredible. One day when we go back to México and people ask me what it was like here, I will tell them those things. I will tell them all the ways I loved this country.

# ACKNOWLEDGMENTS

With deep gratitude to the entire team at Knopf, but especially to Robin Desser, who is the editor of my dreams and who has not only made this a better book, but who has made me a better, wiser, more thoughtful writer; to my agent, the inimitable Julie Barer, or as I sometimes refer to her: "My favorite person in the world"; to everyone who read at various stages along the way—Kate Sullivan, Diana Spechler, Tita Ramírez, and Jennifer Kurdyla; to my mom, for too many things to name, not least of which is sharing the story that helped set this book in motion; to my dad, not only for inspiring me to write this book, but for inspiring me, period; and to my husband and children, who are, in the truest definition of the word that I can think of, my home.

This book was set in Caledonia, a Linotype face designed by W. A. Dwiggins (1880–1956). It belongs to the family of printing types called "modern face" by printers—a term used to mark the change in style of the type letters that occurred around 1800. Caledonia borders on the general design of Scotch Roman but it is more freely drawn than that letter.

# A TALE FOR THE TIME BEING

## RUTH OZEKI

C

· THE CANONS ·

CANON GATE